DARK GRAPHIC NOVELS

DARK GRAPHIC TALES
BY EDGAR ALLAN POE

THE GOLD BUG
THE SYSTEM OF DOCTOR TARR AND PROFESSOR FETHER
THE FALL OF THE HOUSE OF USHER

ADAPTATION
DENISE DESPEYROUX

ILLUSTRATIONS
MIQUEL SERRATOSA

Enslow Publishers, Inc.
40 Industrial Road
Box 398
Berkeley Heights, NJ 07922
USA
http://www.enslow.com

Translated from the Spanish edition by Stacey Juana Pontoriero. Edited and produced by Enslow Publishers, Inc.

Library of Congress Cataloging-in-Publication Data

Despeyroux, Denise.
[Relatos de Poe. English]
Dark graphic tales by Edgar Allan Poe / adaptation, Denise Despeyroux ; illustrations, Miquel Serratosa.
v. cm. — (Dark graphic novels)
Summary: A graphic novel adaptation of three short stories by Edgar Allan Poe.
Includes bibliographical references.
Contents: The gold bug — The system of Doctor Tarr and Professor Fether — The fall of the house of Usher.
ISBN 978-0-7660-4086-1
1. Horror tales, American. 2. Children's stories, American. 3. Graphic novels. [1. Graphic novels. 2. Horror stories. 3. Short stories.] I. Serratosa, Miquel, 1980- ill. II. Poe, Edgar Allan, 1809-1849. III. Title.
PZ7.7.D5055Dar 2012
741.5'946—dc23

2011034273

Future edition:
Paperback ISBN 978-1-4644-0103-9

Originally published in Spanish under the title *Relatos de Poe*.

Published by Parramón Ediciones, S.A., Barcelona, Spain.

Text adapted by: Denise Despeyroux
Illustrator: Miquel Serratosa

Printed in Spain

122011 UNIGRAF, Madrid, Spain

10 9 8 7 6 5 4 3 2 1

To Our Readers: We have done our best to make sure all Internet Addresses in this book were active and appropriate when we went to press. However, the author and the publishers have no control over and assume no liability for the material available on those Internet sites or on other Web sites they may link to. Any comments or suggestions can be sent by e-mail to comments@enslow.com or to the address on the back cover.

THE GOLD BUG

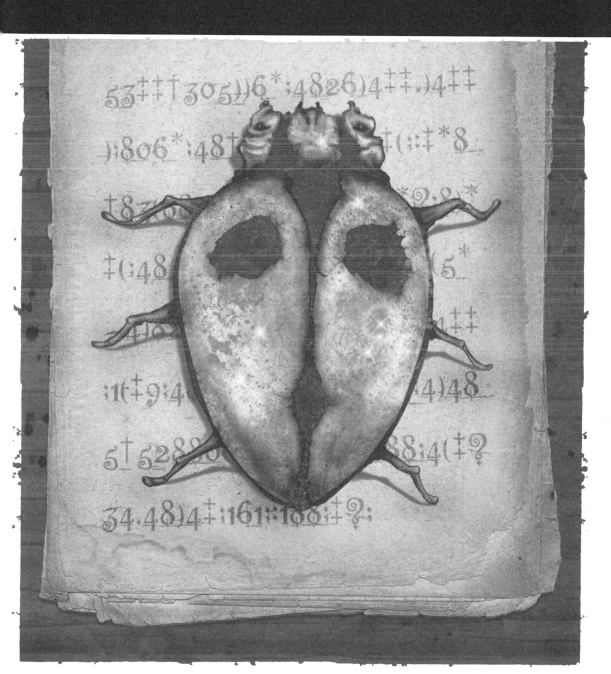

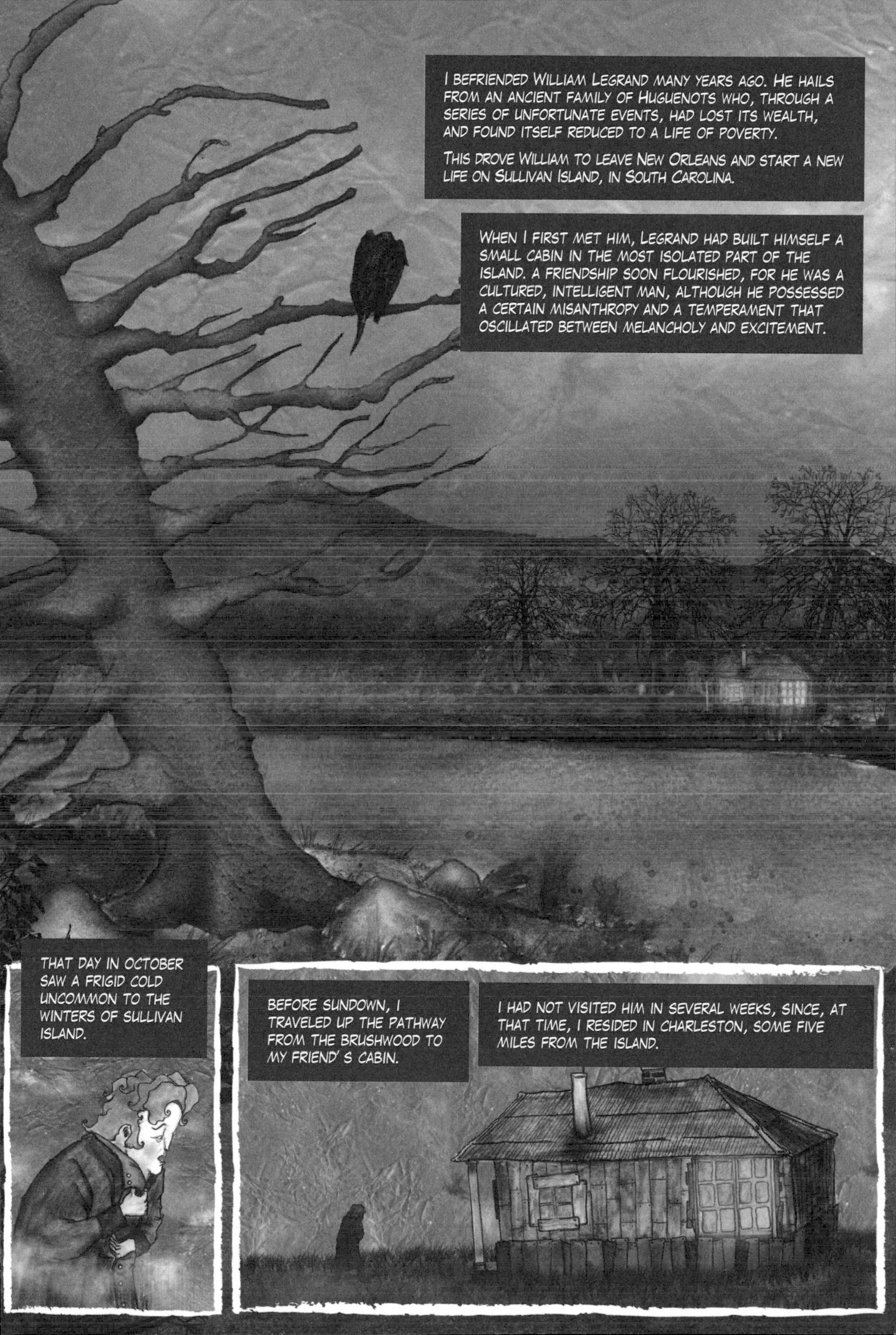
I BEFRIENDED WILLIAM LEGRAND MANY YEARS AGO. HE HAILS FROM AN ANCIENT FAMILY OF HUGUENOTS WHO, THROUGH A SERIES OF UNFORTUNATE EVENTS, HAD LOST ITS WEALTH, AND FOUND ITSELF REDUCED TO A LIFE OF POVERTY.
THIS DROVE WILLIAM TO LEAVE NEW ORLEANS AND START A NEW LIFE ON SULLIVAN ISLAND, IN SOUTH CAROLINA.
WHEN I FIRST MET HIM, LEGRAND HAD BUILT HIMSELF A SMALL CABIN IN THE MOST ISOLATED PART OF THE ISLAND. A FRIENDSHIP SOON FLOURISHED, FOR HE WAS A CULTURED, INTELLIGENT MAN, ALTHOUGH HE POSSESSED A CERTAIN MISANTHROPY AND A TEMPERAMENT THAT OSCILLATED BETWEEN MELANCHOLY AND EXCITEMENT.
THAT DAY IN OCTOBER SAW A FRIGID COLD UNCOMMON TO THE WINTERS OF SULLIVAN ISLAND.
BEFORE SUNDOWN, I TRAVELED UP THE PATHWAY FROM THE BRUSHWOOD TO MY FRIEND' S CABIN.
I HAD NOT VISITED HIM IN SEVERAL WEEKS, SINCE, AT THAT TIME, I RESIDED IN CHARLESTON, SOME FIVE MILES FROM THE ISLAND.

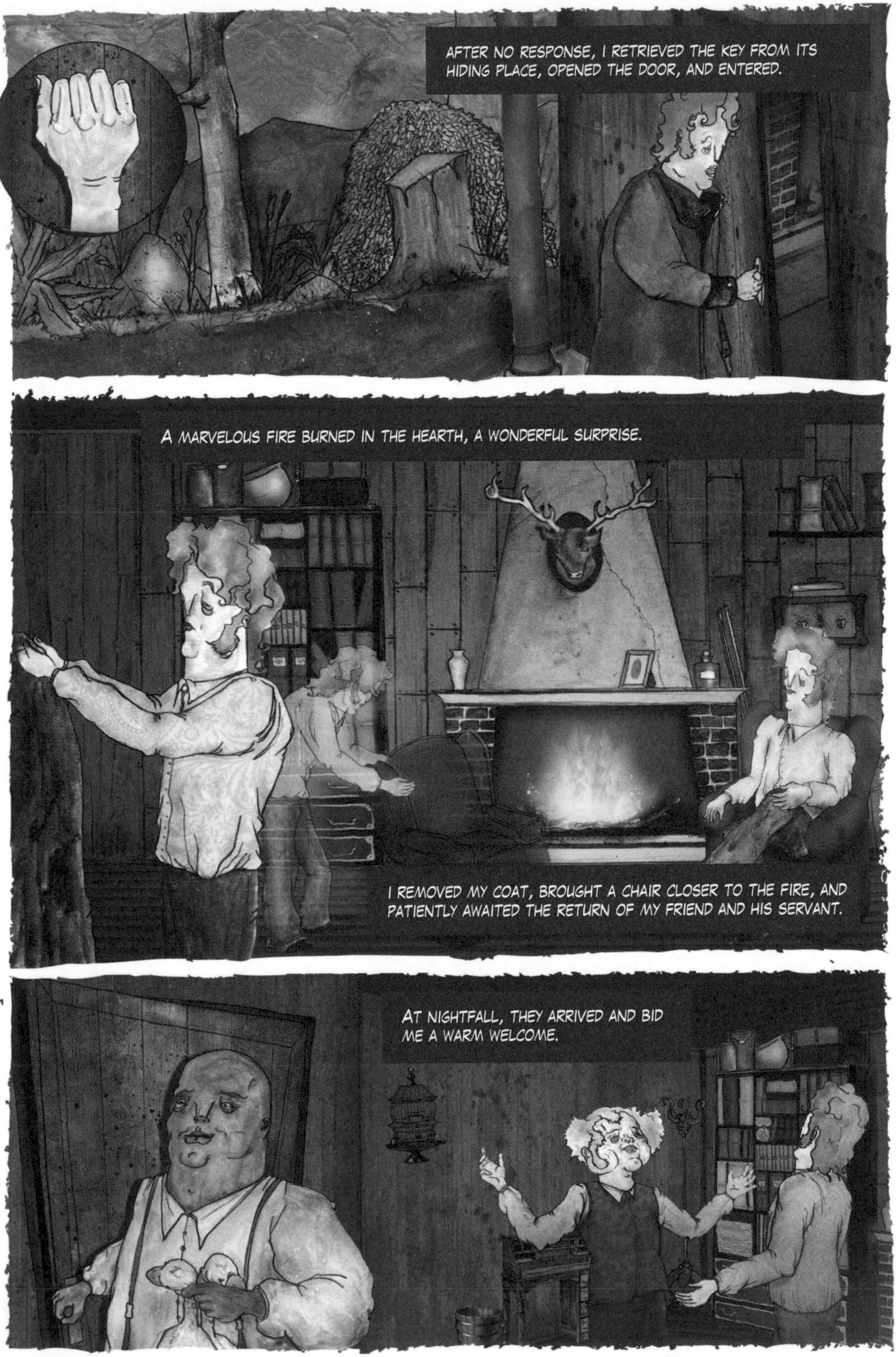
AFTER NO RESPONSE, I RETRIEVED THE KEY FROM ITS HIDING PLACE, OPENED THE DOOR, AND ENTERED.
A MARVELOUS FIRE BURNED IN THE HEARTH, A WONDERFUL SURPRISE.
I REMOVED MY COAT, BROUGHT A CHAIR CLOSER TO THE FIRE, AND PATIENTLY AWAITED THE RETURN OF MY FRIEND AND HIS SERVANT.
AT NIGHTFALL, THEY ARRIVED AND BID ME A WARM WELCOME.

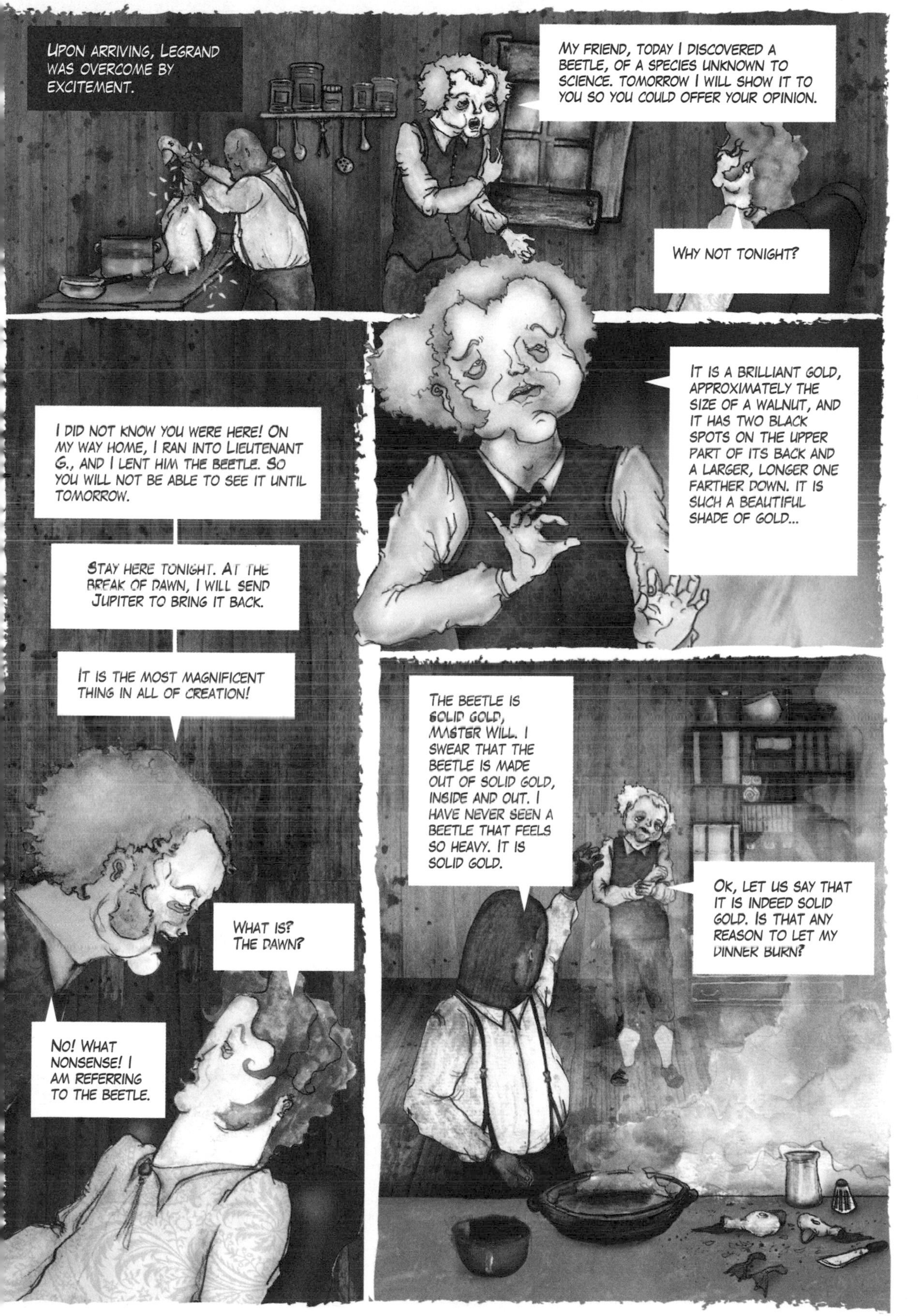
Upon arriving, Legrand was overcome by excitement.
My friend, today I discovered a beetle, of a species unknown to science. Tomorrow I will show it to you so you could offer your opinion.
Why not tonight?
It is a brilliant gold, approximately the size of a walnut, and it has two black spots on the upper part of its back and a larger, longer one farther down. It is such a beautiful shade of gold...
I did not know you were here! On my way home, I ran into Lieutenant G., and I lent him the beetle. So you will not be able to see it until tomorrow.
Stay here tonight. At the break of dawn, I will send Jupiter to bring it back.
It is the most magnificent thing in all of creation!
What is? The dawn?
No! What nonsense! I am referring to the beetle.
The beetle is solid gold, Master Will. I swear that the beetle is made out of solid gold, inside and out. I have never seen a beetle that feels so heavy. It is solid gold.
Ok, let us say that it is indeed solid gold. Is that any reason to let my dinner burn?

THE BEETLE'S COLOR IS ENOUGH TO SUPPORT JUPITER'S THEORY. NEVER HAVE YOU SEEN SUCH A BRILLIANT GOLD. UNFORTUNATELY I CANNOT SHOW YOU RIGHT NOW, BUT LET ME DRAW IT FOR YOU SO YOU HAVE AN IDEA OF WHAT THE INSECT LOOKS LIKE.

NOW WHERE IS SOME PAPER?

NO MATTER, THIS PIECE OF PARCHMENT WILL DO.

AS SOON AS HE GAVE ME THE SKETCH, WE HEARD A LOUD NOISE AT THE DOOR.

GRRRRRRRRRR

JUPITER OPENED THE DOOR, AND A HUGE NEWFOUNDLAND, BELONGING TO LEGRAND, HAPPILY JUMPED ON TOP OF ME TO EXPRESS HIS AFFECTION.

ONCE THE DOG CALMED DOWN AND I WAS ABLE TO LOOK AT THE SKETCH, I WAS A BIT PERPLEXED.

THIS IS INDEED A STRANGE BEETLE. I ADMIT I HAVE NEVER SEEN ANYTHING LIKE IT. I WOULD SAY IT LOOKS MORE LIKE A SKULL THAN AN INSECT.

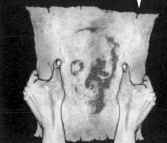

A SKULL? WELL... I SUPPOSE IT COULD RESEMBLE ONE ON PAPER. THE TWO SMALL BLACK SPOTS MAY LOOK LIKE EYES AND THE LONGER ONE BELOW THEM, A MOUTH. BUT LOOK AT THE SKETCH MORE CLOSELY, YOU WILL SEE THAT IT IS NOT A SKULL, BUT, IN FACT, A BEETLE.

I TAKE IT THAT YOU ARE NO ARTIST, LEGRAND. I WILL HAVE TO WAIT TO SEE THE INSECT MYSELF TO HAVE AN IDEA OF WHAT IT IS LIKE.

THAT SAID, I HELD OUT THE SKETCH FOR HIM TO TAKE. I WAS SUPRISED AT HIS TAKING OFFENSE AT MY COMMENTS ABOUT THE DRAWING.

LEGRAND WAS ABOUT TO TOSS THE PAPER INTO THE FIRE, BUT SUDDENLY HE STOPPED HIMSELF. IN AN INSTANT, HIS FACE WENT FROM BRIGHT RED TO GHOSTLY WHITE.

NEXT, HE TOOK A CANDLE AND WENT TO GO SIT ON A CHEST ON THE OTHER SIDE OF THE ROOM. THERE HE SPENT SEVERAL MINUTES CLOSELY EXAMINING THE DRAWING IN GREAT DETAIL WHILE ANXIOUSLY TURNING IT IN ALL DIRECTIONS.

HE THEN TOOK HIS WALLET OUT OF HIS POCKET, STUCK THE DRAWING IN IT, AND PUT EVERYTHING INSIDE A DRAWER, WHICH HE LOCKED.

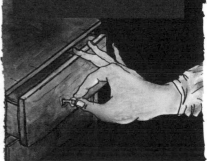

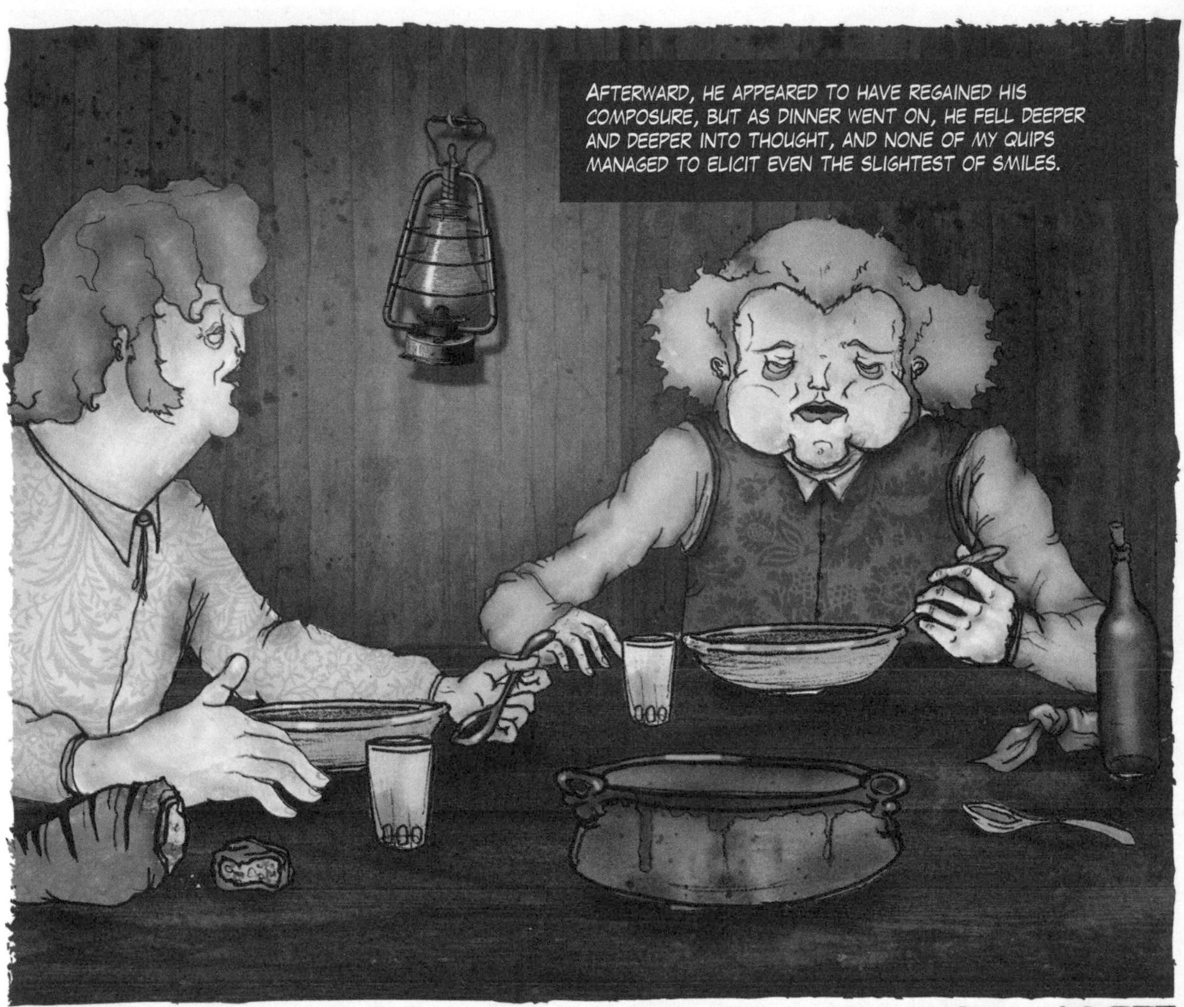
AFTERWARD, HE APPEARED TO HAVE REGAINED HIS COMPOSURE, BUT AS DINNER WENT ON, HE FELL DEEPER AND DEEPER INTO THOUGHT, AND NONE OF MY QUIPS MANAGED TO ELICIT EVEN THE SLIGHTEST OF SMILES.

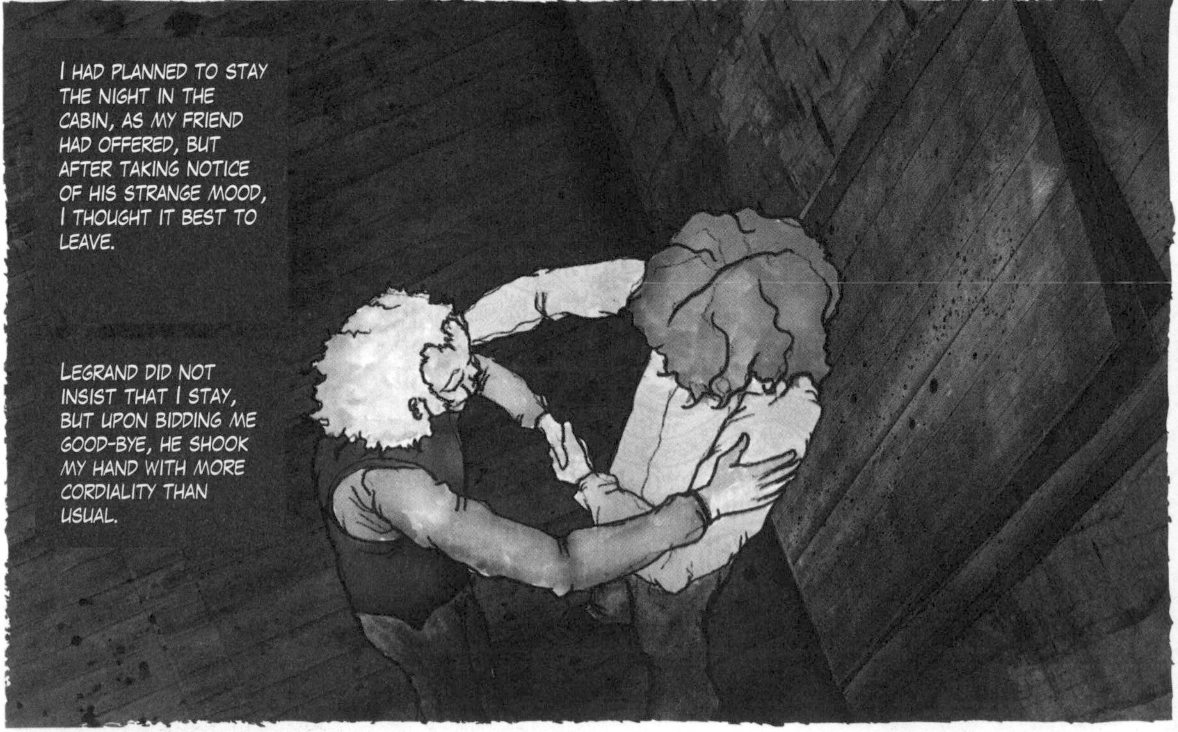
I HAD PLANNED TO STAY THE NIGHT IN THE CABIN, AS MY FRIEND HAD OFFERED, BUT AFTER TAKING NOTICE OF HIS STRANGE MOOD, I THOUGHT IT BEST TO LEAVE.
LEGRAND DID NOT INSIST THAT I STAY, BUT UPON BIDDING ME GOOD-BYE, HE SHOOK MY HAND WITH MORE CORDIALITY THAN USUAL.

ABOUT A MONTH LATER, DURING WHICH I HAD NOT HEARD FROM MY FRIEND, I RECEIVED AN UNEXPECTED VISIT FROM HIS SERVANT JUPITER.

WHAT'S THE MATTER, JUPITER? I HAVE NEVER SEEN YOU SO DEPRESSED. HOW IS YOUR MASTER?

NOT WELL AT ALL, SIR. HE SAYS THERE'S NOTHING WRONG, BUT HE'S VERY SICK, I KNOW IT.

VERY SICK! WHY DIDN'T YOU TELL ME THIS BEFORE? IS HE BEDRIDDEN?

NO SIR, HE'S UP AND DOWN ALL DAY WITH SOME STRANGE NUMBERS WRITTEN ON A SLATE, WHITE AS MILK AND HANGING HIS HEAD.

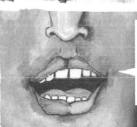

I DON'T UNDERSTAND, JUPITER. DO YOU HAVE ANY IDEA WHY HE IS ACTING THIS WAY? DID SOMETHING BAD HAPPEN?

JUST THE BUG. I SWEAR THAT BUG GOT INTO MASTER WILL'S HEAD.

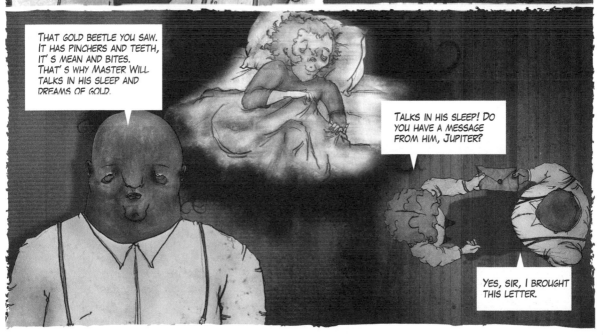

THAT GOLD BEETLE YOU SAW. IT HAS PINCHERS AND TEETH, IT'S MEAN AND BITES. THAT'S WHY MASTER WILL TALKS IN HIS SLEEP AND DREAMS OF GOLD.

TALKS IN HIS SLEEP! DO YOU HAVE A MESSAGE FROM HIM, JUPITER?

YES, SIR, I BROUGHT THIS LETTER.

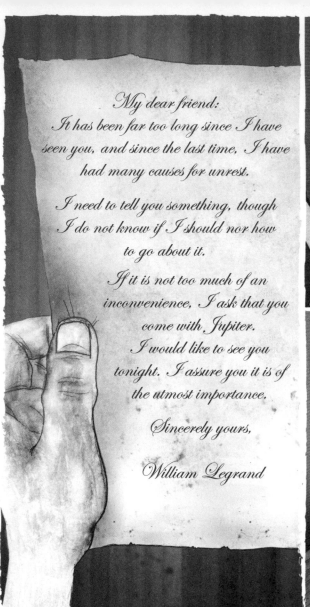

My dear friend:
It has been far too long since I have seen you, and since the last time, I have had many causes for unrest.

I need to tell you something, though I do not know if I should nor how to go about it.

If it is not too much of an inconvenience, I ask that you come with Jupiter.
I would like to see you tonight. I assure you it is of the utmost importance.

Sincerely yours,

William Legrand

SOMETHING ABOUT THE LETTER'S TONE FILLED ME WITH DREAD. I DID NOT RECOGNIZE LEGRAND. WHAT HAD GOTTEN INTO HIS HEAD? WHAT COULD HAVE BEEN OF THE UTMOST IMPORTANCE?

I FEARED THAT SOME MISHAP HAD CAUSED MY FRIEND TO LOSE ALL SENSE OF REASON. WITHOUT A SECOND THOUGHT, I WENT WITH JUPITER.

WE ARRIVED AT THE DOCK, AND I WAS SURPRISED TO SEE A BRAND NEW SCYTHE AND A COUPLE OF SHOVELS IN LEGRAND'S BOAT.

SEEING THAT JUPITER WAS COMPLETELY OBSESSED WITH THE BUG, I DID NOT WANT TO ASK ANY MORE QUESTIONS.

A STEADY BREEZE QUICKLY BROUGHT US TO THE SMALL BAY NORTH OF FORT MOULTRIE.

AFTER A TWO-MILE HIKE, IT WAS THREE IN THE AFTERNOON BY THE TIME WE REACHED THE CABIN.

LEGRAND'S CONDITION WAS ALARMING, AND AFTER I INQUIRED ABOUT THE BEETLE, HE WORRIED ME EVEN MORE.

NOTHING IN THE WORLD CAN SEPARATE ME FROM THIS BEETLE. DID YOU KNOW JUPITER WAS RIGHT ALL ALONG? THAT INSECT IS SOLID GOLD!

THIS BUG WILL MAKE ME RICH! IT WILL RESTORE MY FAMILY'S WEALTH! LOOK! SEE FOR YOURSELF!

IT WAS BEAUTIFUL, A GREAT DISCOVERY FROM A SCIENTIFIC POINT OF VIEW. THE WEIGHT AND THE COLOR SUPPORTED JUPITER'S THEORY, BUT IT SURPRISED ME THAT MY FRIEND DID NOT DISPLAY MORE COMMON SENSE.

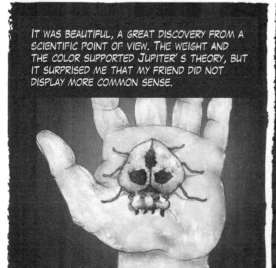

MY FRIEND, FOR ONCE, ALLOW ME TO GIVE YOU SOME ADVICE. THE FIRST THING YOU SHOULD DO IS GO TO BED, YOU NEED TO...

I AM NOT ILL. IF YOU TRULY WANT TO HELP ME, I WILL TELL YOU HOW YOU CAN DO SO. JUPITER AND I ARE GOING ON AN EXPEDITION INTO THE MOUNTAINS, COME WITH US.

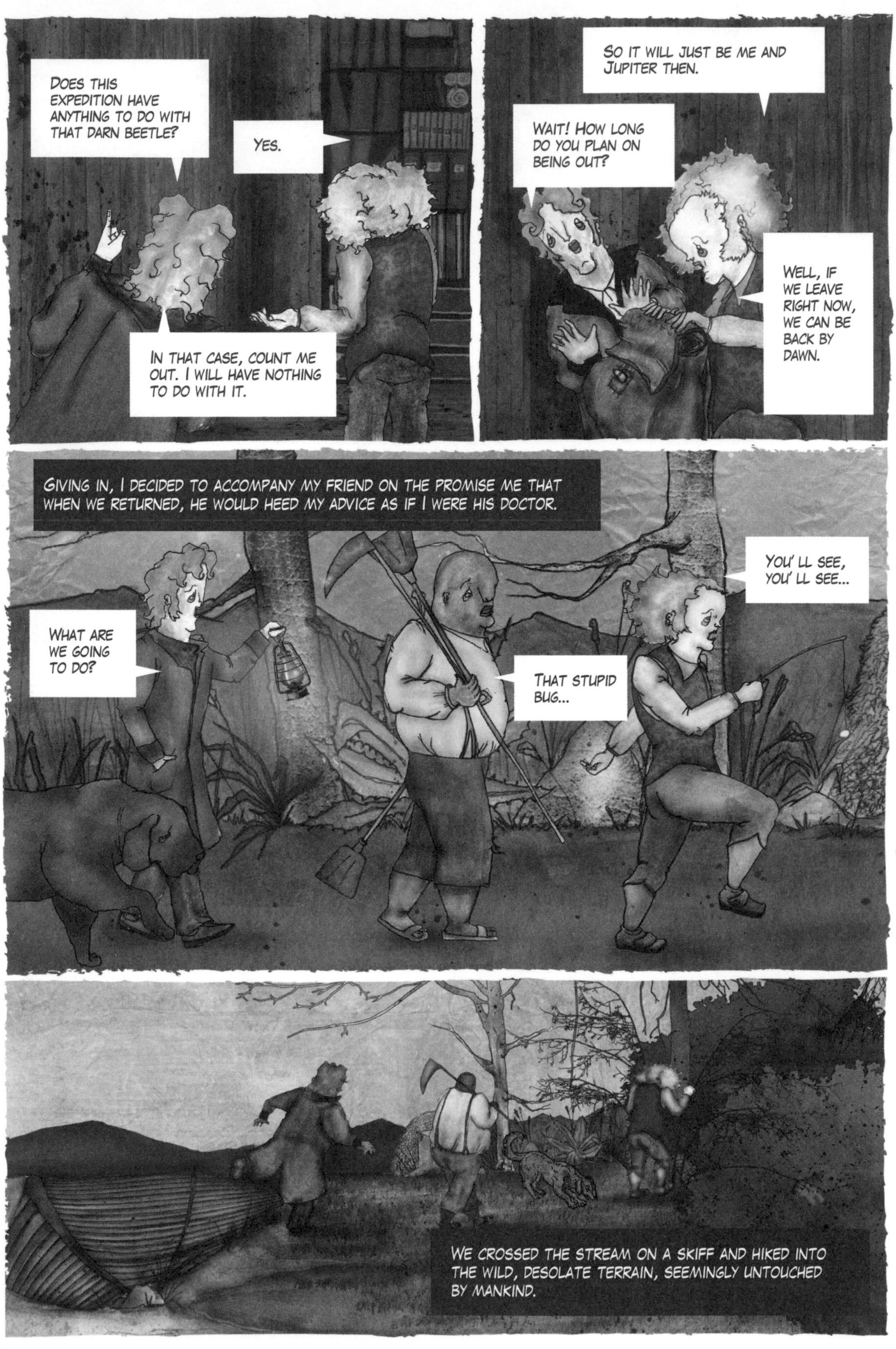
Does this expedition have anything to do with that darn beetle?
Yes.
In that case, count me out. I will have nothing to do with it.
So it will just be me and Jupiter then.
Wait! How long do you plan on being out?
Well, if we leave right now, we can be back by dawn.
Giving in, I decided to accompany my friend on the promise me that when we returned, he would heed my advice as if I were his doctor.
What are we going to do?
That stupid bug...
You'll see, you'll see...
We crossed the stream on a skiff and hiked into the wild, desolate terrain, seemingly untouched by mankind.

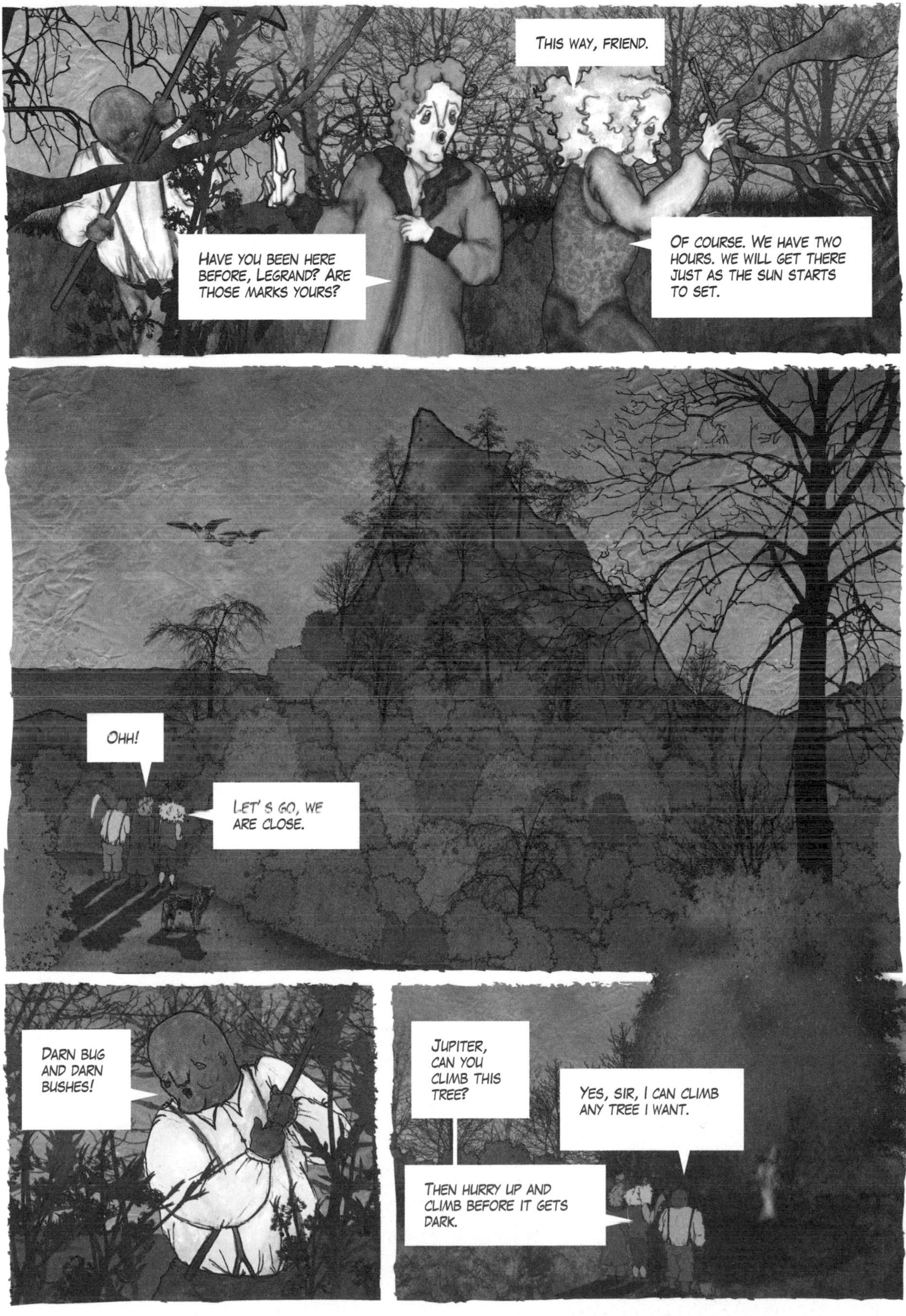

This way, friend.
Have you been here before, Legrand? Are those marks yours?
Of course. We have two hours. We will get there just as the sun starts to set.
Ohh!
Let's go, we are close.
Darn bug and darn bushes!
Jupiter, can you climb this tree?
Yes, sir, I can climb any tree I want.
Then hurry up and climb before it gets dark.

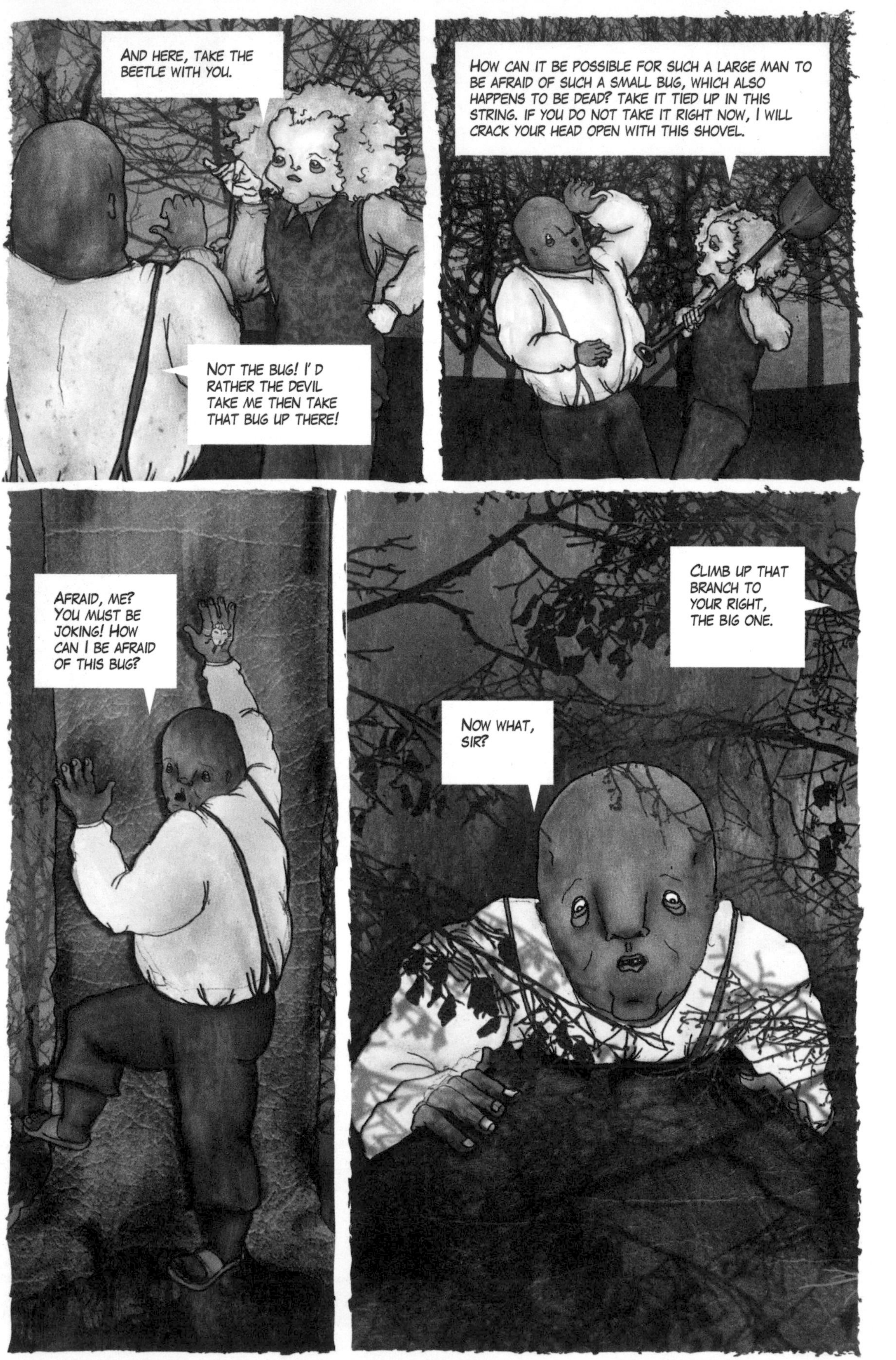
AND HERE, TAKE THE BEETLE WITH YOU.
NOT THE BUG! I' D RATHER THE DEVIL TAKE ME THEN TAKE THAT BUG UP THERE!
HOW CAN IT BE POSSIBLE FOR SUCH A LARGE MAN TO BE AFRAID OF SUCH A SMALL BUG, WHICH ALSO HAPPENS TO BE DEAD? TAKE IT TIED UP IN THIS STRING. IF YOU DO NOT TAKE IT RIGHT NOW, I WILL CRACK YOUR HEAD OPEN WITH THIS SHOVEL.
AFRAID, ME? YOU MUST BE JOKING! HOW CAN I BE AFRAID OF THIS BUG?
CLIMB UP THAT BRANCH TO YOUR RIGHT, THE BIG ONE.
NOW WHAT, SIR?

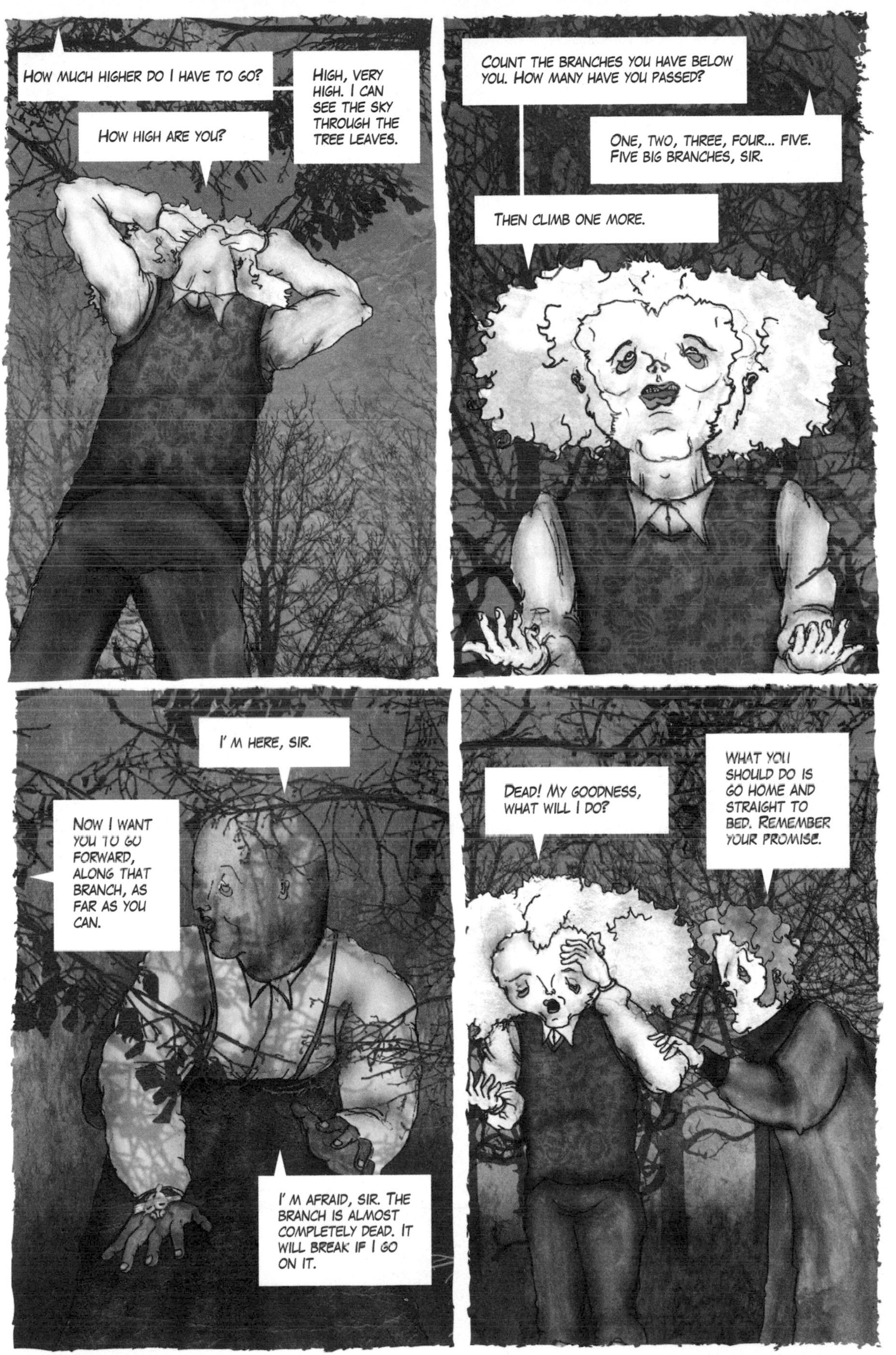
HOW MUCH HIGHER DO I HAVE TO GO?
HOW HIGH ARE YOU?
HIGH, VERY HIGH. I CAN SEE THE SKY THROUGH THE TREE LEAVES.
COUNT THE BRANCHES YOU HAVE BELOW YOU. HOW MANY HAVE YOU PASSED?
ONE, TWO, THREE, FOUR... FIVE. FIVE BIG BRANCHES, SIR.
THEN CLIMB ONE MORE.
I' M HERE, SIR.
NOW I WANT YOU TO GO FORWARD, ALONG THAT BRANCH, AS FAR AS YOU CAN.
I' M AFRAID, SIR. THE BRANCH IS ALMOST COMPLETELY DEAD. IT WILL BREAK IF I GO ON IT.
DEAD! MY GOODNESS, WHAT WILL I DO?
WHAT YOU SHOULD DO IS GO HOME AND STRAIGHT TO BED. REMEMBER YOUR PROMISE.

JUPITER! CAN YOU HEAR ME? STICK THE KNIFE INTO THE WOOD AND TELL ME IF IT IS TRULY ROTTEN.

IT IS ROTTEN, BUT NOT SO MUCH, SIR. I CAN MOVE FORWARD A BIT ALONG THE BRANCH, BUT JUST ME, FOR SURE.

WHAT DO YOU MEAN JUST YOU? WHAT ARE YOU SAYING?

THE BUG IS TOO HEAVY, SIR. I SHOULD DROP IT SO THE BRANCH DOESN'T BREAK.

YES, SIR, BUT PLEASE DON'T YELL AT ME LIKE THAT.

FOOL! IF YOU DROP THE BEETLE, I SWEAR I WILL BREAK YOUR NECK. DO YOU HEAR ME?

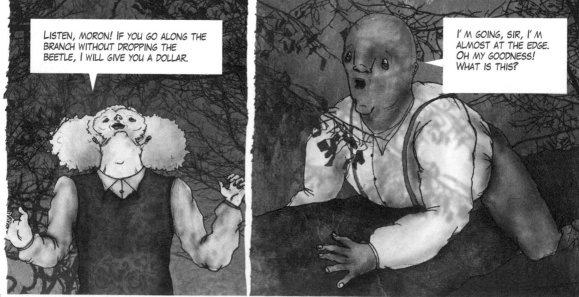

LISTEN, MORON! IF YOU GO ALONG THE BRANCH WITHOUT DROPPING THE BEETLE, I WILL GIVE YOU A DOLLAR.

I'M GOING, SIR, I'M ALMOST AT THE EDGE. OH MY GOODNESS! WHAT IS THIS?

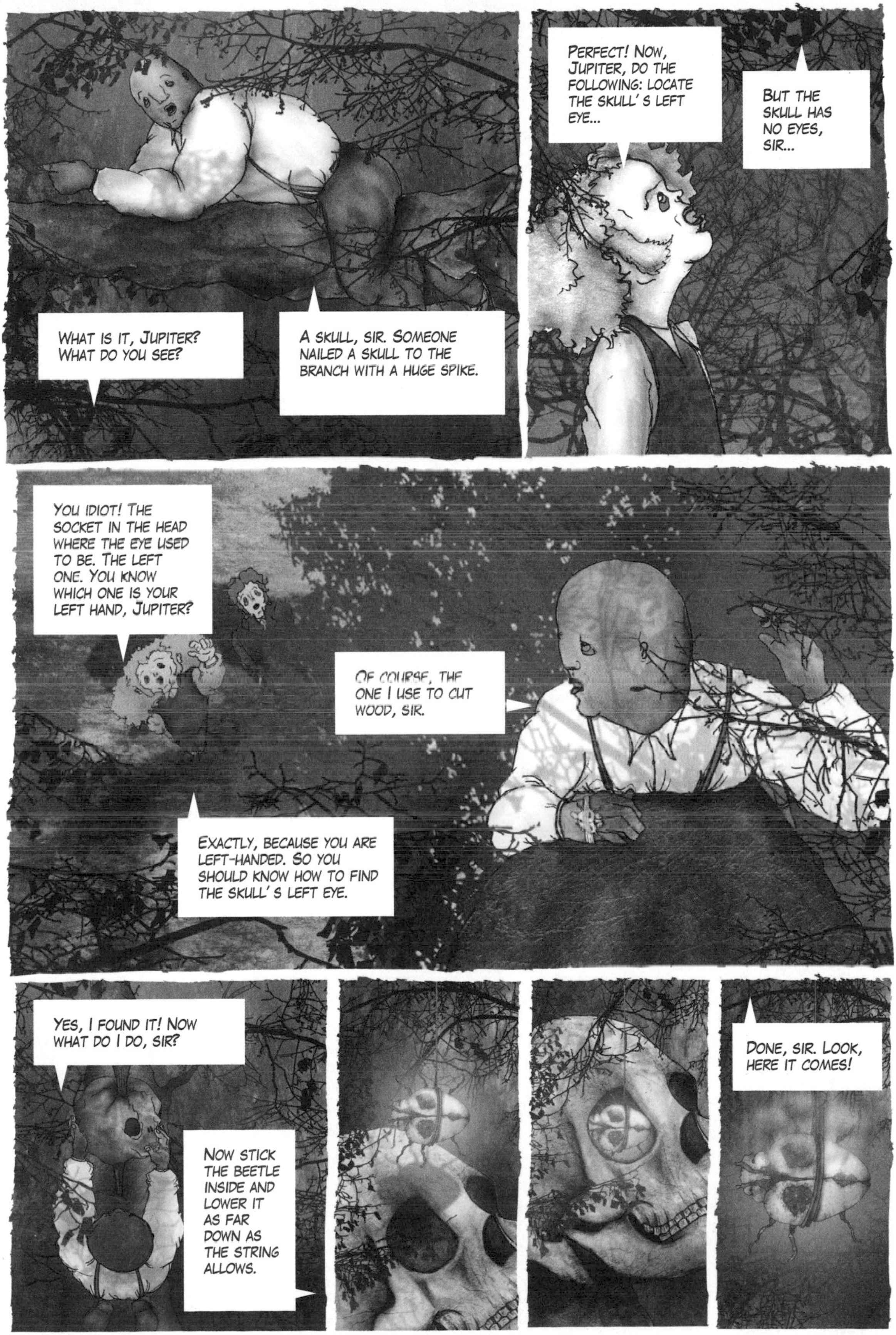
WHAT IS IT, JUPITER? WHAT DO YOU SEE?
A SKULL, SIR. SOMEONE NAILED A SKULL TO THE BRANCH WITH A HUGE SPIKE.
PERFECT! NOW, JUPITER, DO THE FOLLOWING: LOCATE THE SKULL'S LEFT EYE...
BUT THE SKULL HAS NO EYES, SIR...
YOU IDIOT! THE SOCKET IN THE HEAD WHERE THE EYE USED TO BE. THE LEFT ONE. YOU KNOW WHICH ONE IS YOUR LEFT HAND, JUPITER?
OF COURSE, THE ONE I USE TO CUT WOOD, SIR.
EXACTLY, BECAUSE YOU ARE LEFT-HANDED. SO YOU SHOULD KNOW HOW TO FIND THE SKULL'S LEFT EYE.
YES, I FOUND IT! NOW WHAT DO I DO, SIR?
NOW STICK THE BEETLE INSIDE AND LOWER IT AS FAR DOWN AS THE STRING ALLOWS.
DONE, SIR. LOOK, HERE IT COMES!

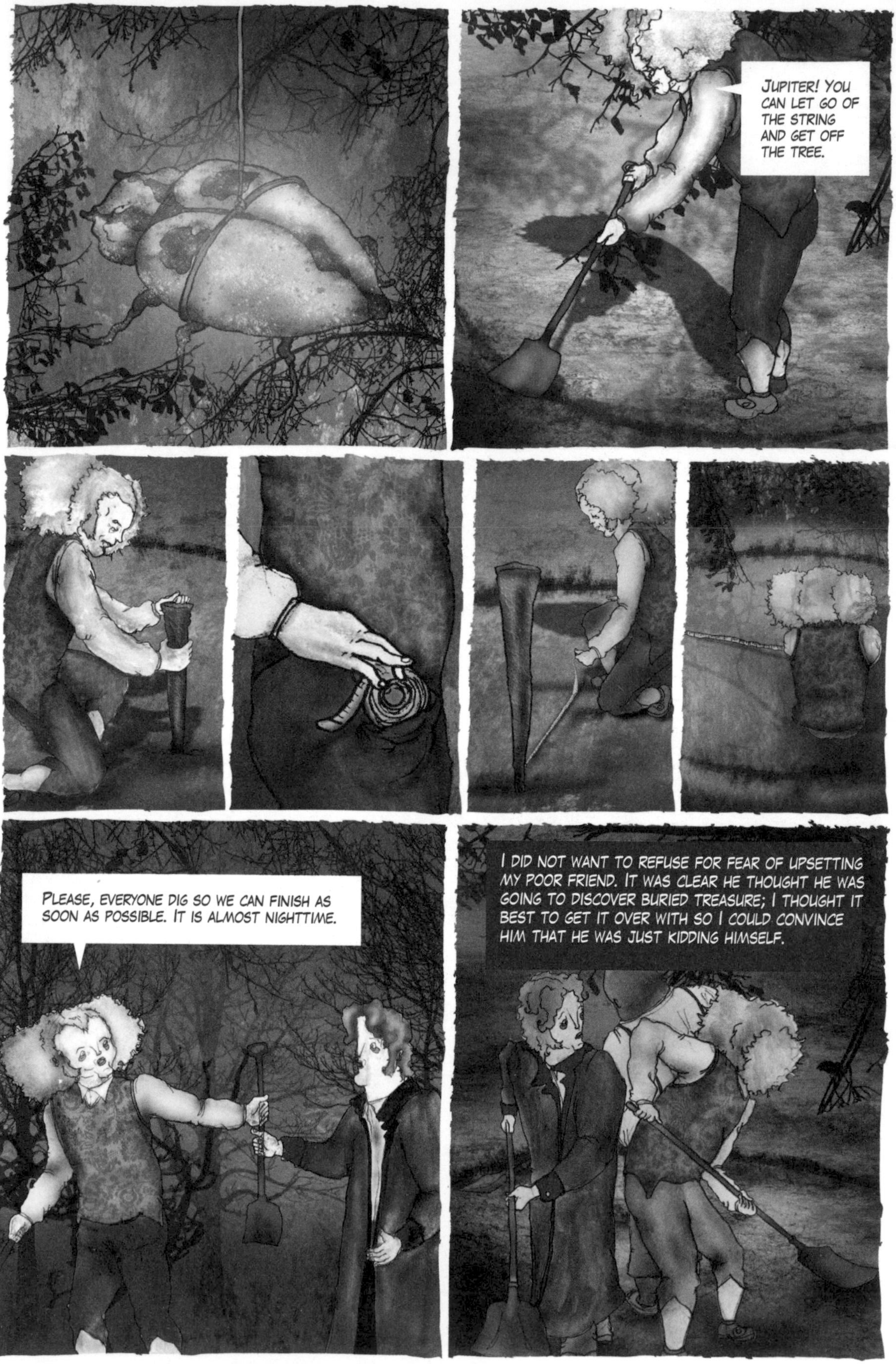
JUPITER! YOU CAN LET GO OF THE STRING AND GET OFF THE TREE.
PLEASE, EVERYONE DIG SO WE CAN FINISH AS SOON AS POSSIBLE. IT IS ALMOST NIGHTTIME.
I DID NOT WANT TO REFUSE FOR FEAR OF UPSETTING MY POOR FRIEND. IT WAS CLEAR HE THOUGHT HE WAS GOING TO DISCOVER BURIED TREASURE; I THOUGHT IT BEST TO GET IT OVER WITH SO I COULD CONVINCE HIM THAT HE WAS JUST KIDDING HIMSELF.

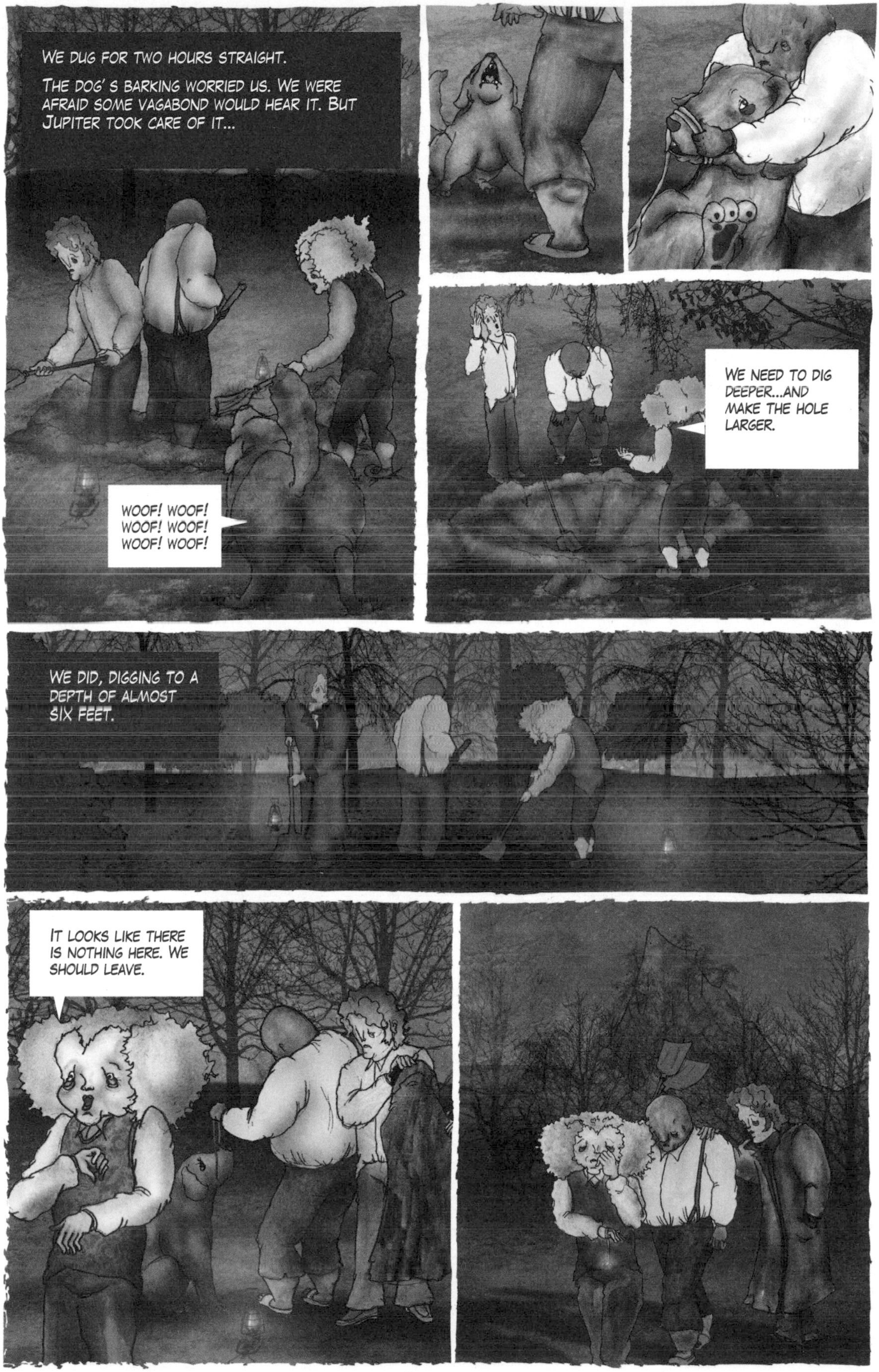
We dug for two hours straight.
The dog's barking worried us. We were afraid some vagabond would hear it. But Jupiter took care of it...
Woof! Woof! Woof! Woof! Woof! Woof!
We need to dig deeper...and make the hole larger.
We did, digging to a depth of almost six feet.
It looks like there is nothing here. We should leave.

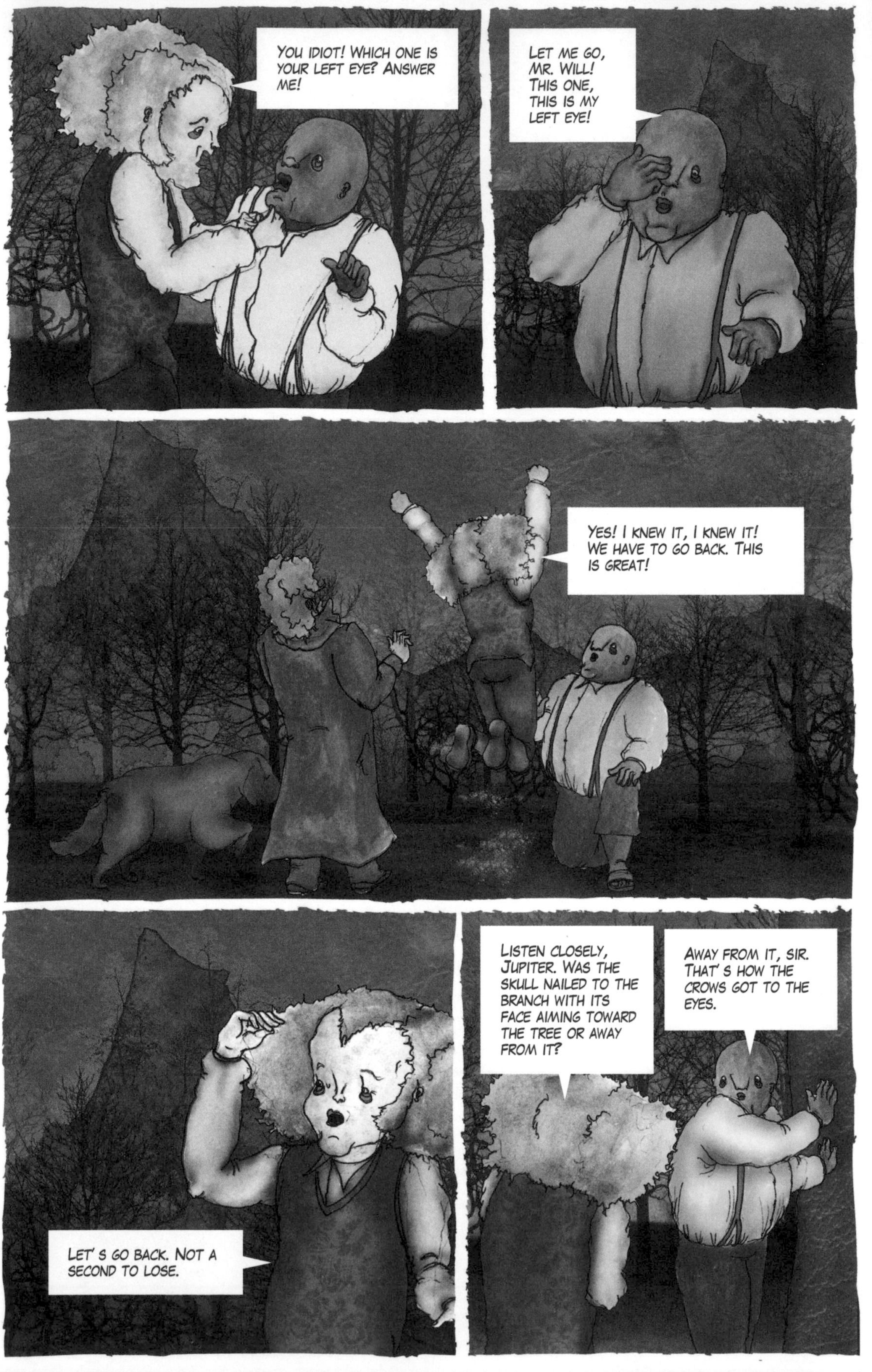
YOU IDIOT! WHICH ONE IS YOUR LEFT EYE? ANSWER ME!
LET ME GO, MR. WILL! THIS ONE, THIS IS MY LEFT EYE!
YES! I KNEW IT, I KNEW IT! WE HAVE TO GO BACK. THIS IS GREAT!
LET'S GO BACK. NOT A SECOND TO LOSE.
LISTEN CLOSELY, JUPITER. WAS THE SKULL NAILED TO THE BRANCH WITH ITS FACE AIMING TOWARD THE TREE OR AWAY FROM IT?
AWAY FROM IT, SIR. THAT'S HOW THE CROWS GOT TO THE EYES.

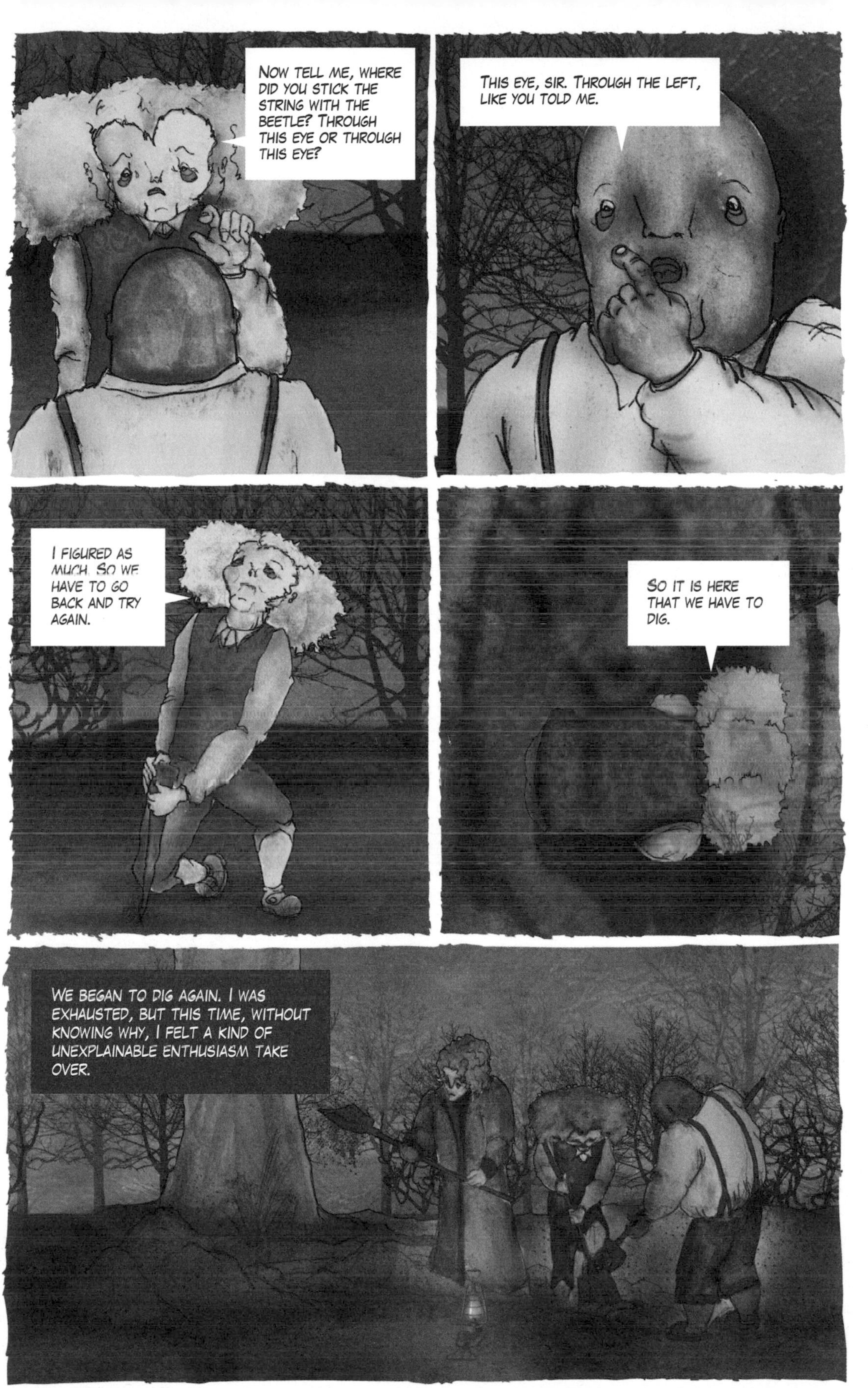
NOW TELL ME, WHERE DID YOU STICK THE STRING WITH THE BEETLE? THROUGH THIS EYE OR THROUGH THIS EYE?
THIS EYE, SIR. THROUGH THE LEFT, LIKE YOU TOLD ME.
I FIGURED AS MUCH. SO WE HAVE TO GO BACK AND TRY AGAIN.
SO IT IS HERE THAT WE HAVE TO DIG.
WE BEGAN TO DIG AGAIN. I WAS EXHAUSTED, BUT THIS TIME, WITHOUT KNOWING WHY, I FELT A KIND OF UNEXPLAINABLE ENTHUSIASM TAKE OVER.

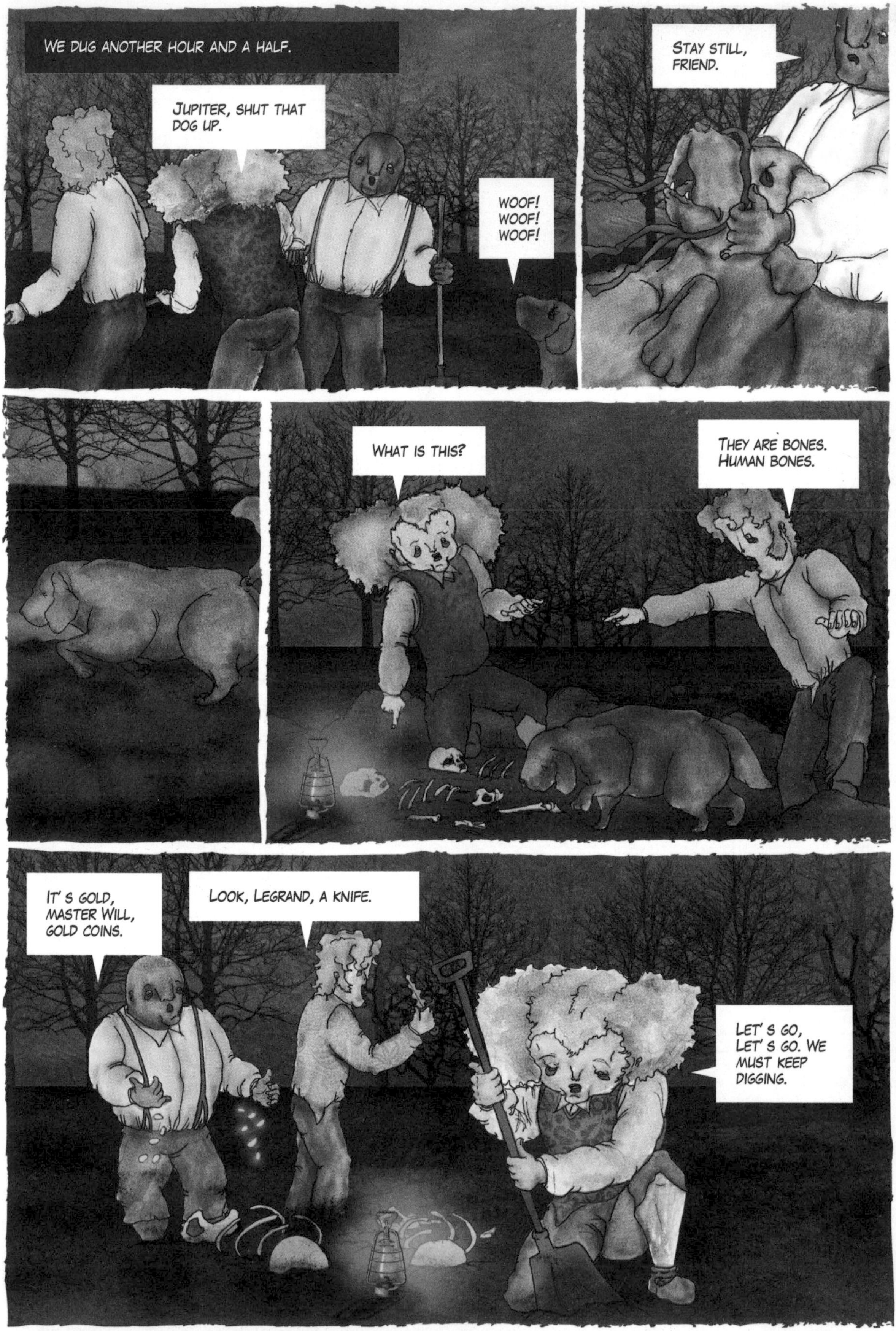

WE DUG ANOTHER HOUR AND A HALF.
JUPITER, SHUT THAT DOG UP.
WOOF! WOOF! WOOF!
STAY STILL, FRIEND.
WHAT IS THIS?
THEY ARE BONES. HUMAN BONES.
IT' S GOLD, MASTER WILL, GOLD COINS.
LOOK, LEGRAND, A KNIFE.
LET' S GO, LET' S GO. WE MUST KEEP DIGGING.

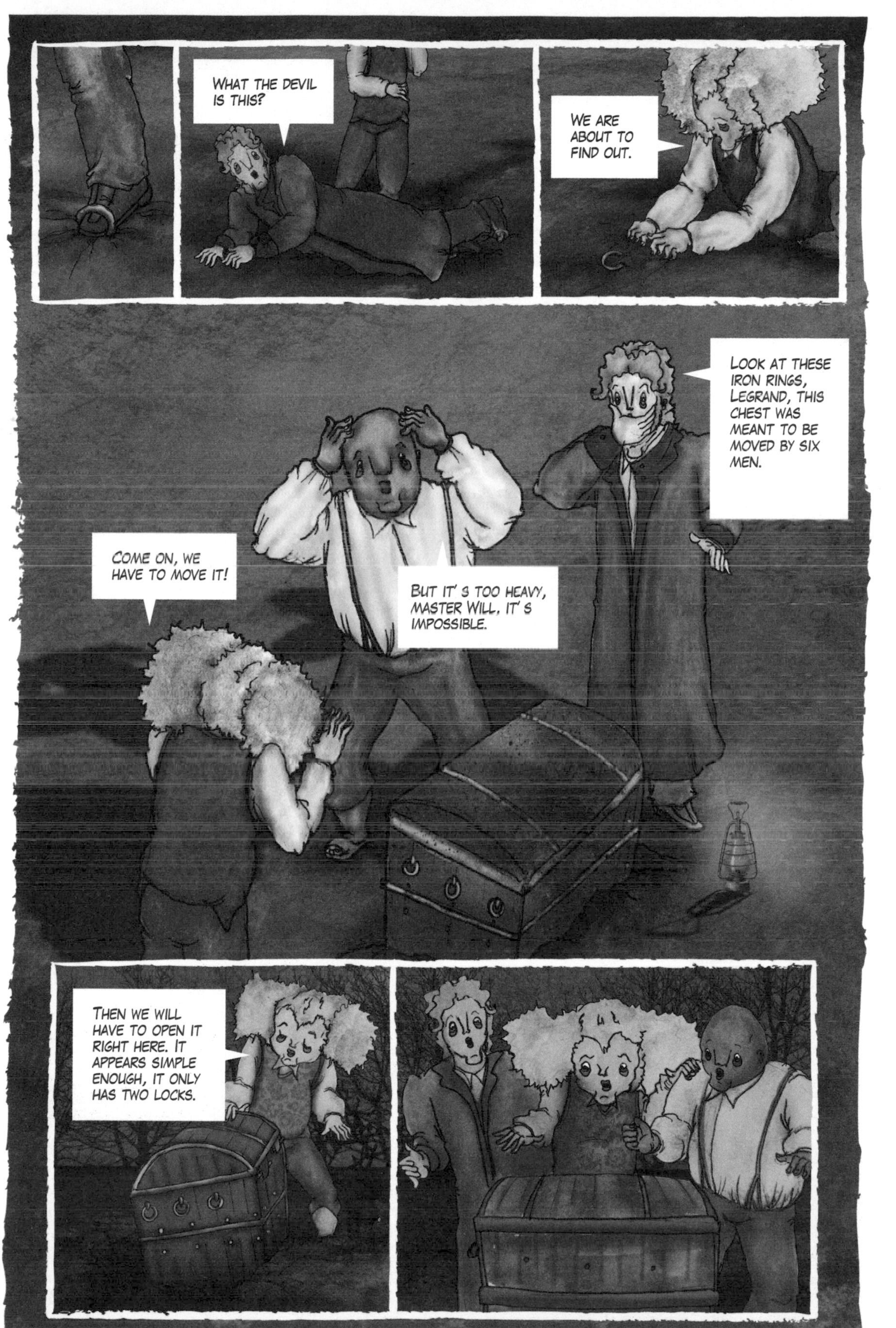
WHAT THE DEVIL IS THIS?
WE ARE ABOUT TO FIND OUT.
LOOK AT THESE IRON RINGS, LEGRAND, THIS CHEST WAS MEANT TO BE MOVED BY SIX MEN.
COME ON, WE HAVE TO MOVE IT!
BUT IT'S TOO HEAVY, MASTER WILL, IT'S IMPOSSIBLE.
THEN WE WILL HAVE TO OPEN IT RIGHT HERE. IT APPEARS SIMPLE ENOUGH, IT ONLY HAS TWO LOCKS.

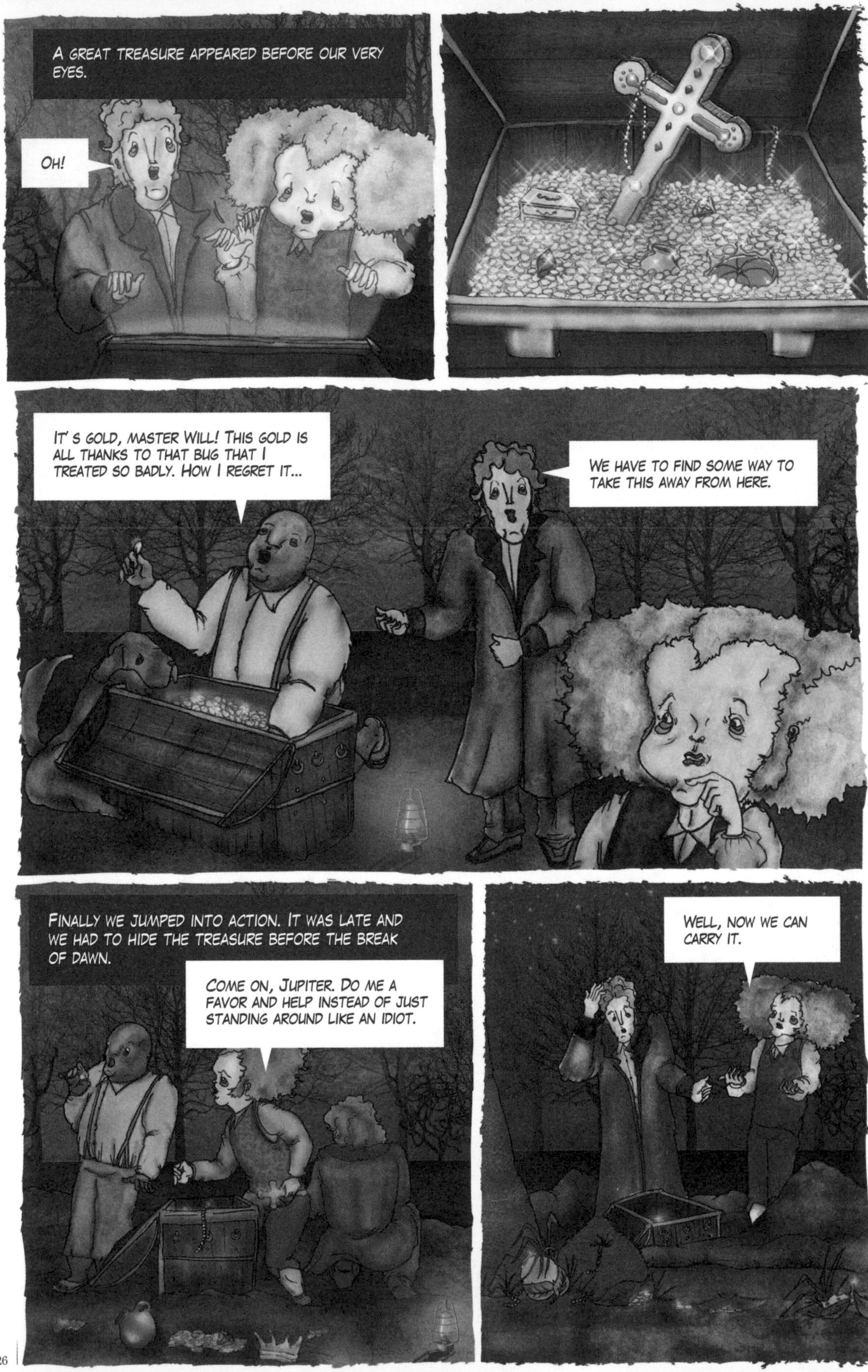
A GREAT TREASURE APPEARED BEFORE OUR VERY EYES.
OH!
IT' S GOLD, MASTER WILL! THIS GOLD IS ALL THANKS TO THAT BUG THAT I TREATED SO BADLY. HOW I REGRET IT...
WE HAVE TO FIND SOME WAY TO TAKE THIS AWAY FROM HERE.
FINALLY WE JUMPED INTO ACTION. IT WAS LATE AND WE HAD TO HIDE THE TREASURE BEFORE THE BREAK OF DAWN.
COME ON, JUPITER. DO ME A FAVOR AND HELP INSTEAD OF JUST STANDING AROUND LIKE AN IDIOT.
WELL, NOW WE CAN CARRY IT.

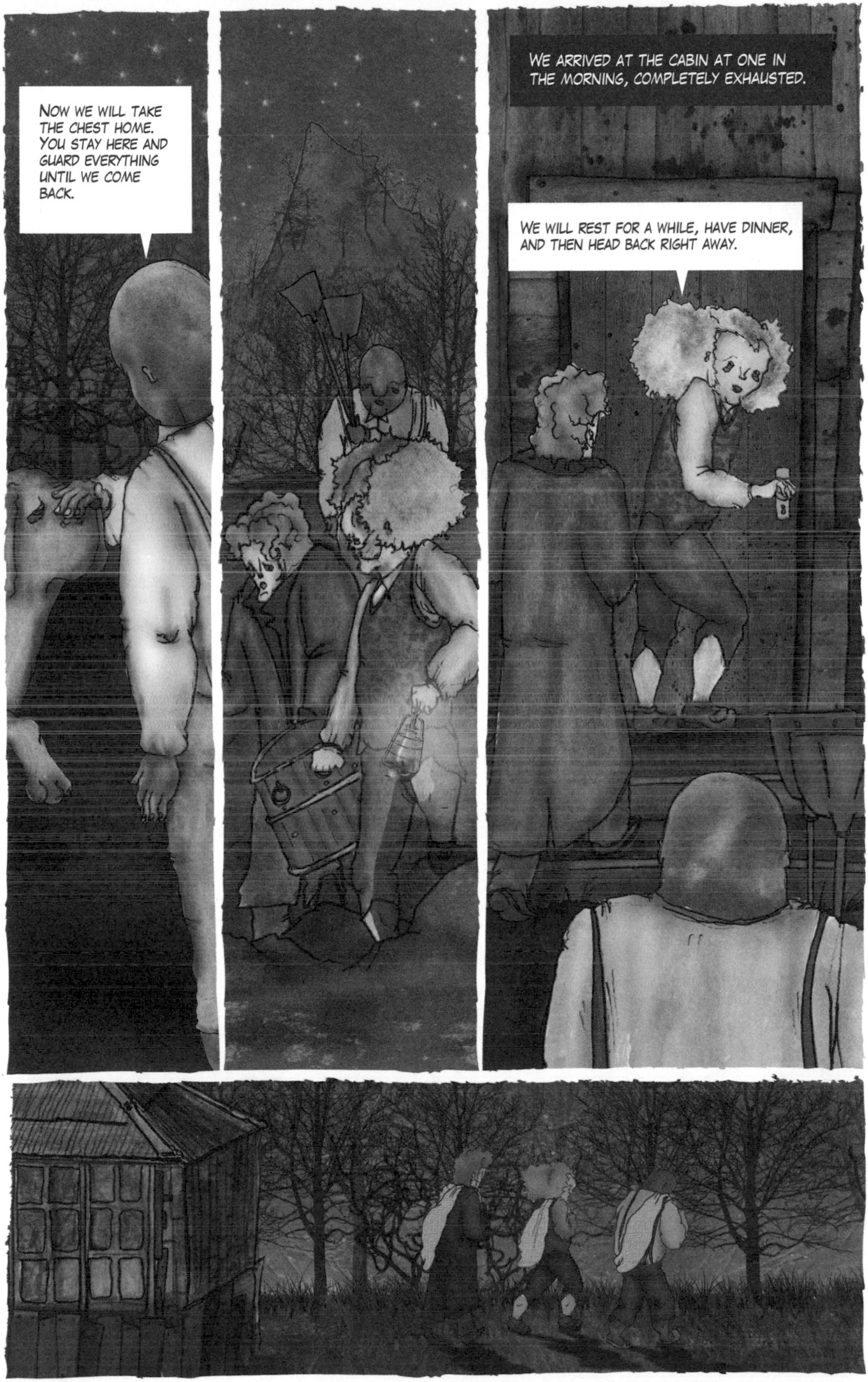
NOW WE WILL TAKE THE CHEST HOME. YOU STAY HERE AND GUARD EVERYTHING UNTIL WE COME BACK.
WE ARRIVED AT THE CABIN AT ONE IN THE MORNING, COMPLETELY EXHAUSTED.
WE WILL REST FOR A WHILE, HAVE DINNER, AND THEN HEAD BACK RIGHT AWAY.

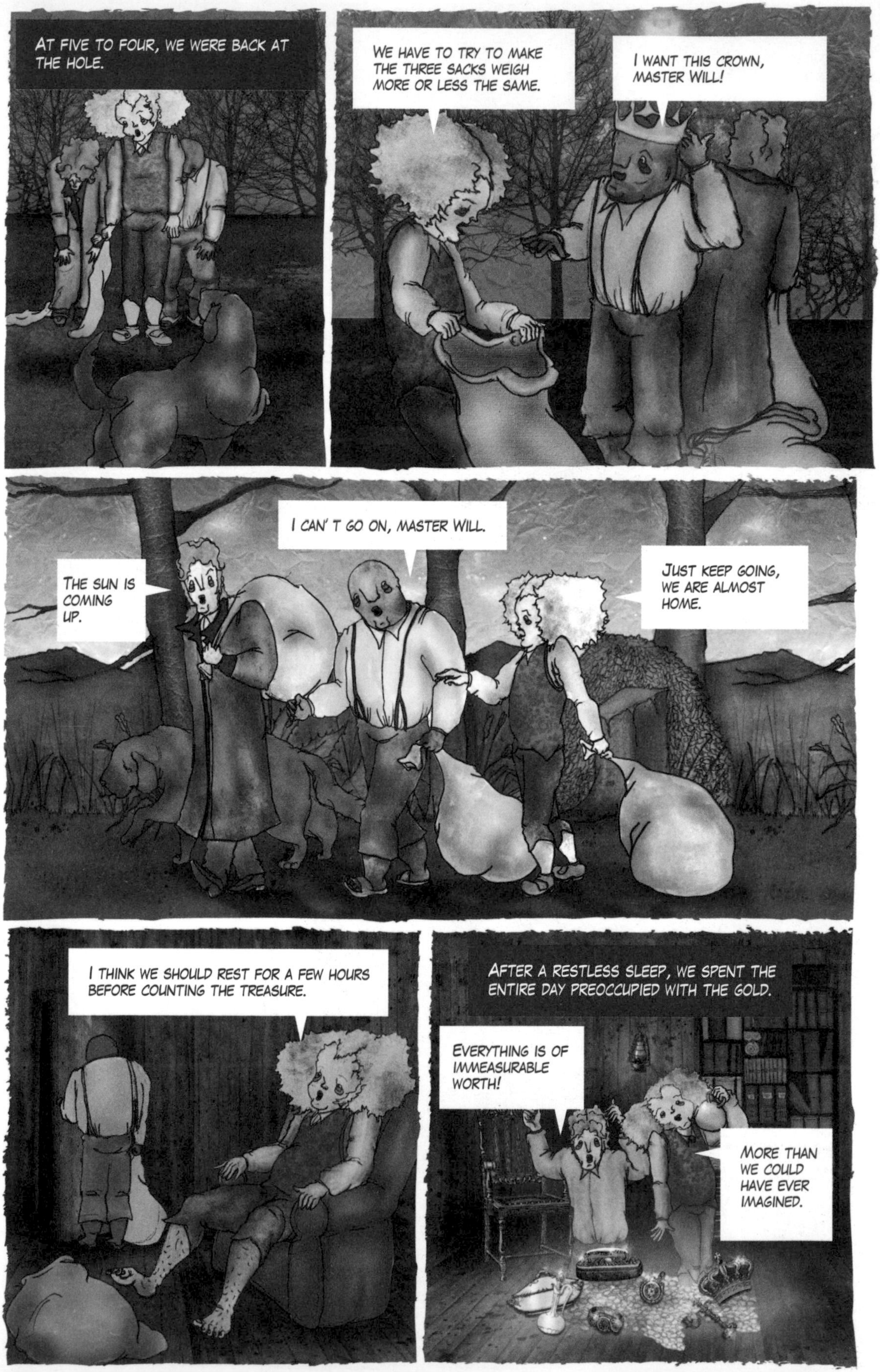
AT FIVE TO FOUR, WE WERE BACK AT THE HOLE.
WE HAVE TO TRY TO MAKE THE THREE SACKS WEIGH MORE OR LESS THE SAME.
I WANT THIS CROWN, MASTER WILL!
THE SUN IS COMING UP.
I CAN' T GO ON, MASTER WILL.
JUST KEEP GOING, WE ARE ALMOST HOME.
I THINK WE SHOULD REST FOR A FEW HOURS BEFORE COUNTING THE TREASURE.
AFTER A RESTLESS SLEEP, WE SPENT THE ENTIRE DAY PREOCCUPIED WITH THE GOLD.
EVERYTHING IS OF IMMEASURABLE WORTH!
MORE THAN WE COULD HAVE EVER IMAGINED.

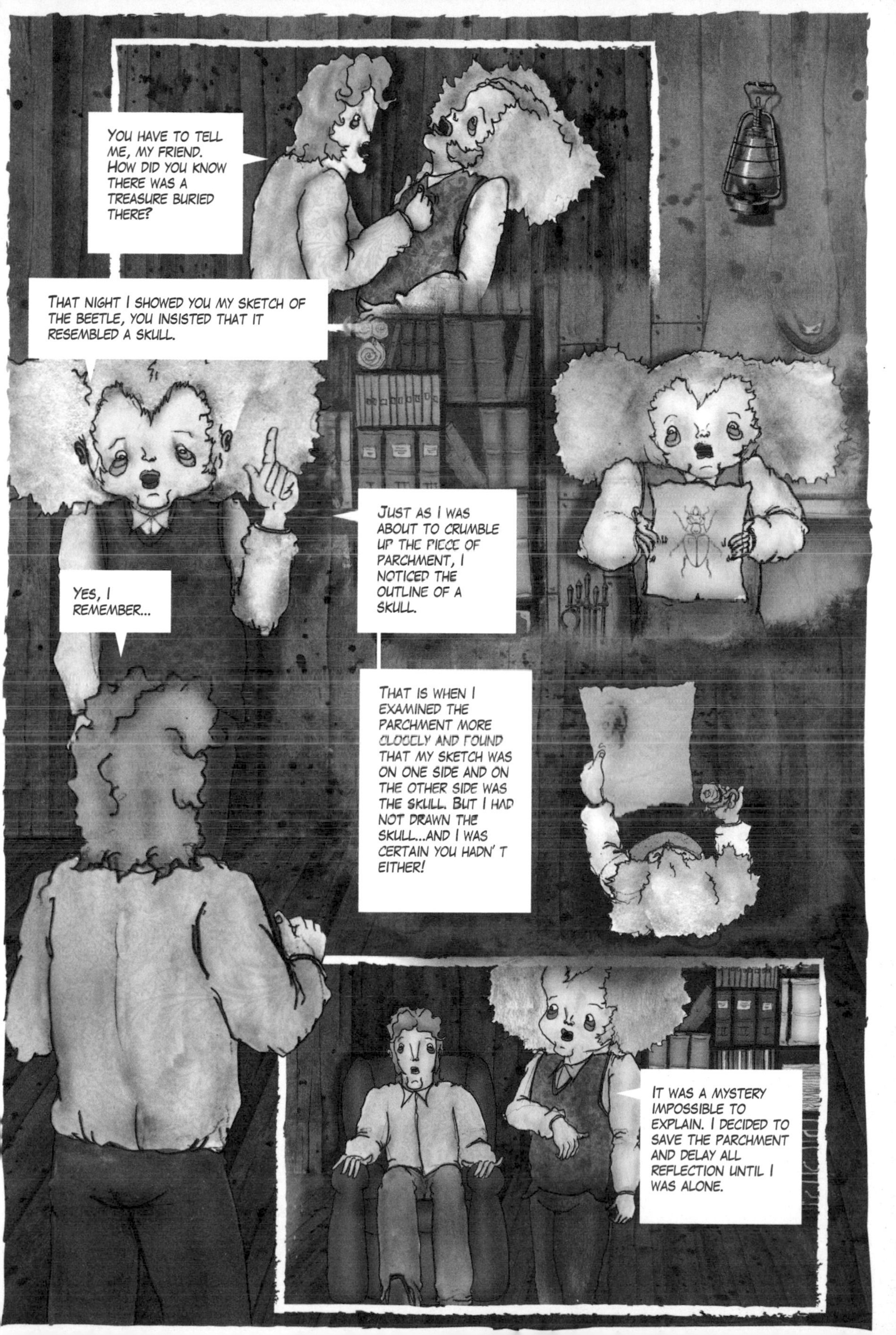
YOU HAVE TO TELL ME, MY FRIEND. HOW DID YOU KNOW THERE WAS A TREASURE BURIED THERE?
THAT NIGHT I SHOWED YOU MY SKETCH OF THE BEETLE, YOU INSISTED THAT IT RESEMBLED A SKULL.
YES, I REMEMBER...
JUST AS I WAS ABOUT TO CRUMBLE UP THE PIECE OF PARCHMENT, I NOTICED THE OUTLINE OF A SKULL.
THAT IS WHEN I EXAMINED THE PARCHMENT MORE CLOSELY AND FOUND THAT MY SKETCH WAS ON ONE SIDE AND ON THE OTHER SIDE WAS THE SKULL. BUT I HAD NOT DRAWN THE SKULL...AND I WAS CERTAIN YOU HADN' T EITHER!
IT WAS A MYSTERY IMPOSSIBLE TO EXPLAIN. I DECIDED TO SAVE THE PARCHMENT AND DELAY ALL REFLECTION UNTIL I WAS ALONE.

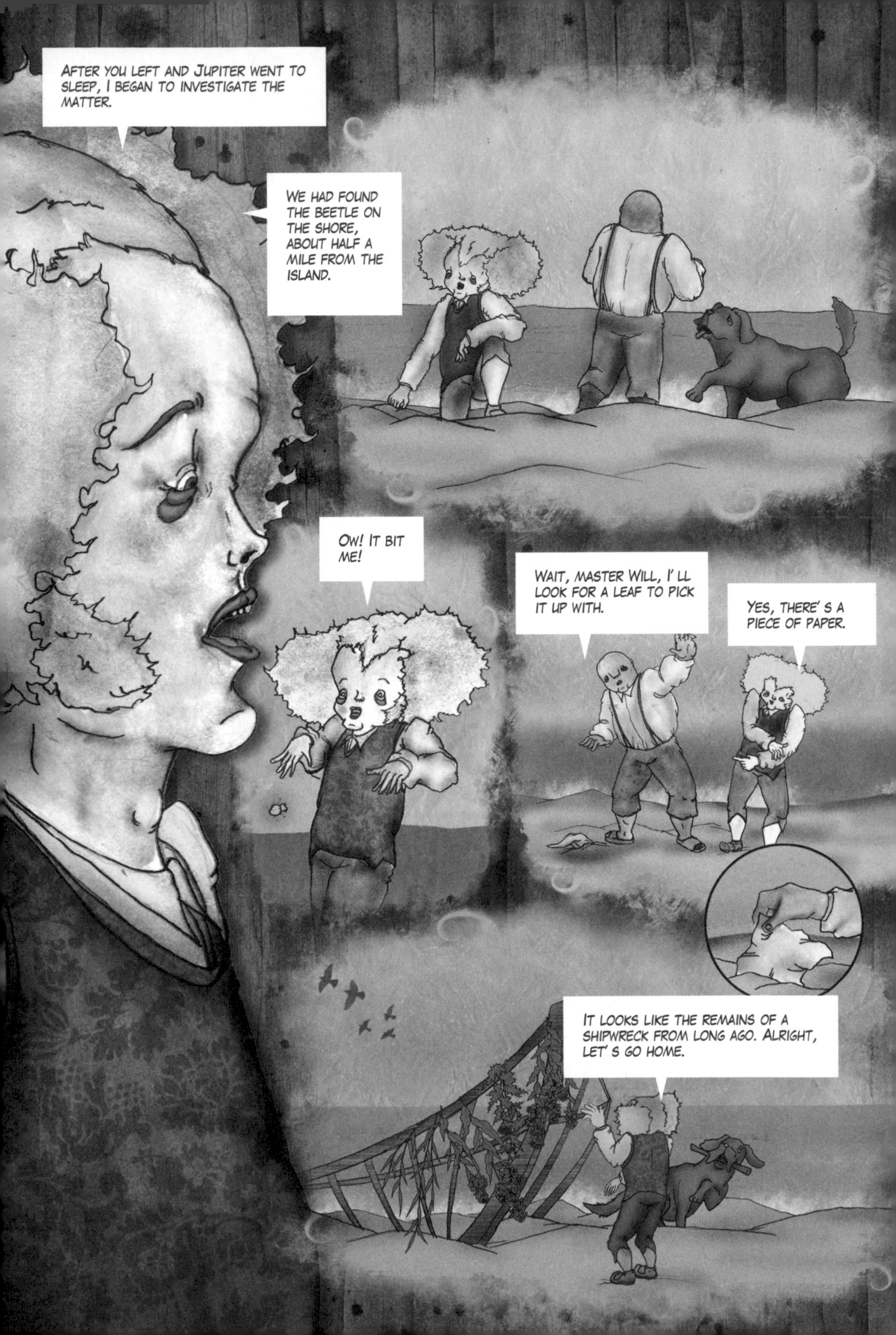
AFTER YOU LEFT AND JUPITER WENT TO SLEEP, I BEGAN TO INVESTIGATE THE MATTER.
WE HAD FOUND THE BEETLE ON THE SHORE, ABOUT HALF A MILE FROM THE ISLAND.
OW! IT BIT ME!
WAIT, MASTER WILL, I' LL LOOK FOR A LEAF TO PICK IT UP WITH.
YES, THERE' S A PIECE OF PAPER.
IT LOOKS LIKE THE REMAINS OF A SHIPWRECK FROM LONG AGO. ALRIGHT, LET' S GO HOME.

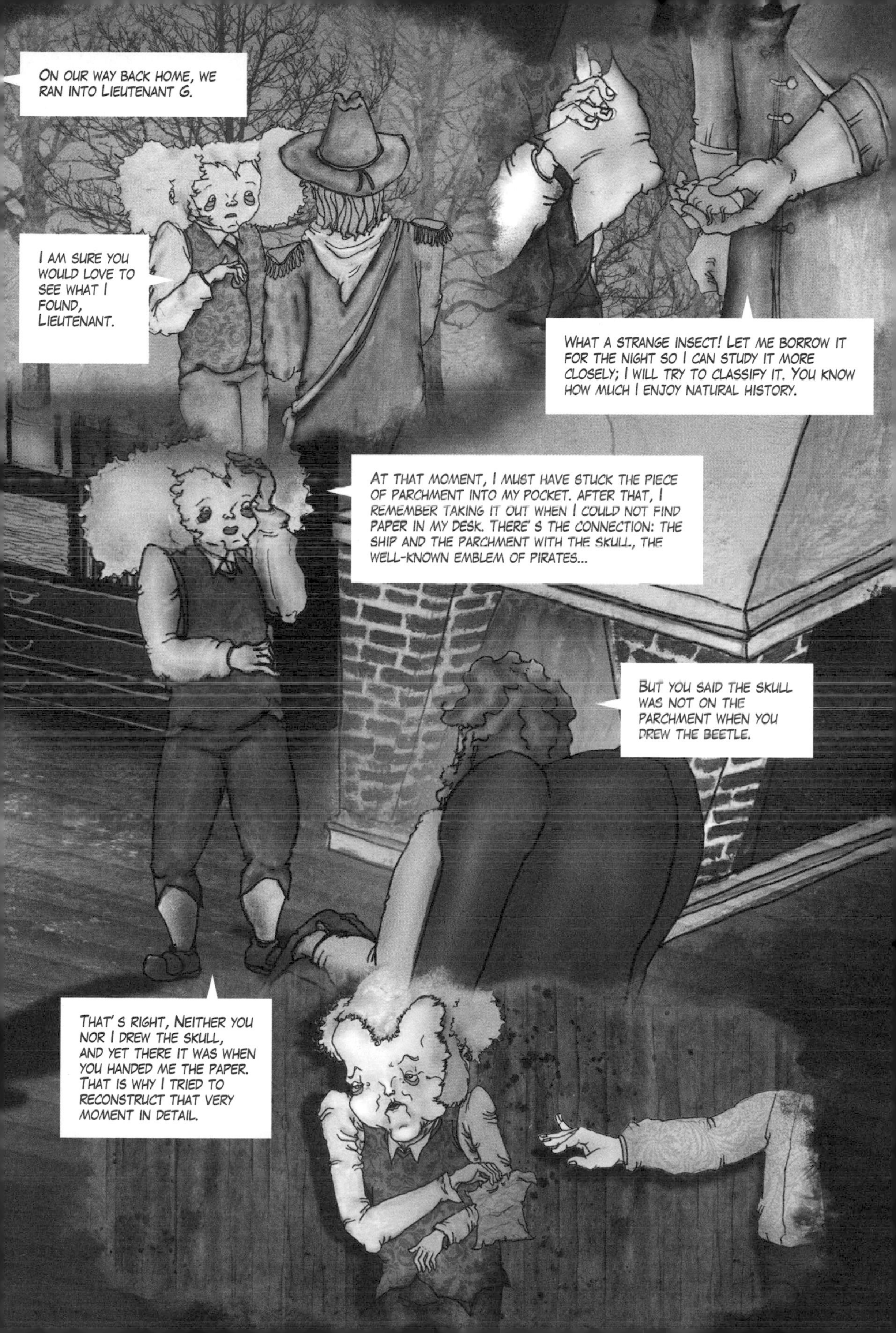

ON OUR WAY BACK HOME, WE RAN INTO LIEUTENANT G.
I AM SURE YOU WOULD LOVE TO SEE WHAT I FOUND, LIEUTENANT.
WHAT A STRANGE INSECT! LET ME BORROW IT FOR THE NIGHT SO I CAN STUDY IT MORE CLOSELY; I WILL TRY TO CLASSIFY IT. YOU KNOW HOW MUCH I ENJOY NATURAL HISTORY.
AT THAT MOMENT, I MUST HAVE STUCK THE PIECE OF PARCHMENT INTO MY POCKET. AFTER THAT, I REMEMBER TAKING IT OUT WHEN I COULD NOT FIND PAPER IN MY DESK. THERE'S THE CONNECTION: THE SHIP AND THE PARCHMENT WITH THE SKULL, THE WELL-KNOWN EMBLEM OF PIRATES...
BUT YOU SAID THE SKULL WAS NOT ON THE PARCHMENT WHEN YOU DREW THE BEETLE.
THAT'S RIGHT, NEITHER YOU NOR I DREW THE SKULL, AND YET THERE IT WAS WHEN YOU HANDED ME THE PAPER. THAT IS WHY I TRIED TO RECONSTRUCT THAT VERY MOMENT IN DETAIL.

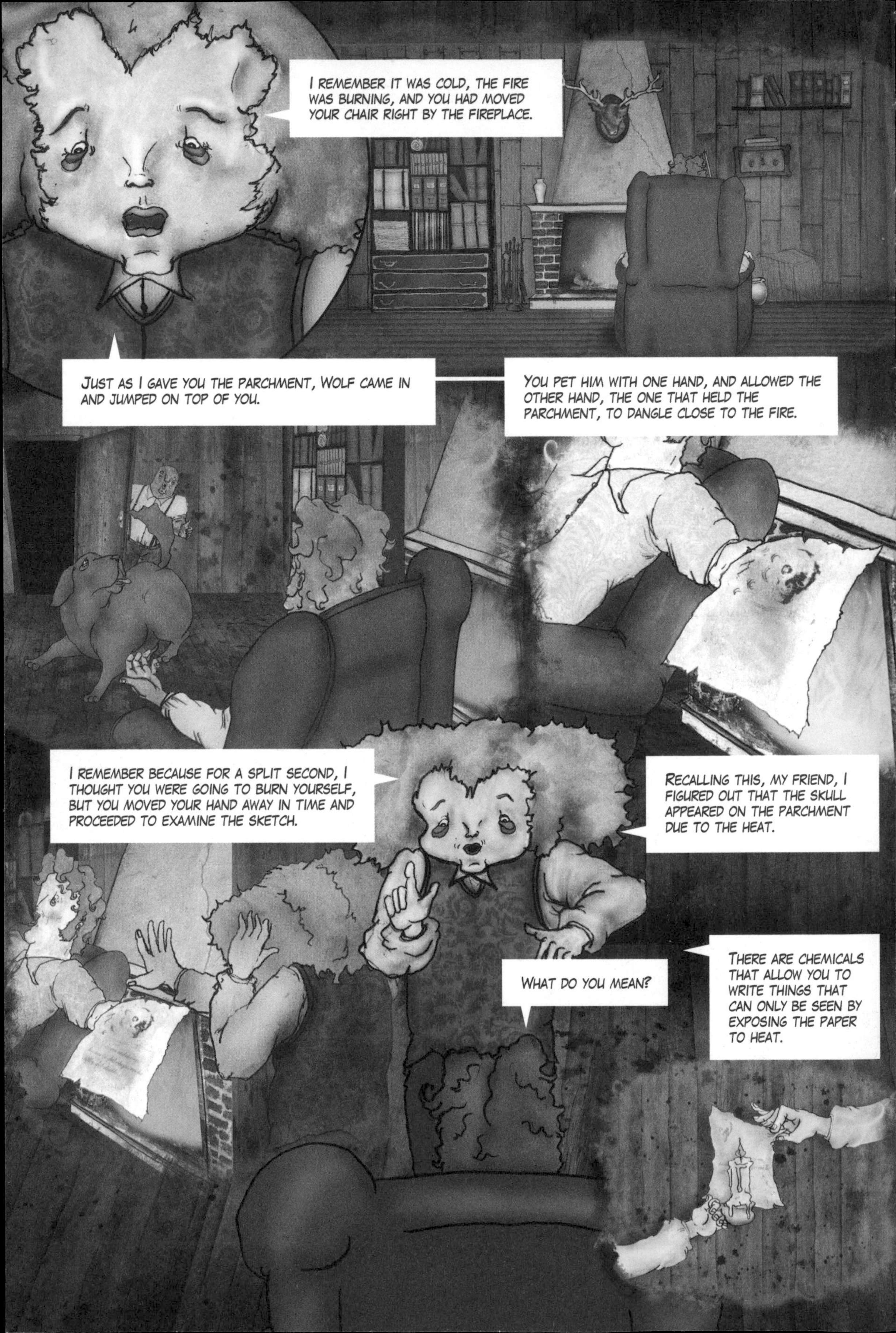
I REMEMBER IT WAS COLD, THE FIRE WAS BURNING, AND YOU HAD MOVED YOUR CHAIR RIGHT BY THE FIREPLACE.
JUST AS I GAVE YOU THE PARCHMENT, WOLF CAME IN AND JUMPED ON TOP OF YOU.
YOU PET HIM WITH ONE HAND, AND ALLOWED THE OTHER HAND, THE ONE THAT HELD THE PARCHMENT, TO DANGLE CLOSE TO THE FIRE.
I REMEMBER BECAUSE FOR A SPLIT SECOND, I THOUGHT YOU WERE GOING TO BURN YOURSELF, BUT YOU MOVED YOUR HAND AWAY IN TIME AND PROCEEDED TO EXAMINE THE SKETCH.
RECALLING THIS, MY FRIEND, I FIGURED OUT THAT THE SKULL APPEARED ON THE PARCHMENT DUE TO THE HEAT.
WHAT DO YOU MEAN?
THERE ARE CHEMICALS THAT ALLOW YOU TO WRITE THINGS THAT CAN ONLY BE SEEN BY EXPOSING THE PAPER TO HEAT.

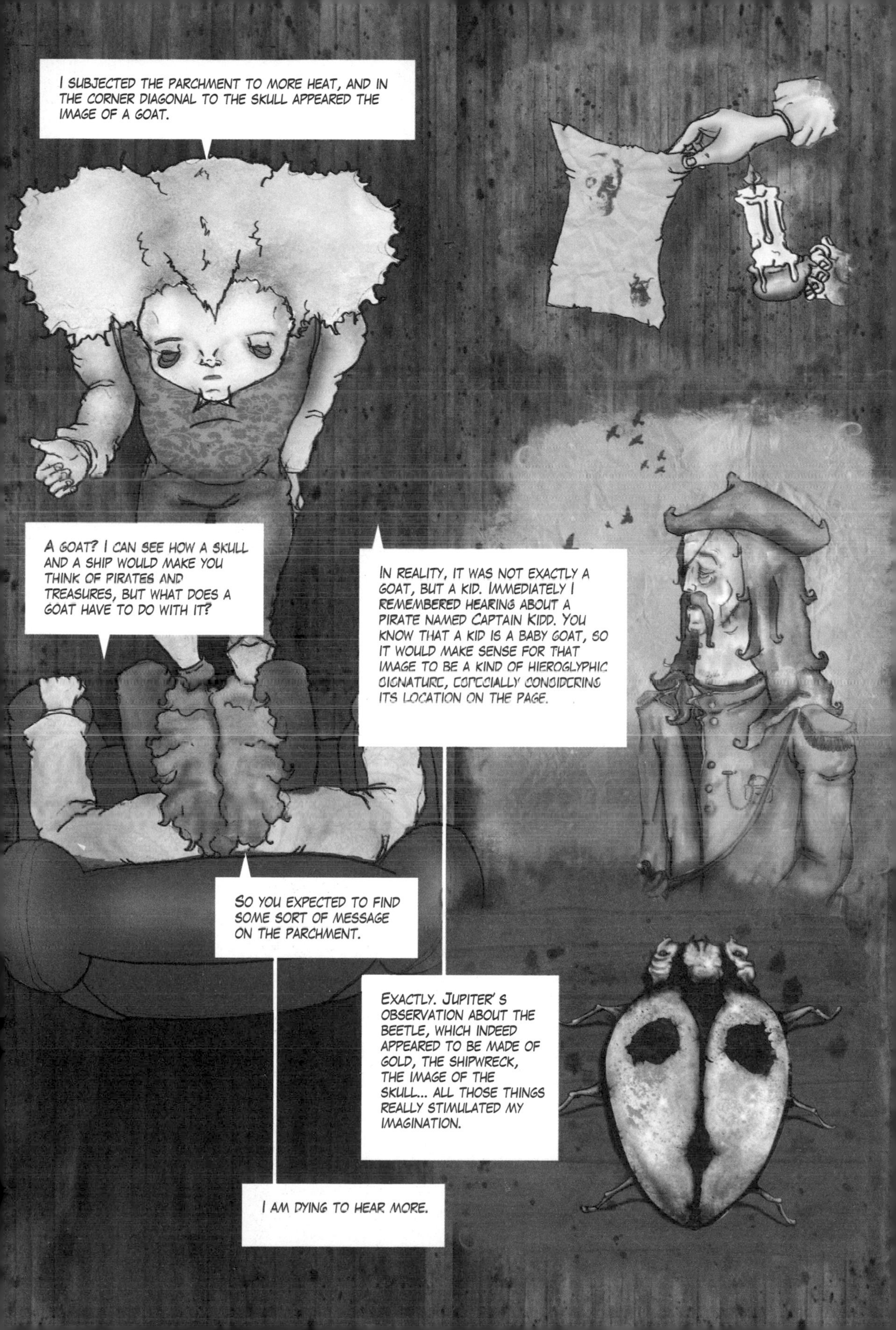
I subjected the parchment to more heat, and in the corner diagonal to the skull appeared the image of a goat.
A goat? I can see how a skull and a ship would make you think of pirates and treasures, but what does a goat have to do with it?
In reality, it was not exactly a goat, but a kid. Immediately I remembered hearing about a pirate named Captain Kidd. You know that a kid is a baby goat, so it would make sense for that image to be a kind of hieroglyphic signature, especially considering its location on the page.
So you expected to find some sort of message on the parchment.
Exactly. Jupiter's observation about the beetle, which indeed appeared to be made of gold, the shipwreck, the image of the skull... all those things really stimulated my imagination.
I am dying to hear more.

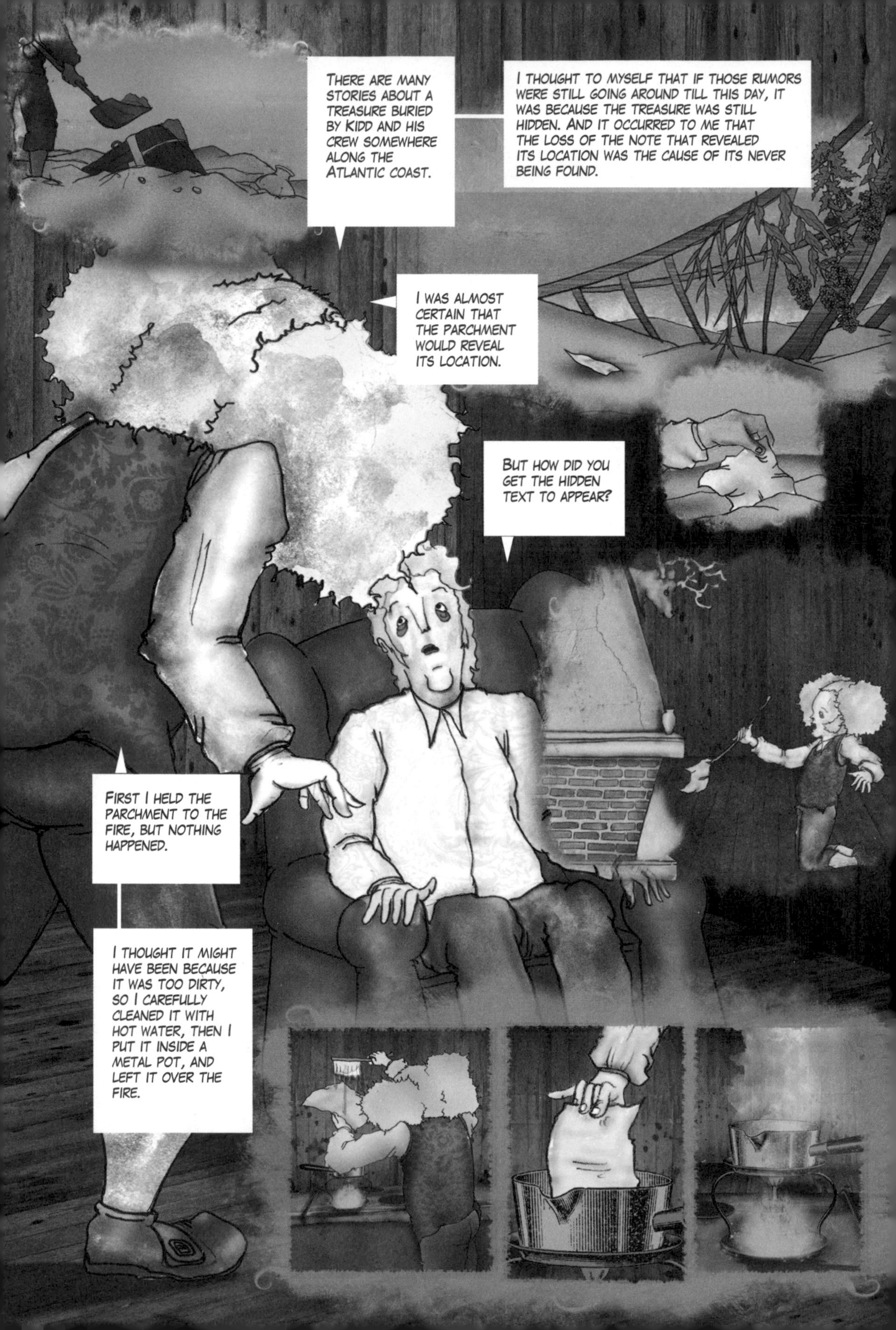
There are many stories about a treasure buried by Kidd and his crew somewhere along the Atlantic coast.
I thought to myself that if those rumors were still going around till this day, it was because the treasure was still hidden. And it occurred to me that the loss of the note that revealed its location was the cause of its never being found.
I was almost certain that the parchment would reveal its location.
But how did you get the hidden text to appear?
First I held the parchment to the fire, but nothing happened.
I thought it might have been because it was too dirty, so I carefully cleaned it with hot water, then I put it inside a metal pot, and left it over the fire.

LEGRAND THEN PROCEEDED TO REHEAT THE PARCHMENT AND GAVE IT TO ME TO INSPECT. WHAT I SAW LEFT ME COMPLETELY CONFUSED.

AND NOW YOU WILL SEE WHAT APPEARED.

DESPITE HAVING BEARED WITNESS TO THE DISCOVERY OF THE MOST VALUABLE TREASURE IN THE WORLD, I AM INCAPABLE OF DECODING WHAT THIS SAYS.

53‡‡†305))6*; 4826)4‡.)
4‡);806*;48†8¶60))85; 1‡
(;:‡*8†83(88)5*†;46 (;8
8*96*?;8)*‡(;485); 5*†
2:*‡(;4956*2(5*—4) 8¶
8*;4069285);)6†8) 4‡‡
;1(‡9;48081;8:8‡1;48†
85;4)485†528806*81(‡
9;48;(88;4(‡?34;48)4‡
;161;:188;‡?;

RIGHT AWAY I DID NOT THINK THAT FINDING THE SOLUTION WOULD PROVE TOO DIFFICULT. FROM WHAT I HEARD ABOUT KIDD, HE DID NOT SEEM CAPABLE OF CONSTRUCTING COMPLICATED CRYPTOGRAMS.

SO YOU WERE ABLE TO SOLVE IT?

I HAVE SOLVED PUZZLES THAT WERE TEN THOUSAND TIMES MORE DIFFICULT. HAS ONE HUMAN MIND EVER CONSTRUCTED AN ENIGMA THAT ANOTHER HUMAN MIND COULD NOT ULTIMATELY SOLVE?

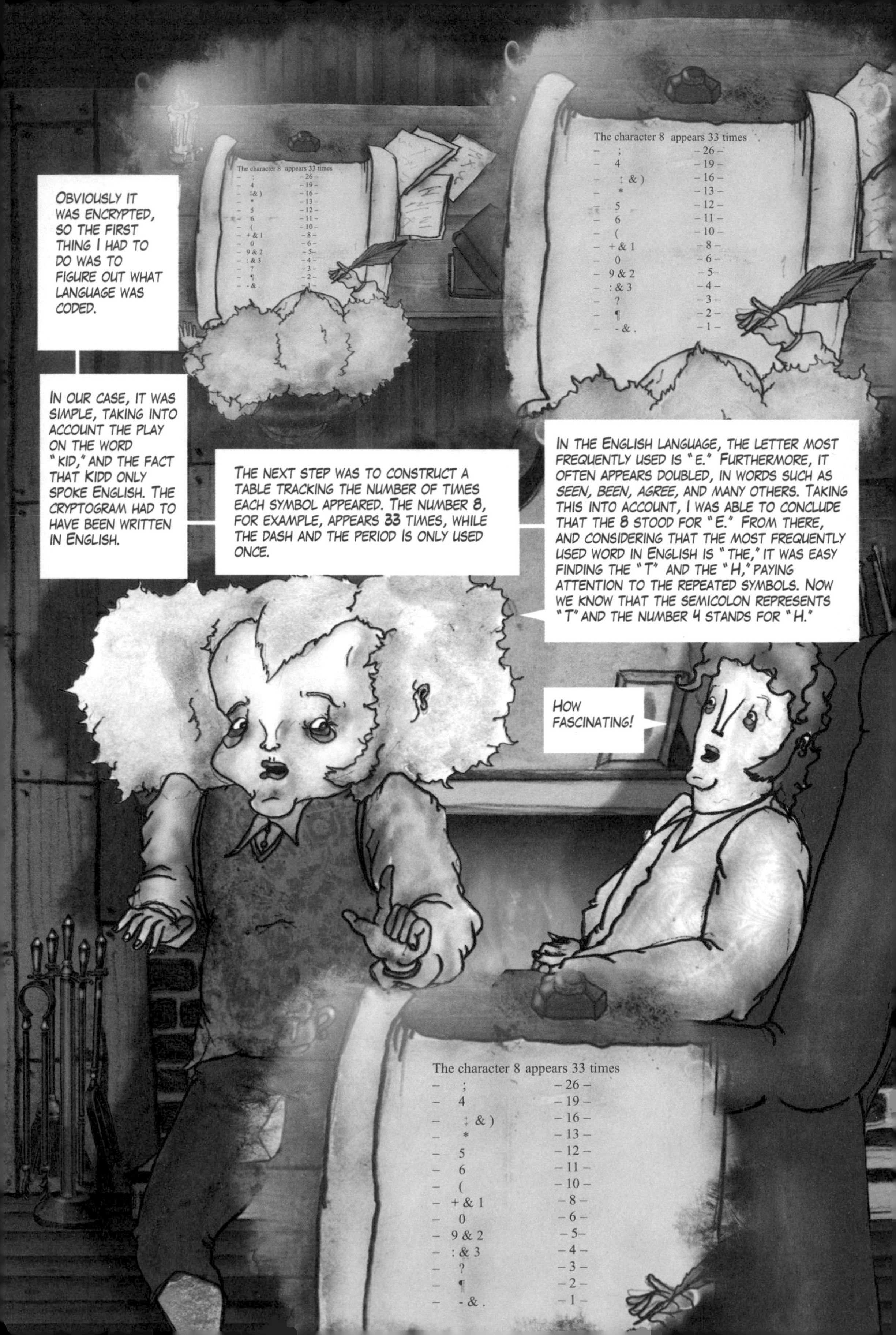

OBVIOUSLY IT WAS ENCRYPTED, SO THE FIRST THING I HAD TO DO WAS TO FIGURE OUT WHAT LANGUAGE WAS CODED.
IN OUR CASE, IT WAS SIMPLE, TAKING INTO ACCOUNT THE PLAY ON THE WORD "KID," AND THE FACT THAT KIDD ONLY SPOKE ENGLISH. THE CRYPTOGRAM HAD TO HAVE BEEN WRITTEN IN ENGLISH.
THE NEXT STEP WAS TO CONSTRUCT A TABLE TRACKING THE NUMBER OF TIMES EACH SYMBOL APPEARED. THE NUMBER 8, FOR EXAMPLE, APPEARS 33 TIMES, WHILE THE DASH AND THE PERIOD IS ONLY USED ONCE.
IN THE ENGLISH LANGUAGE, THE LETTER MOST FREQUENTLY USED IS "E." FURTHERMORE, IT OFTEN APPEARS DOUBLED, IN WORDS SUCH AS SEEN, BEEN, AGREE, AND MANY OTHERS. TAKING THIS INTO ACCOUNT, I WAS ABLE TO CONCLUDE THAT THE 8 STOOD FOR "E." FROM THERE, AND CONSIDERING THAT THE MOST FREQUENTLY USED WORD IN ENGLISH IS "THE," IT WAS EASY FINDING THE "T" AND THE "H," PAYING ATTENTION TO THE REPEATED SYMBOLS. NOW WE KNOW THAT THE SEMICOLON REPRESENTS "T" AND THE NUMBER 4 STANDS FOR "H."
HOW FASCINATING!
The character 8 appears 33 times
– ; – 26 –
– 4 – 19 –
– ‡ &) – 16 –
– * – 13 –
– 5 – 12 –
– 6 – 11 –
– (– 10 –
– + & 1 – 8 –
– 0 – 6 –
– 9 & 2 – 5–
– : & 3 – 4 –
– ? – 3 –
– ¶ – 2 –
– - & . – 1 –

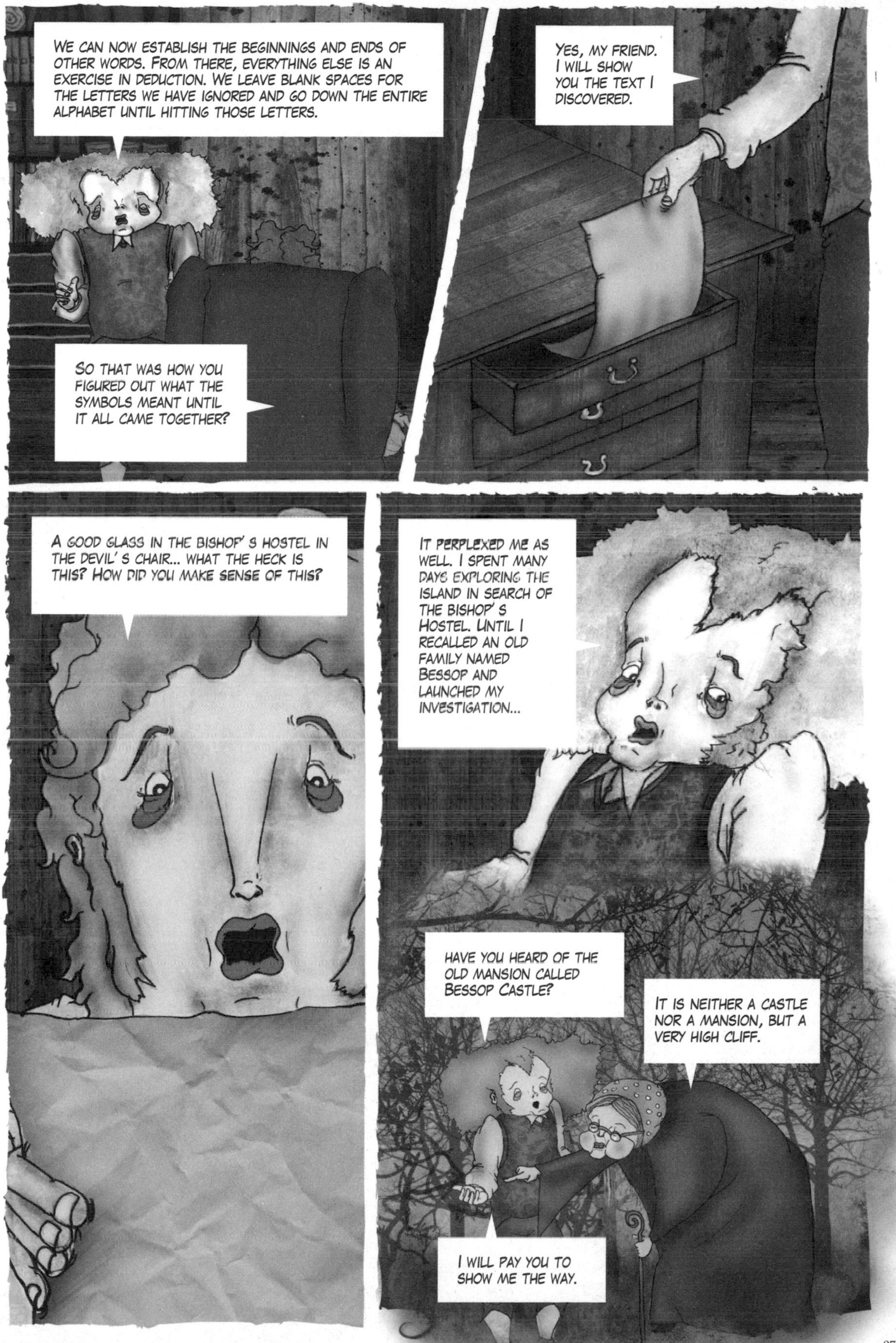
WE CAN NOW ESTABLISH THE BEGINNINGS AND ENDS OF OTHER WORDS. FROM THERE, EVERYTHING ELSE IS AN EXERCISE IN DEDUCTION. WE LEAVE BLANK SPACES FOR THE LETTERS WE HAVE IGNORED AND GO DOWN THE ENTIRE ALPHABET UNTIL HITTING THOSE LETTERS.
SO THAT WAS HOW YOU FIGURED OUT WHAT THE SYMBOLS MEANT UNTIL IT ALL CAME TOGETHER?
YES, MY FRIEND. I WILL SHOW YOU THE TEXT I DISCOVERED.
A GOOD GLASS IN THE BISHOP' S HOSTEL IN THE DEVIL' S CHAIR... WHAT THE HECK IS THIS? HOW DID YOU MAKE SENSE OF THIS?
IT PERPLEXED ME AS WELL. I SPENT MANY DAYS EXPLORING THE ISLAND IN SEARCH OF THE BISHOP' S HOSTEL. UNTIL I RECALLED AN OLD FAMILY NAMED BESSOP AND LAUNCHED MY INVESTIGATION...
HAVE YOU HEARD OF THE OLD MANSION CALLED BESSOP CASTLE?
IT IS NEITHER A CASTLE NOR A MANSION, BUT A VERY HIGH CLIFF.
I WILL PAY YOU TO SHOW ME THE WAY.

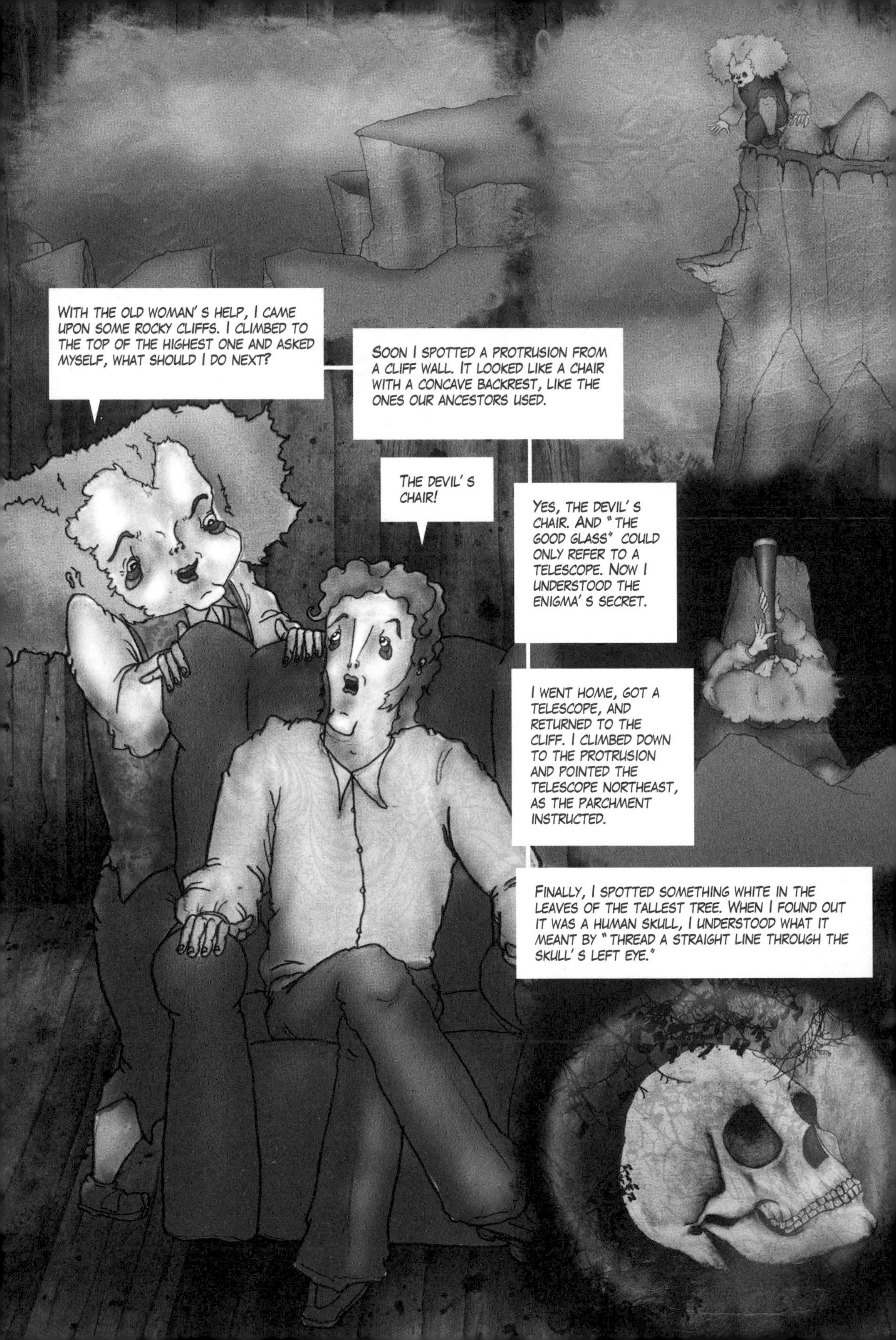
WITH THE OLD WOMAN'S HELP, I CAME UPON SOME ROCKY CLIFFS. I CLIMBED TO THE TOP OF THE HIGHEST ONE AND ASKED MYSELF, WHAT SHOULD I DO NEXT?
SOON I SPOTTED A PROTRUSION FROM A CLIFF WALL. IT LOOKED LIKE A CHAIR WITH A CONCAVE BACKREST, LIKE THE ONES OUR ANCESTORS USED.
THE DEVIL'S CHAIR!
YES, THE DEVIL'S CHAIR. AND "THE GOOD GLASS" COULD ONLY REFER TO A TELESCOPE. NOW I UNDERSTOOD THE ENIGMA'S SECRET.
I WENT HOME, GOT A TELESCOPE, AND RETURNED TO THE CLIFF. I CLIMBED DOWN TO THE PROTRUSION AND POINTED THE TELESCOPE NORTHEAST, AS THE PARCHMENT INSTRUCTED.
FINALLY, I SPOTTED SOMETHING WHITE IN THE LEAVES OF THE TALLEST TREE. WHEN I FOUND OUT IT WAS A HUMAN SKULL, I UNDERSTOOD WHAT IT MEANT BY "THREAD A STRAIGHT LINE THROUGH THE SKULL'S LEFT EYE."

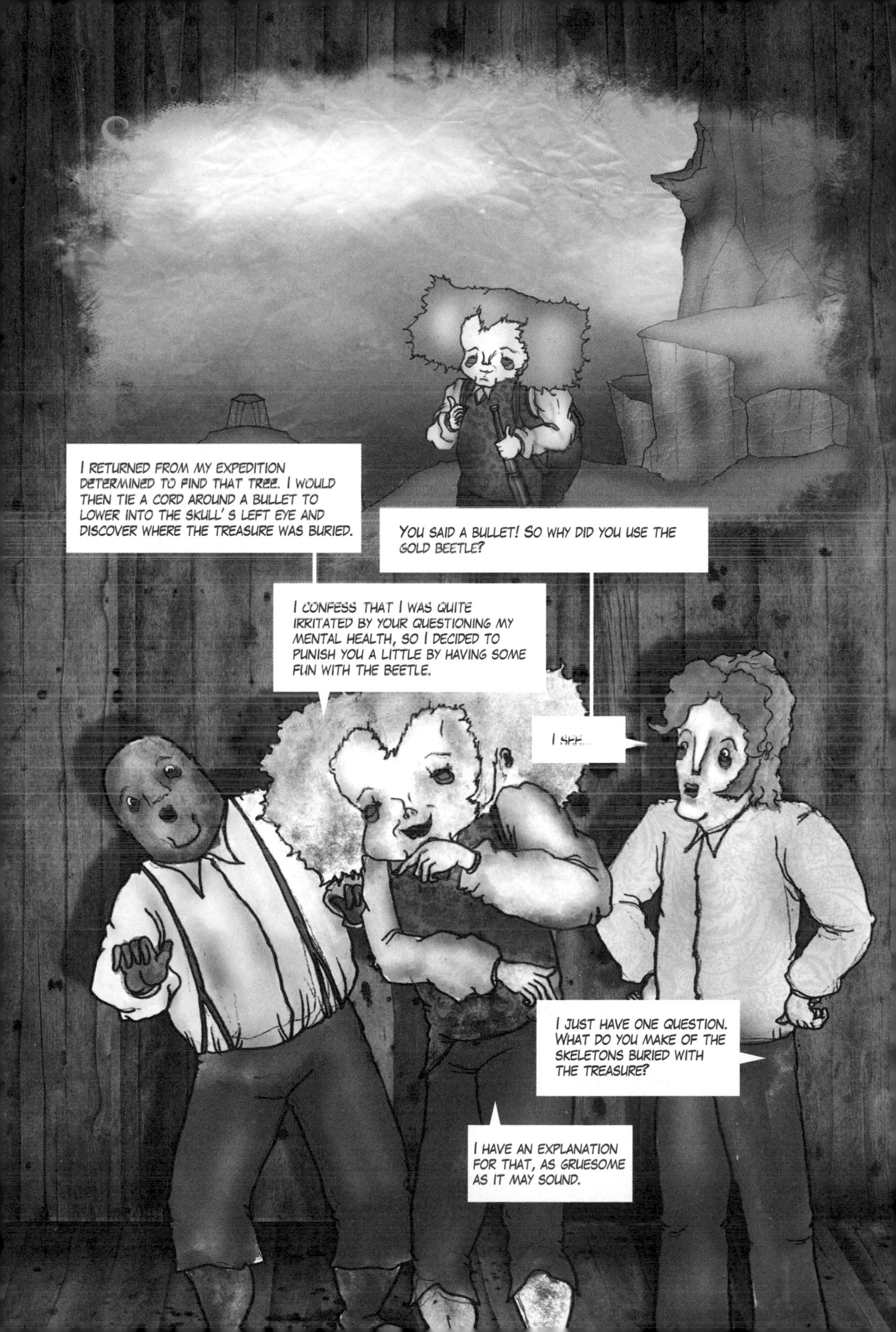
I RETURNED FROM MY EXPEDITION DETERMINED TO FIND THAT TREE. I WOULD THEN TIE A CORD AROUND A BULLET TO LOWER INTO THE SKULL'S LEFT EYE AND DISCOVER WHERE THE TREASURE WAS BURIED.
YOU SAID A BULLET! SO WHY DID YOU USE THE GOLD BEETLE?
I CONFESS THAT I WAS QUITE IRRITATED BY YOUR QUESTIONING MY MENTAL HEALTH, SO I DECIDED TO PUNISH YOU A LITTLE BY HAVING SOME FUN WITH THE BEETLE.
I SEE...
I JUST HAVE ONE QUESTION. WHAT DO YOU MAKE OF THE SKELETONS BURIED WITH THE TREASURE?
I HAVE AN EXPLANATION FOR THAT, AS GRUESOME AS IT MAY SOUND.

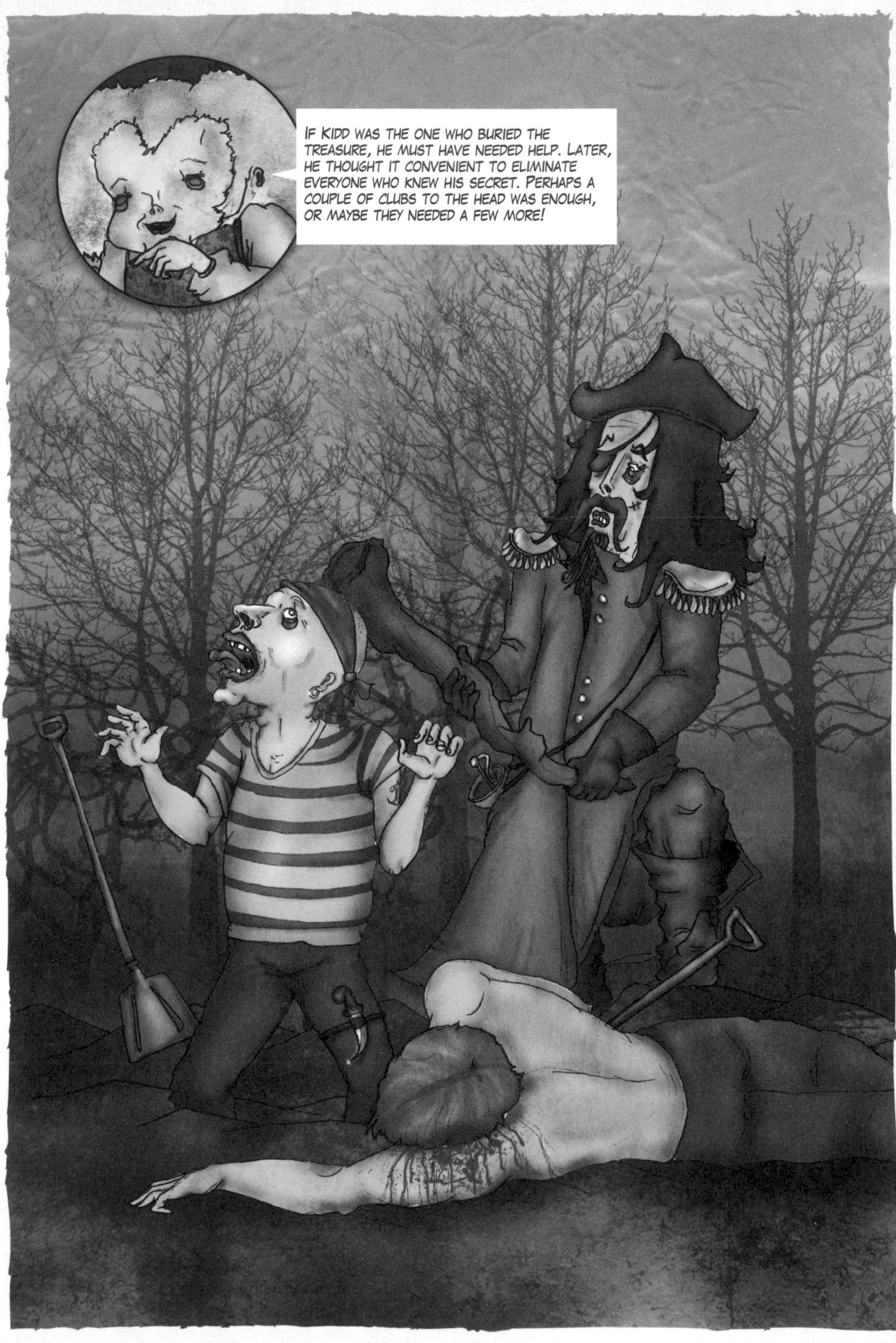
IF KIDD WAS THE ONE WHO BURIED THE TREASURE, HE MUST HAVE NEEDED HELP. LATER, HE THOUGHT IT CONVENIENT TO ELIMINATE EVERYONE WHO KNEW HIS SECRET. PERHAPS A COUPLE OF CLUBS TO THE HEAD WAS ENOUGH, OR MAYBE THEY NEEDED A FEW MORE!

THE SYSTEM OF DOCTOR TARR AND PROFESSOR FETHER

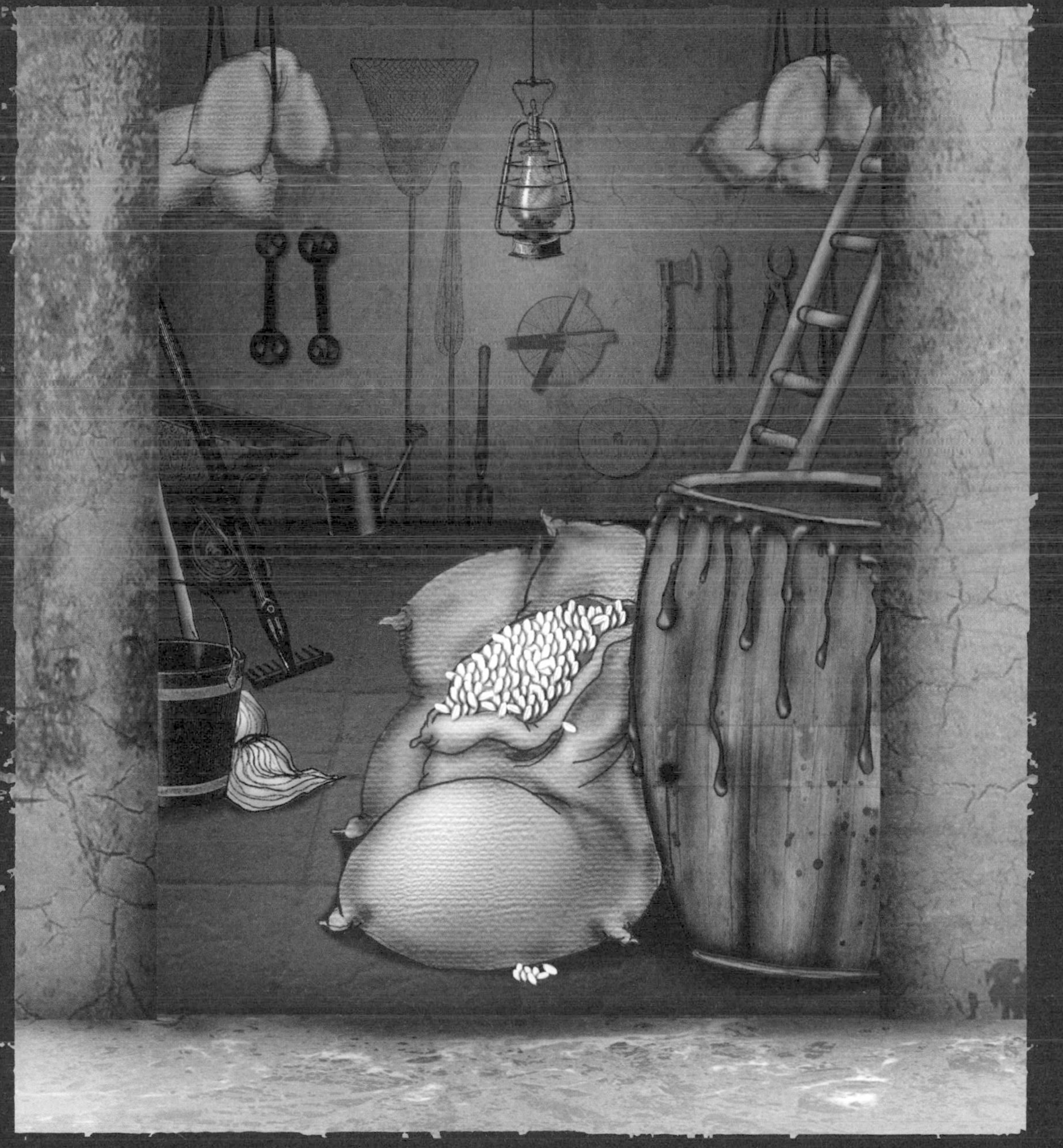

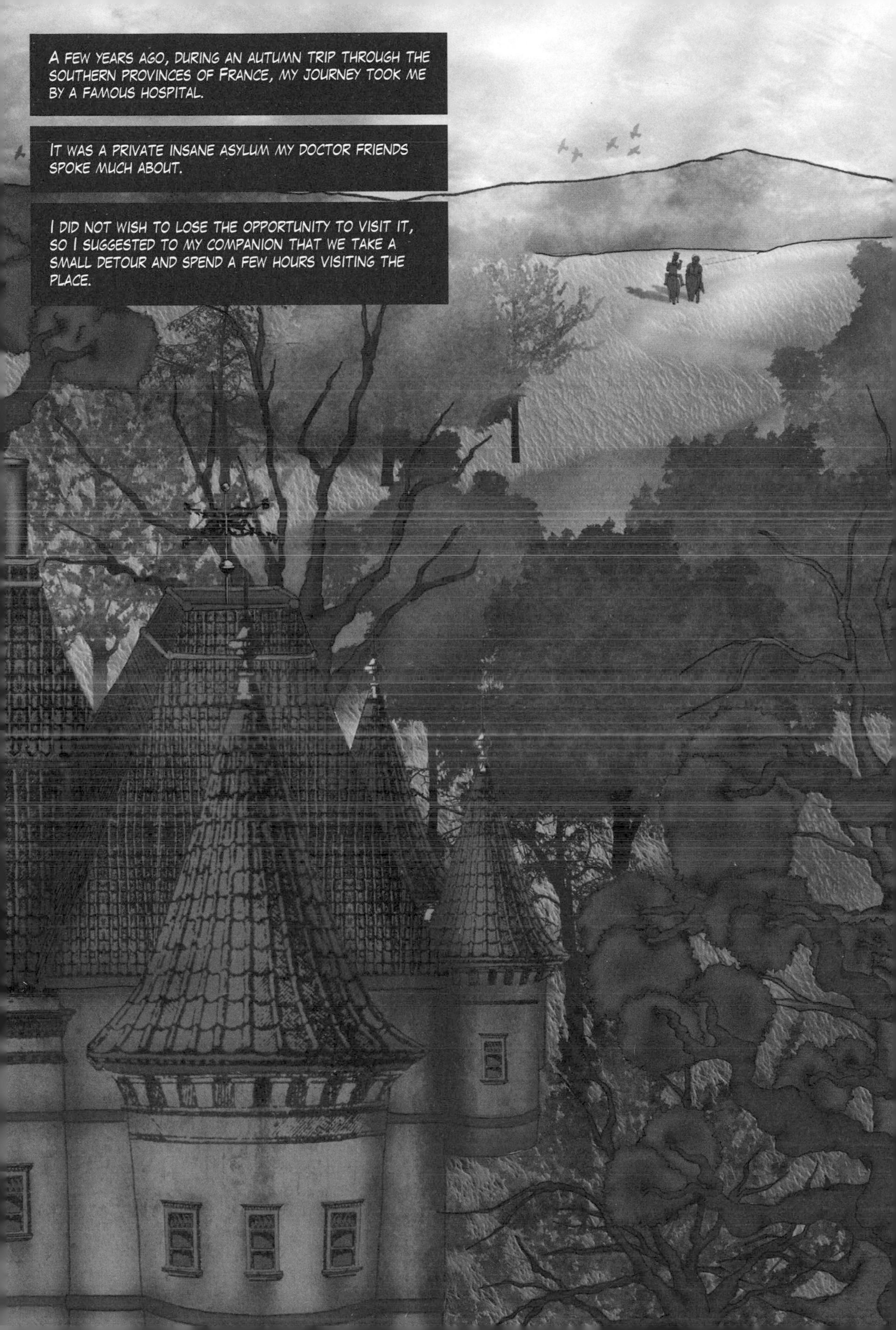
A few years ago, during an autumn trip through the southern provinces of France, my journey took me by a famous hospital.
It was a private insane asylum my doctor friends spoke much about.
I did not wish to lose the opportunity to visit it, so I suggested to my companion that we take a small detour and spend a few hours visiting the place.

I'M SORRY, MY FRIEND, BUT I MUST CONFESS THAT I WOULD NOT LIKE TO CROSS PATHS WITH A LUNATIC. HOWEVER, PLEASE FEEL FREE TO SATISFY YOUR CURIOSITY. I WILL RIDE SLOWLY SO YOU CAN CATCH UP LATER TODAY OR PERHAPS TOMORROW.

NOW THAT I THINK ABOUT IT, I REALIZE IT WILL PROBABLY BE DIFFICULT TO ENTER THE INSTITUTION.

THAT'S RIGHT, FRIEND. UNLESS YOU HAVE OFFICIAL WRITTEN PERMISSION OR YOU KNOW THE DIRECTOR, MONSIEUR MAILLARD, THEY WILL NOT LET YOU IN. THE RULES IN PRIVATE MENTAL INSTITUTIONS ARE STRICTER THAN THE ONES IN PUBLIC ASYLUMS.

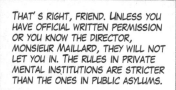

I SUPPOSE I SHOULD JUST FORGET ABOUT VISITING THEN.

NOT SO FAST. I MET MAILLARD A FEW YEARS AGO. I WILL ACCOMPANY YOU TO THE ENTRANCE TO INTRODUCE YOU, THOUGH I HAVE NO INTENTION OF GOING INSIDE. I HAVE ALREADY MADE IT KNOWN THAT I HAVE NO INTEREST IN BEING IN THE COMPANY OF THE DEMENTED.

WE LEFT THE MAIN ROAD AND FOLLOWED A HEAVILY WOODED PATH THAT EVENTUALLY LEAD INTO A THICK FOREST.

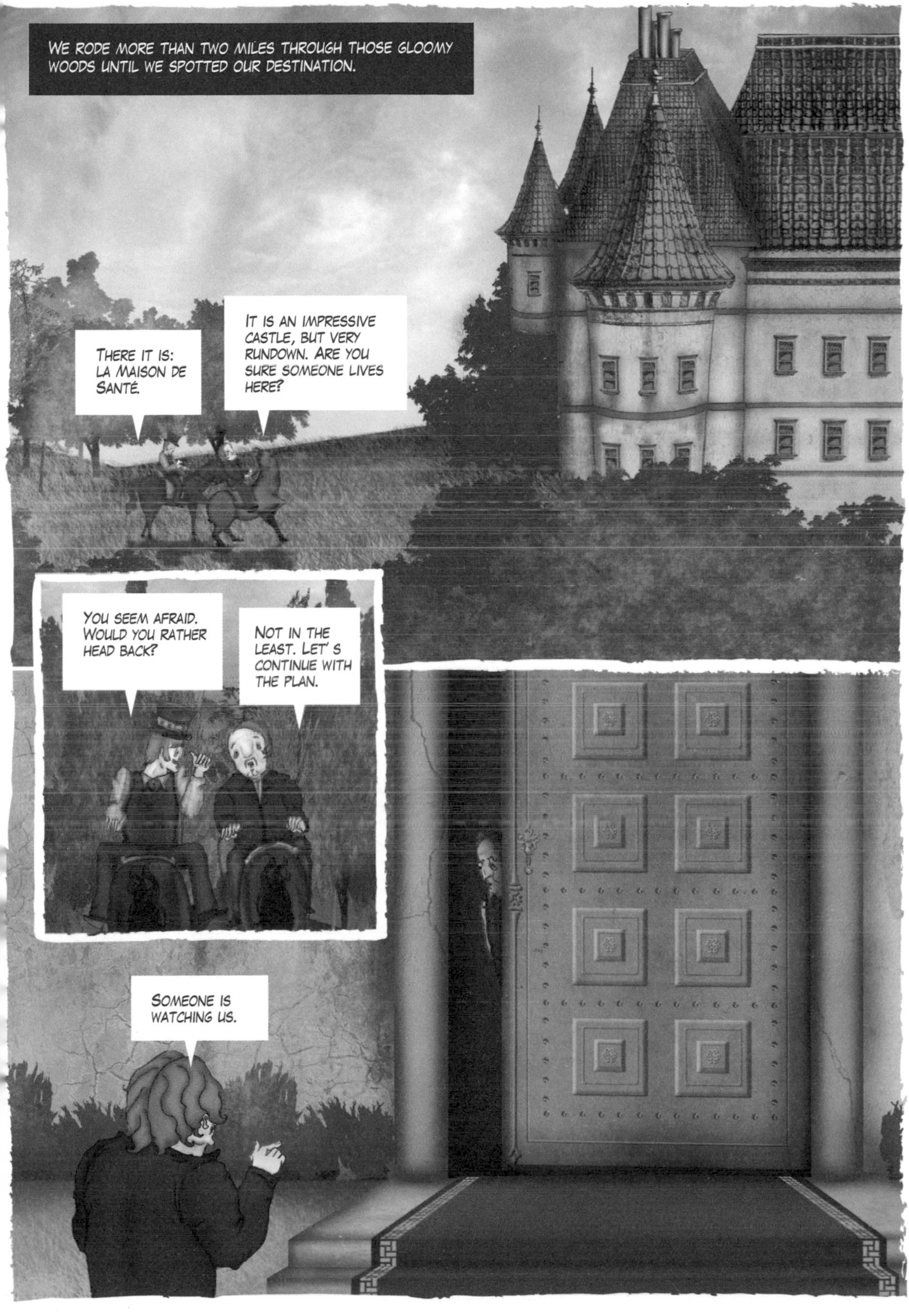
WE RODE MORE THAN TWO MILES THROUGH THOSE GLOOMY WOODS UNTIL WE SPOTTED OUR DESTINATION.
THERE IT IS: LA MAISON DE SANTÉ.
IT IS AN IMPRESSIVE CASTLE, BUT VERY RUNDOWN. ARE YOU SURE SOMEONE LIVES HERE?
YOU SEEM AFRAID. WOULD YOU RATHER HEAD BACK?
NOT IN THE LEAST. LET'S CONTINUE WITH THE PLAN.
SOMEONE IS WATCHING US.

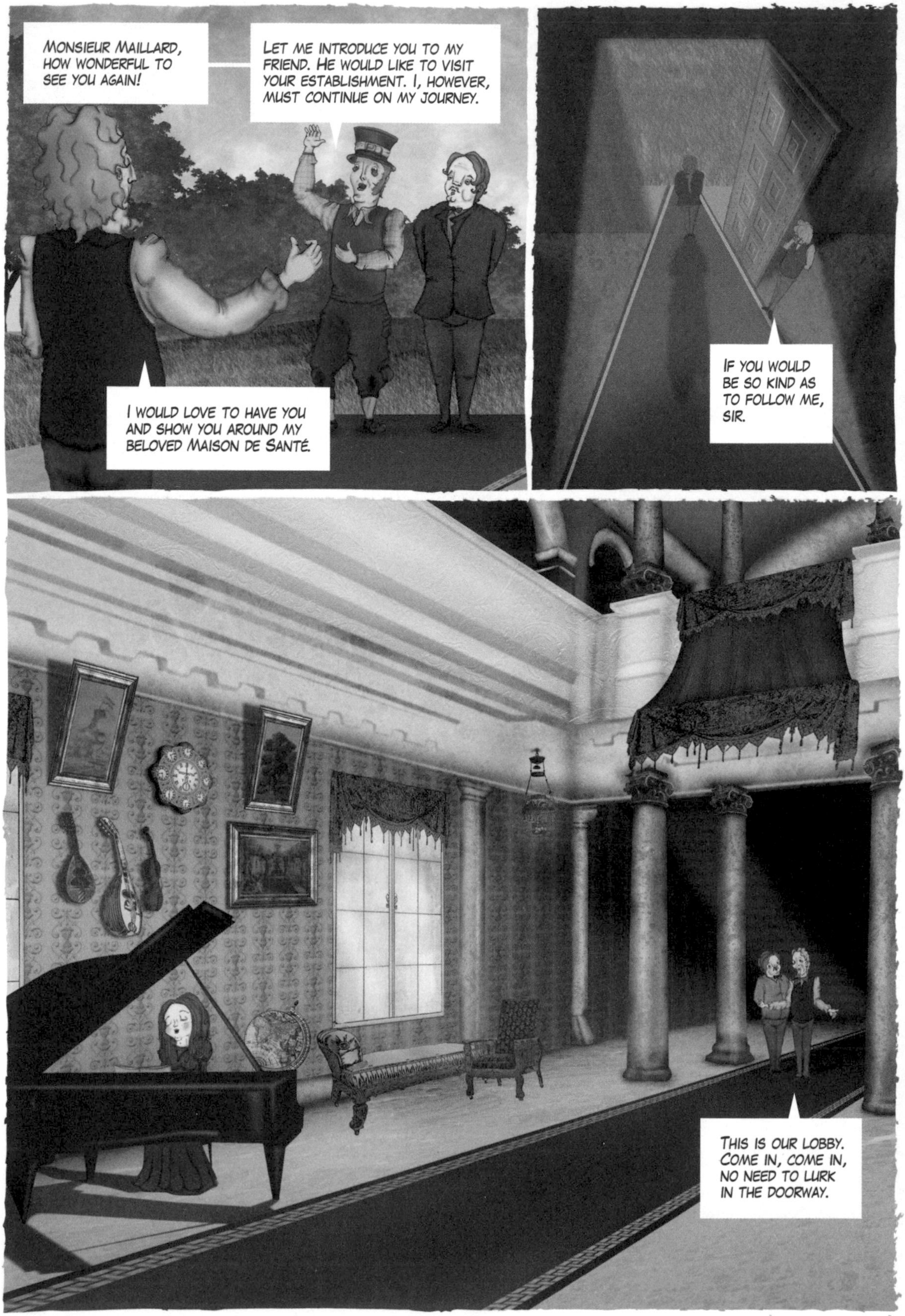
MONSIEUR MAILLARD, HOW WONDERFUL TO SEE YOU AGAIN!
LET ME INTRODUCE YOU TO MY FRIEND. HE WOULD LIKE TO VISIT YOUR ESTABLISHMENT. I, HOWEVER, MUST CONTINUE ON MY JOURNEY.
I WOULD LOVE TO HAVE YOU AND SHOW YOU AROUND MY BELOVED MAISON DE SANTÉ.
IF YOU WOULD BE SO KIND AS TO FOLLOW ME, SIR.
THIS IS OUR LOBBY. COME IN, COME IN, NO NEED TO LURK IN THE DOORWAY.

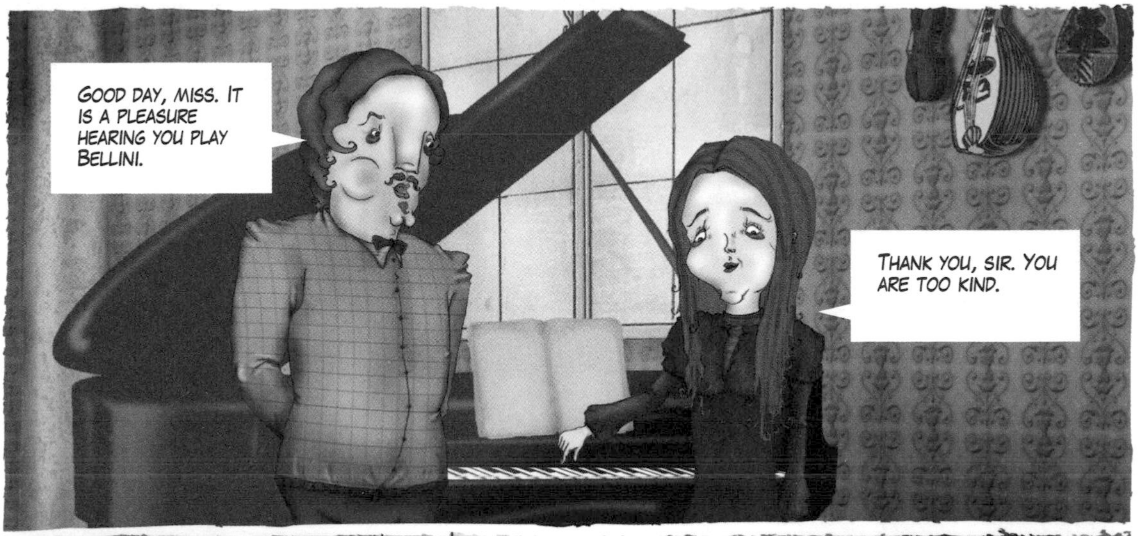
GOOD DAY, MISS. IT IS A PLEASURE HEARING YOU PLAY BELLINI.
THANK YOU, SIR. YOU ARE TOO KIND.

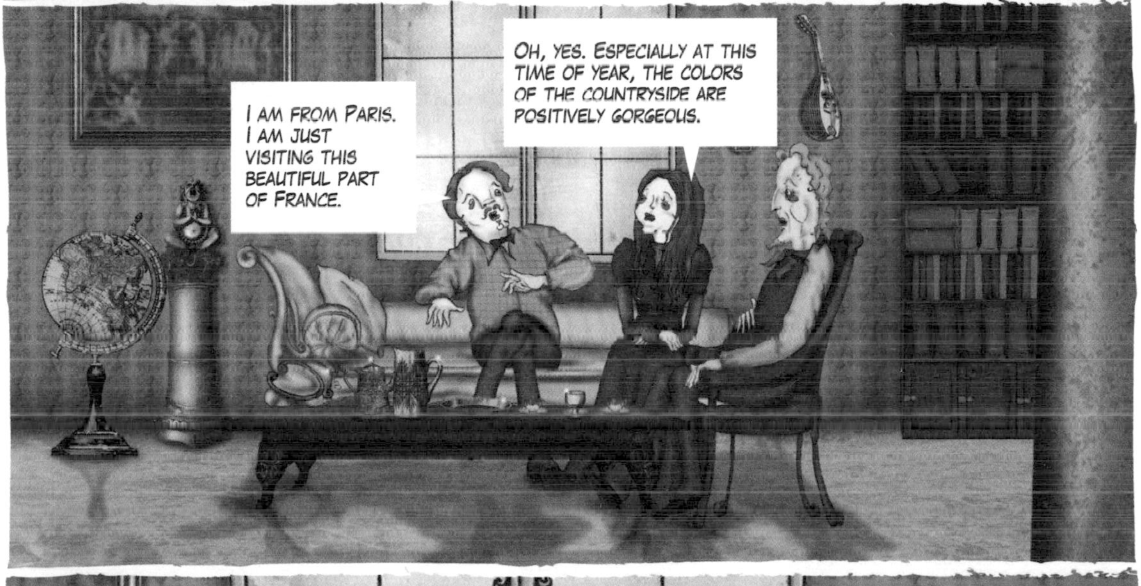
I AM FROM PARIS. I AM JUST VISITING THIS BEAUTIFUL PART OF FRANCE.
OH, YES. ESPECIALLY AT THIS TIME OF YEAR, THE COLORS OF THE COUNTRYSIDE ARE POSITIVELY GORGEOUS.

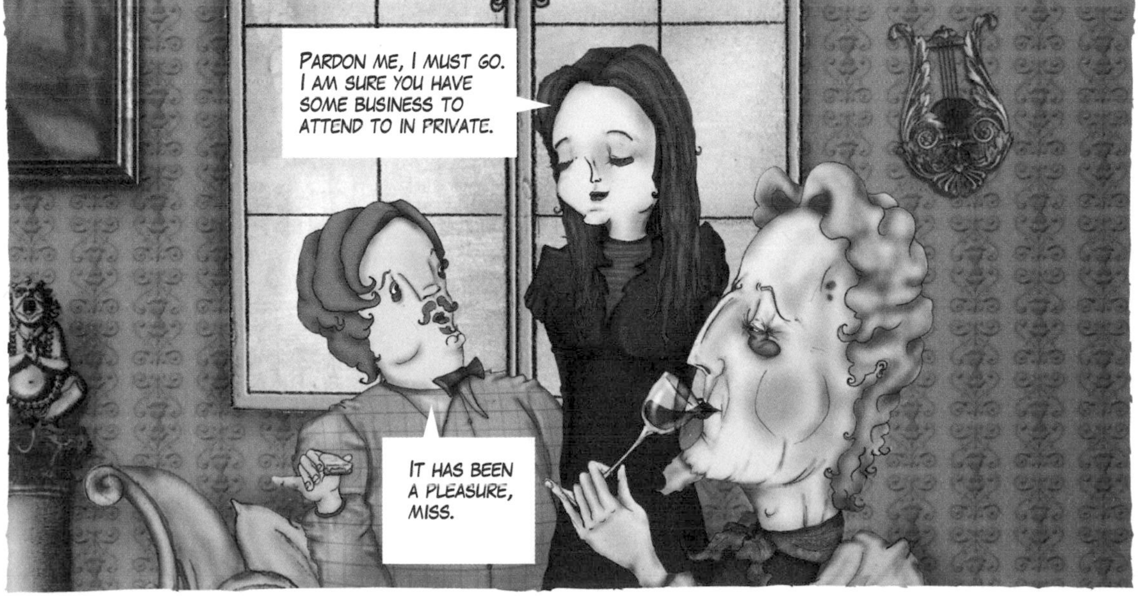
PARDON ME, I MUST GO. I AM SURE YOU HAVE SOME BUSINESS TO ATTEND TO IN PRIVATE.
IT HAS BEEN A PLEASURE, MISS.

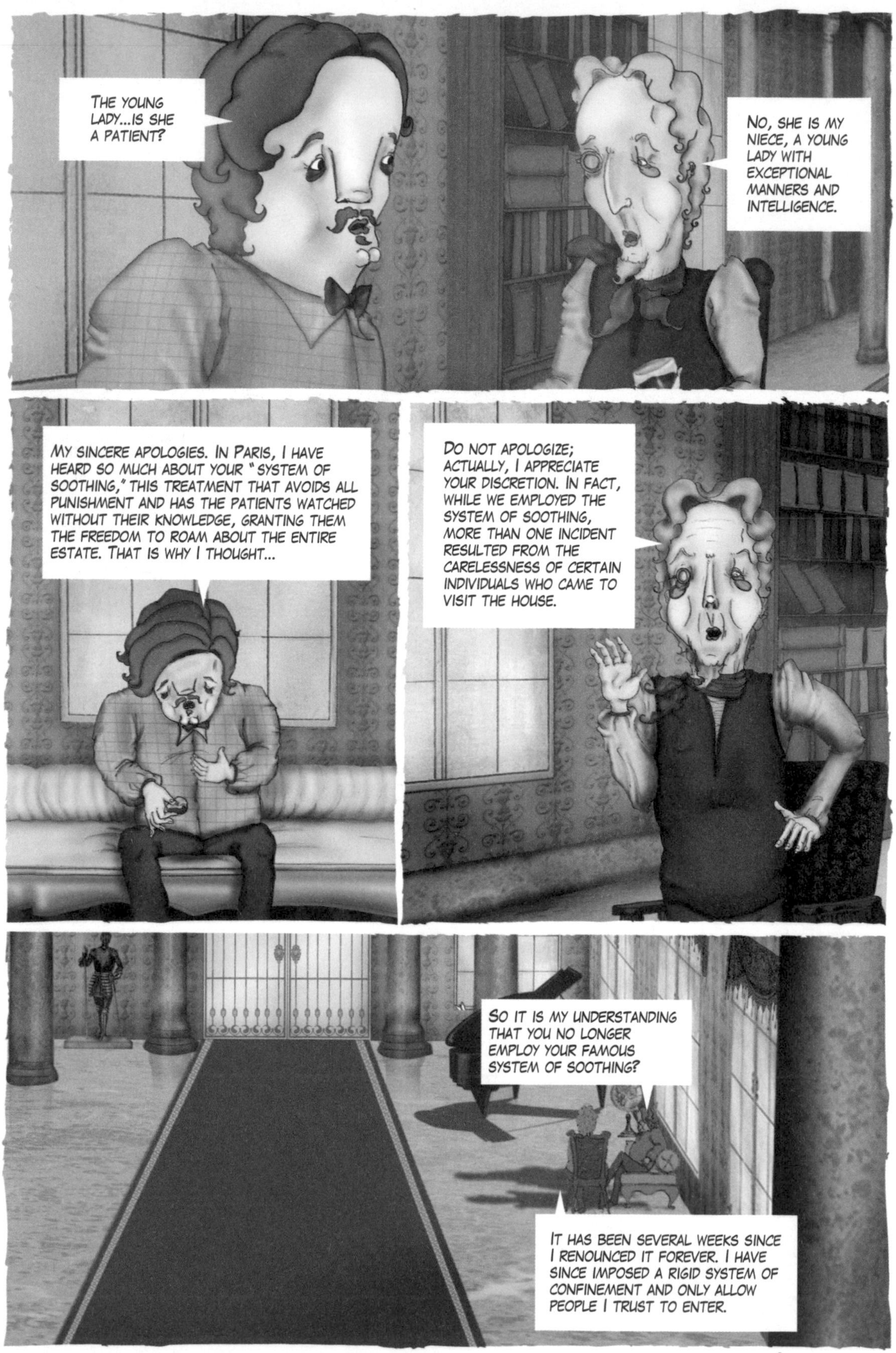
THE YOUNG LADY...IS SHE A PATIENT?
NO, SHE IS MY NIECE, A YOUNG LADY WITH EXCEPTIONAL MANNERS AND INTELLIGENCE.
MY SINCERE APOLOGIES. IN PARIS, I HAVE HEARD SO MUCH ABOUT YOUR "SYSTEM OF SOOTHING," THIS TREATMENT THAT AVOIDS ALL PUNISHMENT AND HAS THE PATIENTS WATCHED WITHOUT THEIR KNOWLEDGE, GRANTING THEM THE FREEDOM TO ROAM ABOUT THE ENTIRE ESTATE. THAT IS WHY I THOUGHT...
DO NOT APOLOGIZE; ACTUALLY, I APPRECIATE YOUR DISCRETION. IN FACT, WHILE WE EMPLOYED THE SYSTEM OF SOOTHING, MORE THAN ONE INCIDENT RESULTED FROM THE CARELESSNESS OF CERTAIN INDIVIDUALS WHO CAME TO VISIT THE HOUSE.
SO IT IS MY UNDERSTANDING THAT YOU NO LONGER EMPLOY YOUR FAMOUS SYSTEM OF SOOTHING?
IT HAS BEEN SEVERAL WEEKS SINCE I RENOUNCED IT FOREVER. I HAVE SINCE IMPOSED A RIGID SYSTEM OF CONFINEMENT AND ONLY ALLOW PEOPLE I TRUST TO ENTER.

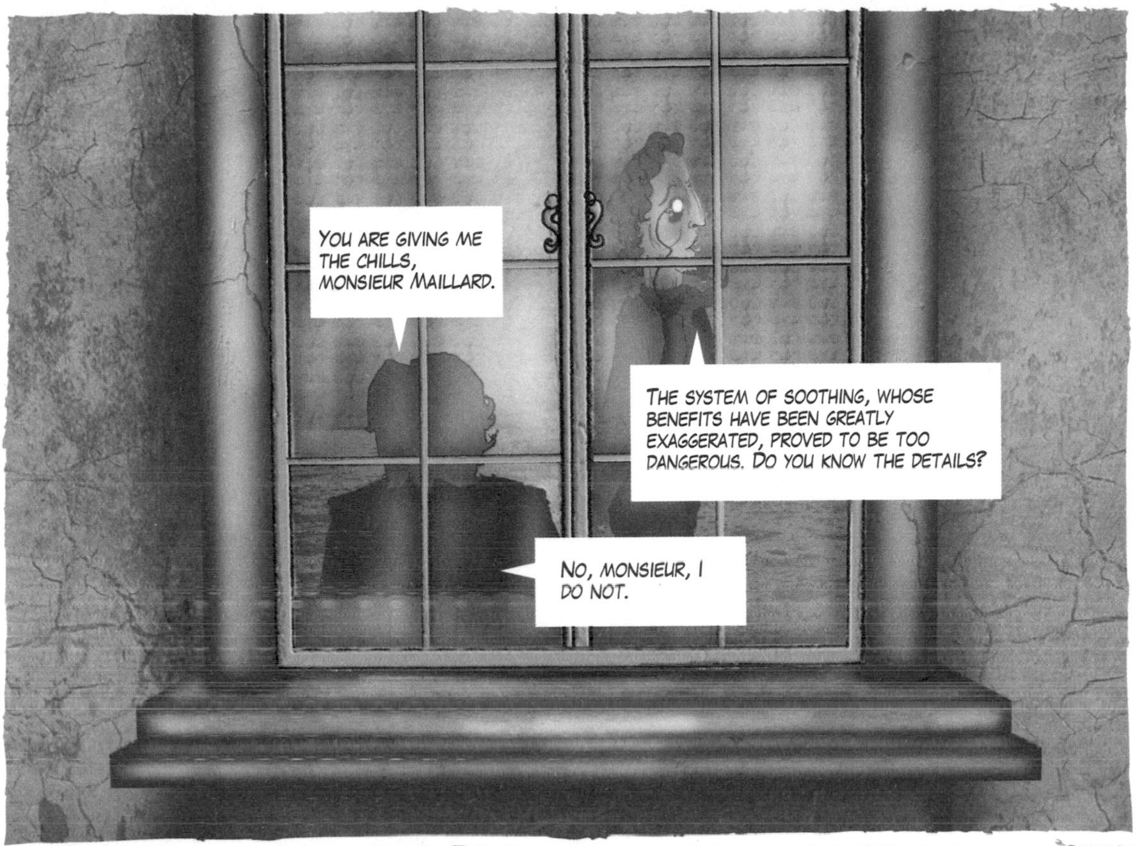
YOU ARE GIVING ME THE CHILLS, MONSIEUR MAILLARD.
THE SYSTEM OF SOOTHING, WHOSE BENEFITS HAVE BEEN GREATLY EXAGGERATED, PROVED TO BE TOO DANGEROUS. DO YOU KNOW THE DETAILS?
NO, MONSIEUR, I DO NOT.

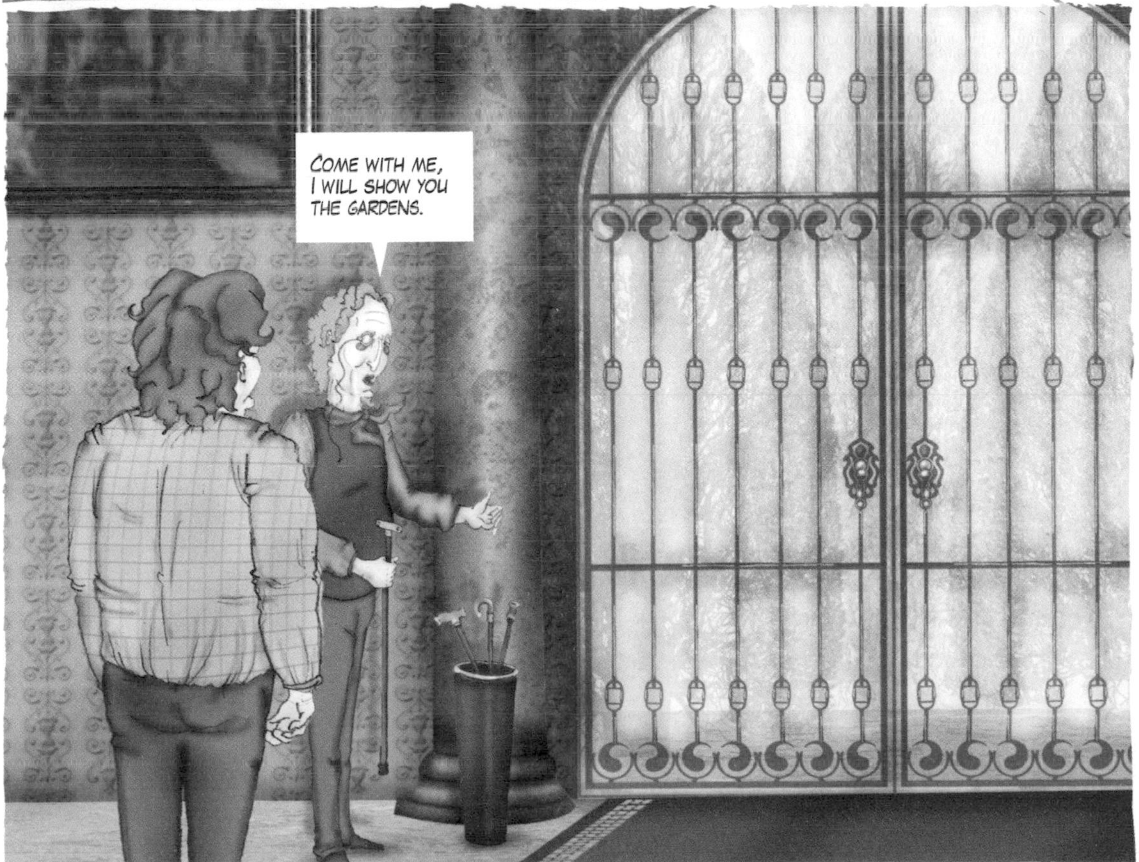
COME WITH ME, I WILL SHOW YOU THE GARDENS.

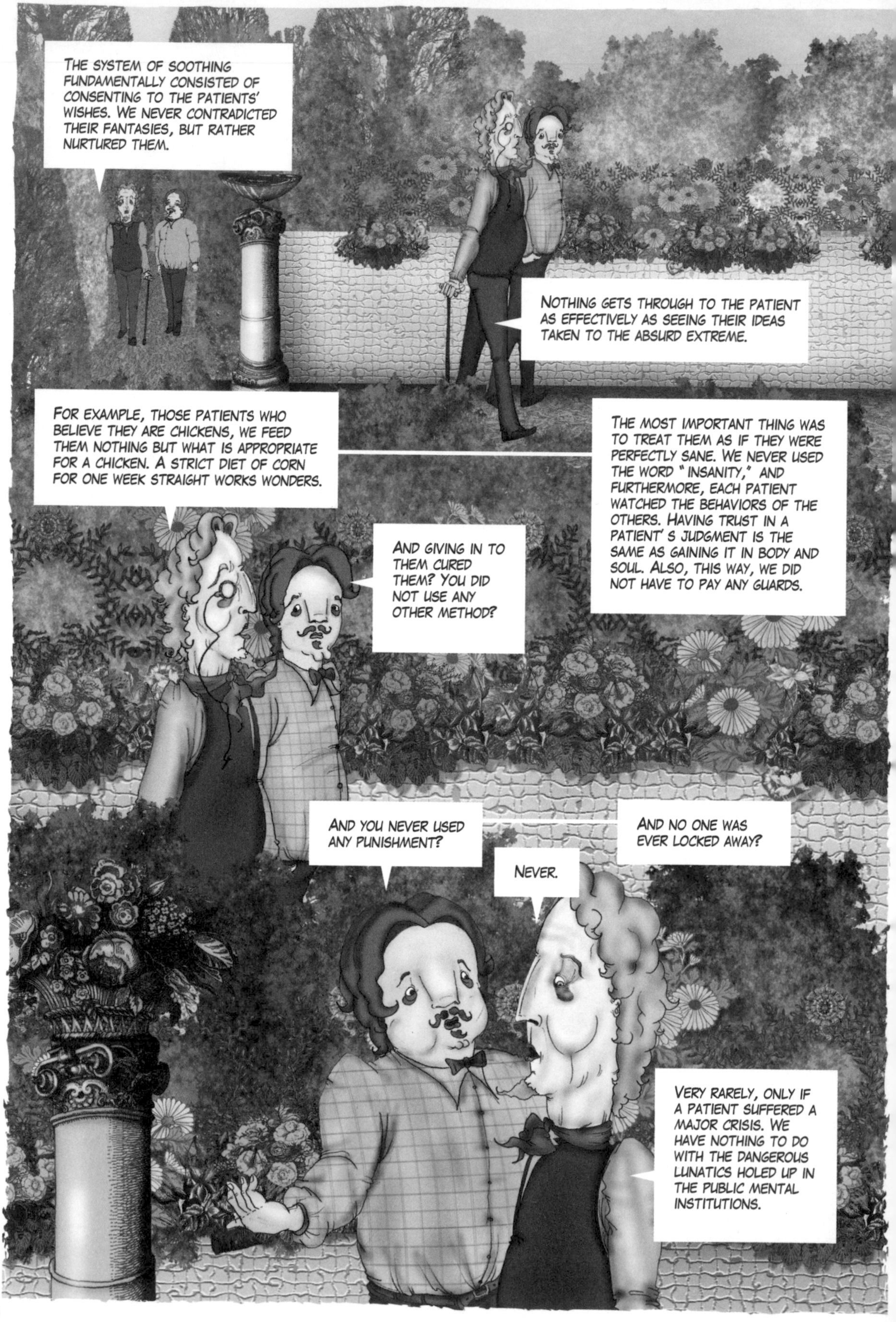
THE SYSTEM OF SOOTHING FUNDAMENTALLY CONSISTED OF CONSENTING TO THE PATIENTS' WISHES. WE NEVER CONTRADICTED THEIR FANTASIES, BUT RATHER NURTURED THEM.
NOTHING GETS THROUGH TO THE PATIENT AS EFFECTIVELY AS SEEING THEIR IDEAS TAKEN TO THE ABSURD EXTREME.
FOR EXAMPLE, THOSE PATIENTS WHO BELIEVE THEY ARE CHICKENS, WE FEED THEM NOTHING BUT WHAT IS APPROPRIATE FOR A CHICKEN. A STRICT DIET OF CORN FOR ONE WEEK STRAIGHT WORKS WONDERS.
THE MOST IMPORTANT THING WAS TO TREAT THEM AS IF THEY WERE PERFECTLY SANE. WE NEVER USED THE WORD "INSANITY," AND FURTHERMORE, EACH PATIENT WATCHED THE BEHAVIORS OF THE OTHERS. HAVING TRUST IN A PATIENT'S JUDGMENT IS THE SAME AS GAINING IT IN BODY AND SOUL. ALSO, THIS WAY, WE DID NOT HAVE TO PAY ANY GUARDS.
AND GIVING IN TO THEM CURED THEM? YOU DID NOT USE ANY OTHER METHOD?
AND YOU NEVER USED ANY PUNISHMENT?
AND NO ONE WAS EVER LOCKED AWAY?
NEVER.
VERY RARELY, ONLY IF A PATIENT SUFFERED A MAJOR CRISIS. WE HAVE NOTHING TO DO WITH THE DANGEROUS LUNATICS HOLED UP IN THE PUBLIC MENTAL INSTITUTIONS.

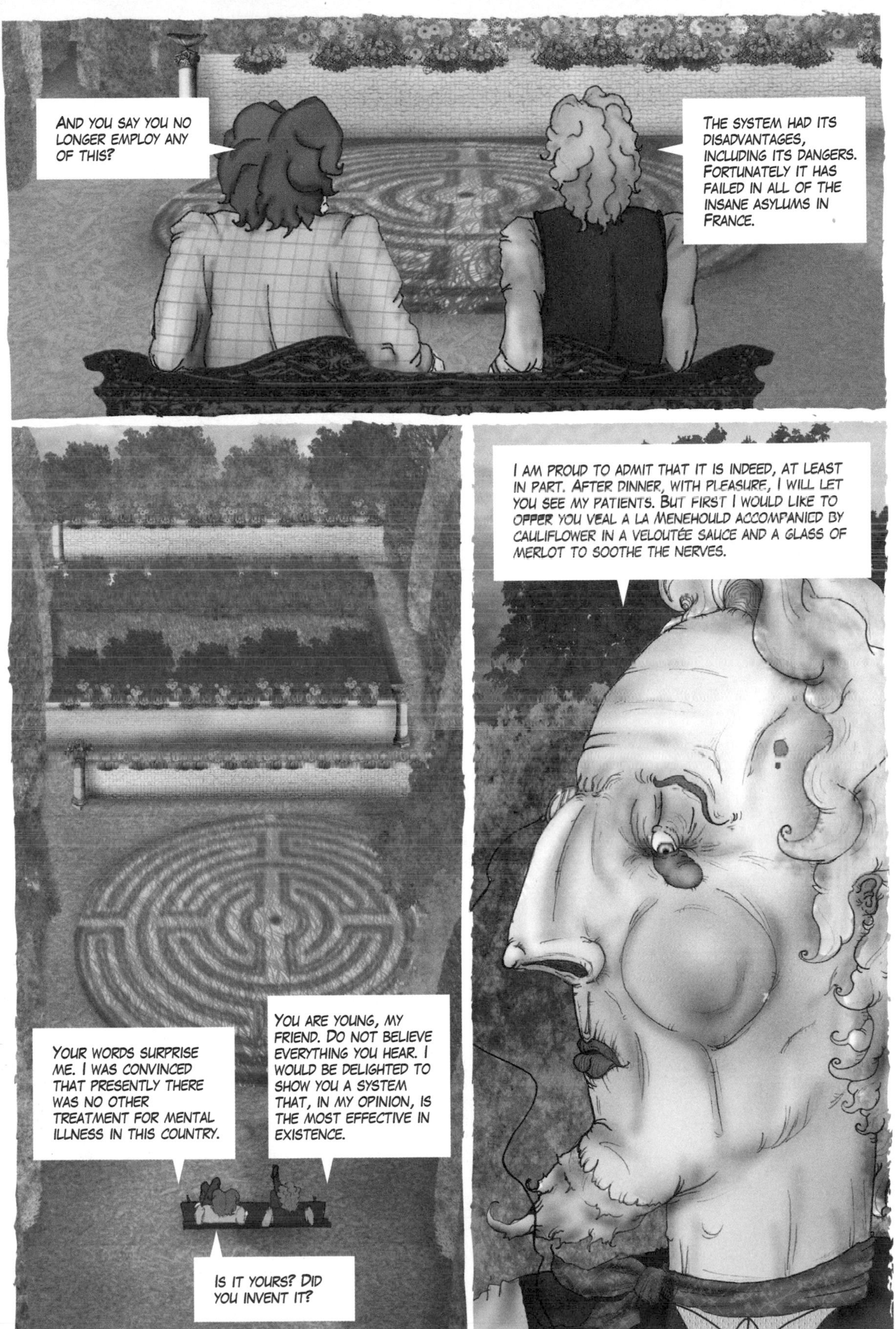
AND YOU SAY YOU NO LONGER EMPLOY ANY OF THIS?
THE SYSTEM HAD ITS DISADVANTAGES, INCLUDING ITS DANGERS. FORTUNATELY IT HAS FAILED IN ALL OF THE INSANE ASYLUMS IN FRANCE.
YOUR WORDS SURPRISE ME. I WAS CONVINCED THAT PRESENTLY THERE WAS NO OTHER TREATMENT FOR MENTAL ILLNESS IN THIS COUNTRY.
YOU ARE YOUNG, MY FRIEND. DO NOT BELIEVE EVERYTHING YOU HEAR. I WOULD BE DELIGHTED TO SHOW YOU A SYSTEM THAT, IN MY OPINION, IS THE MOST EFFECTIVE IN EXISTENCE.
IS IT YOURS? DID YOU INVENT IT?
I AM PROUD TO ADMIT THAT IT IS INDEED, AT LEAST IN PART. AFTER DINNER, WITH PLEASURE, I WILL LET YOU SEE MY PATIENTS. BUT FIRST I WOULD LIKE TO OFFER YOU VEAL A LA MENEHOULD ACCOMPANIED BY CAULIFLOWER IN A VELOUTÉE SAUCE AND A GLASS OF MERLOT TO SOOTHE THE NERVES.

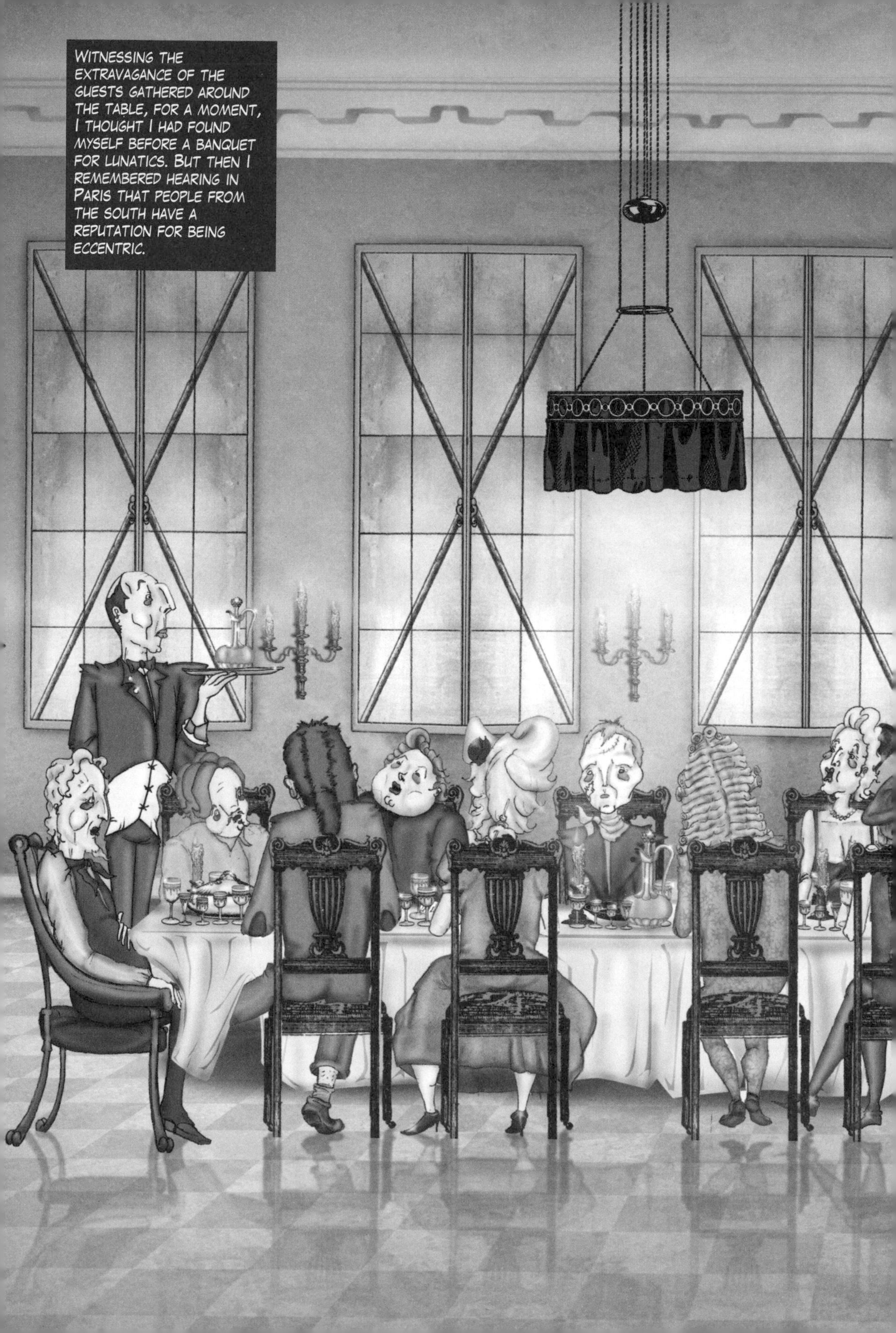
WITNESSING THE EXTRAVAGANCE OF THE GUESTS GATHERED AROUND THE TABLE, FOR A MOMENT, I THOUGHT I HAD FOUND MYSELF BEFORE A BANQUET FOR LUNATICS. BUT THEN I REMEMBERED HEARING IN PARIS THAT PEOPLE FROM THE SOUTH HAVE A REPUTATION FOR BEING ECCENTRIC.

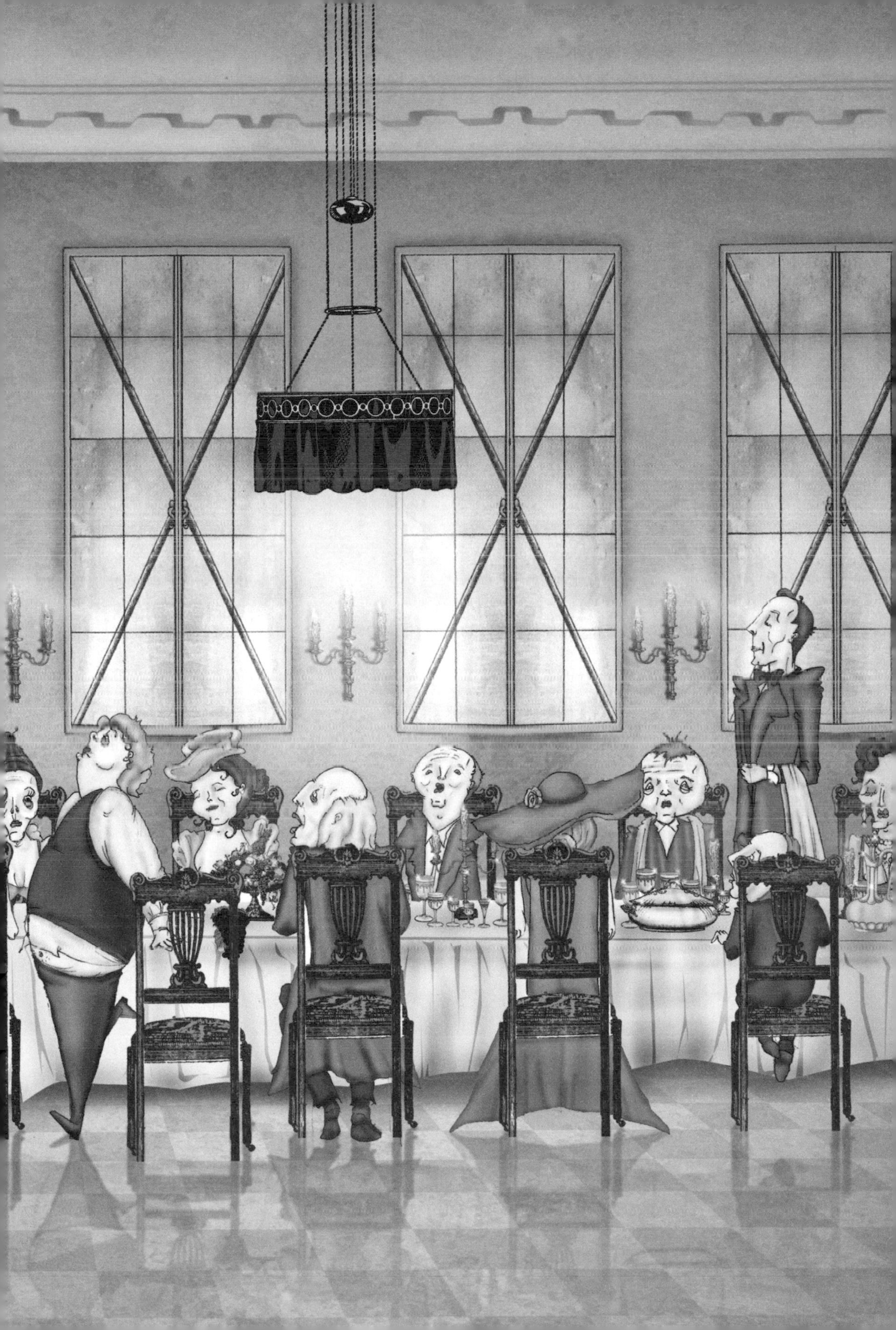

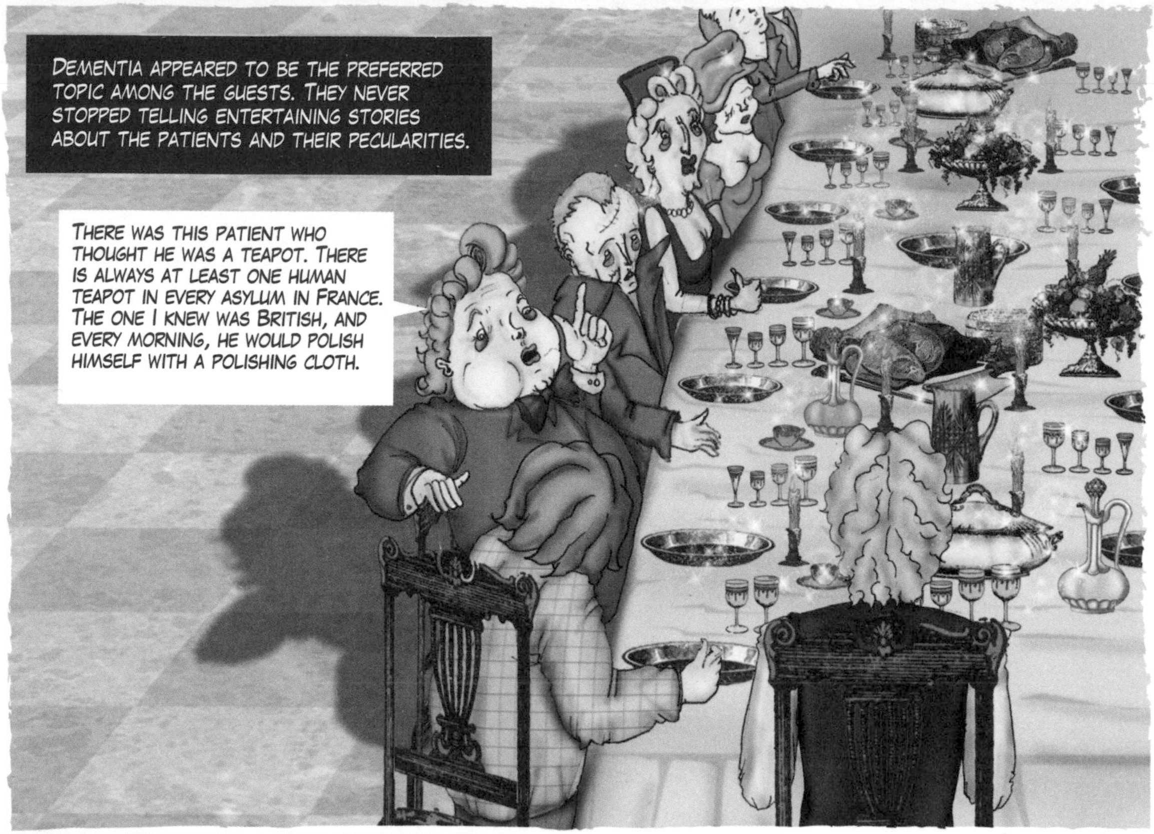
DEMENTIA APPEARED TO BE THE PREFERRED TOPIC AMONG THE GUESTS. THEY NEVER STOPPED TELLING ENTERTAINING STORIES ABOUT THE PATIENTS AND THEIR PECULARITIES.
THERE WAS THIS PATIENT WHO THOUGHT HE WAS A TEAPOT. THERE IS ALWAYS AT LEAST ONE HUMAN TEAPOT IN EVERY ASYLUM IN FRANCE. THE ONE I KNEW WAS BRITISH, AND EVERY MORNING, HE WOULD POLISH HIMSELF WITH A POLISHING CLOTH.

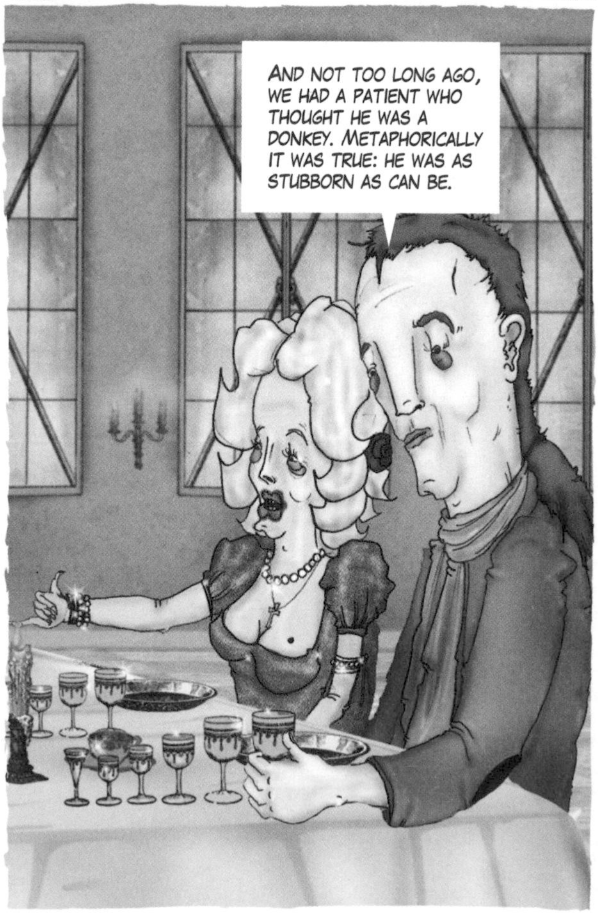
AND NOT TOO LONG AGO, WE HAD A PATIENT WHO THOUGHT HE WAS A DONKEY. METAPHORICALLY IT WAS TRUE: HE WAS AS STUBBORN AS CAN BE.

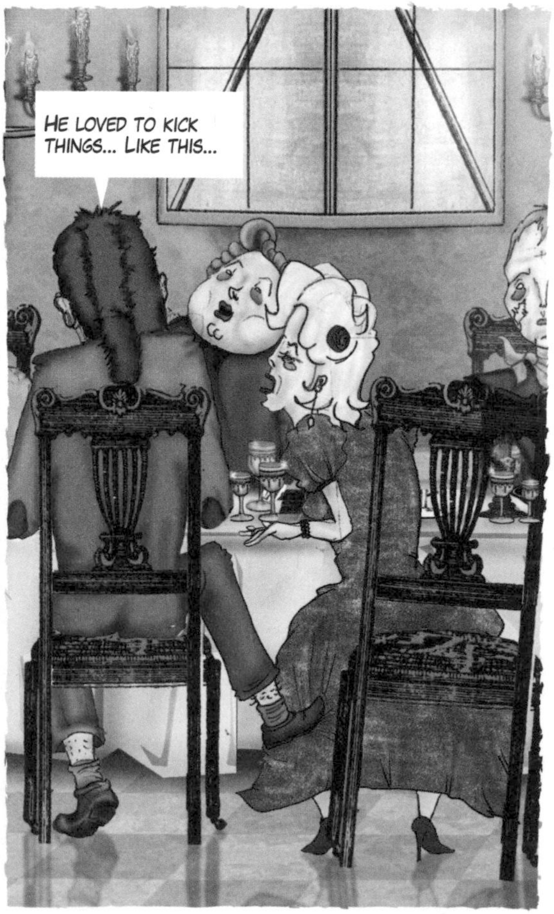
HE LOVED TO KICK THINGS... LIKE THIS...

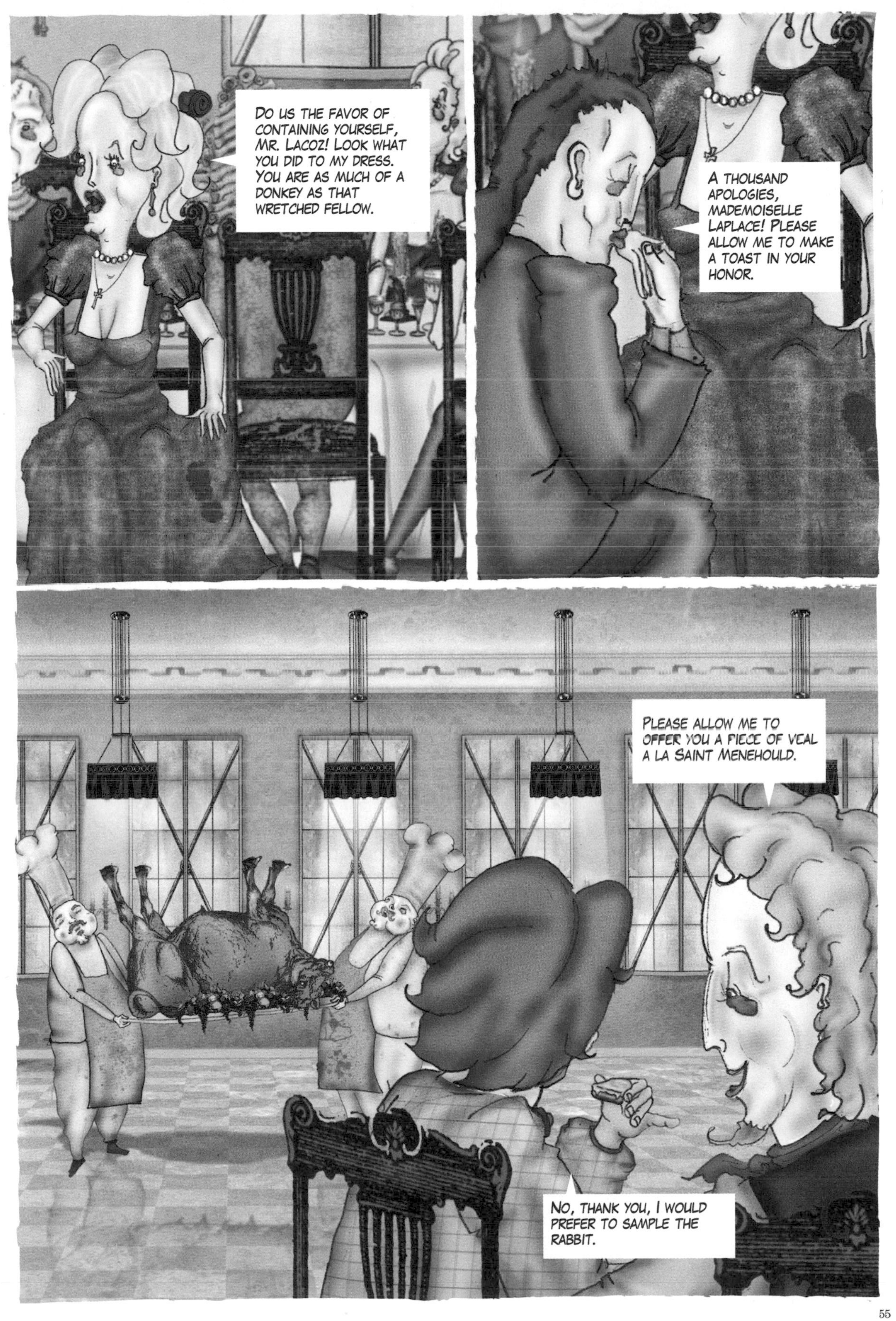
DO US THE FAVOR OF CONTAINING YOURSELF, MR. LACOZ! LOOK WHAT YOU DID TO MY DRESS. YOU ARE AS MUCH OF A DONKEY AS THAT WRETCHED FELLOW.
A THOUSAND APOLOGIES, MADEMOISELLE LAPLACE! PLEASE ALLOW ME TO MAKE A TOAST IN YOUR HONOR.
PLEASE ALLOW ME TO OFFER YOU A PIECE OF VEAL A LA SAINT MENEHOULD.
NO, THANK YOU, I WOULD PREFER TO SAMPLE THE RABBIT.

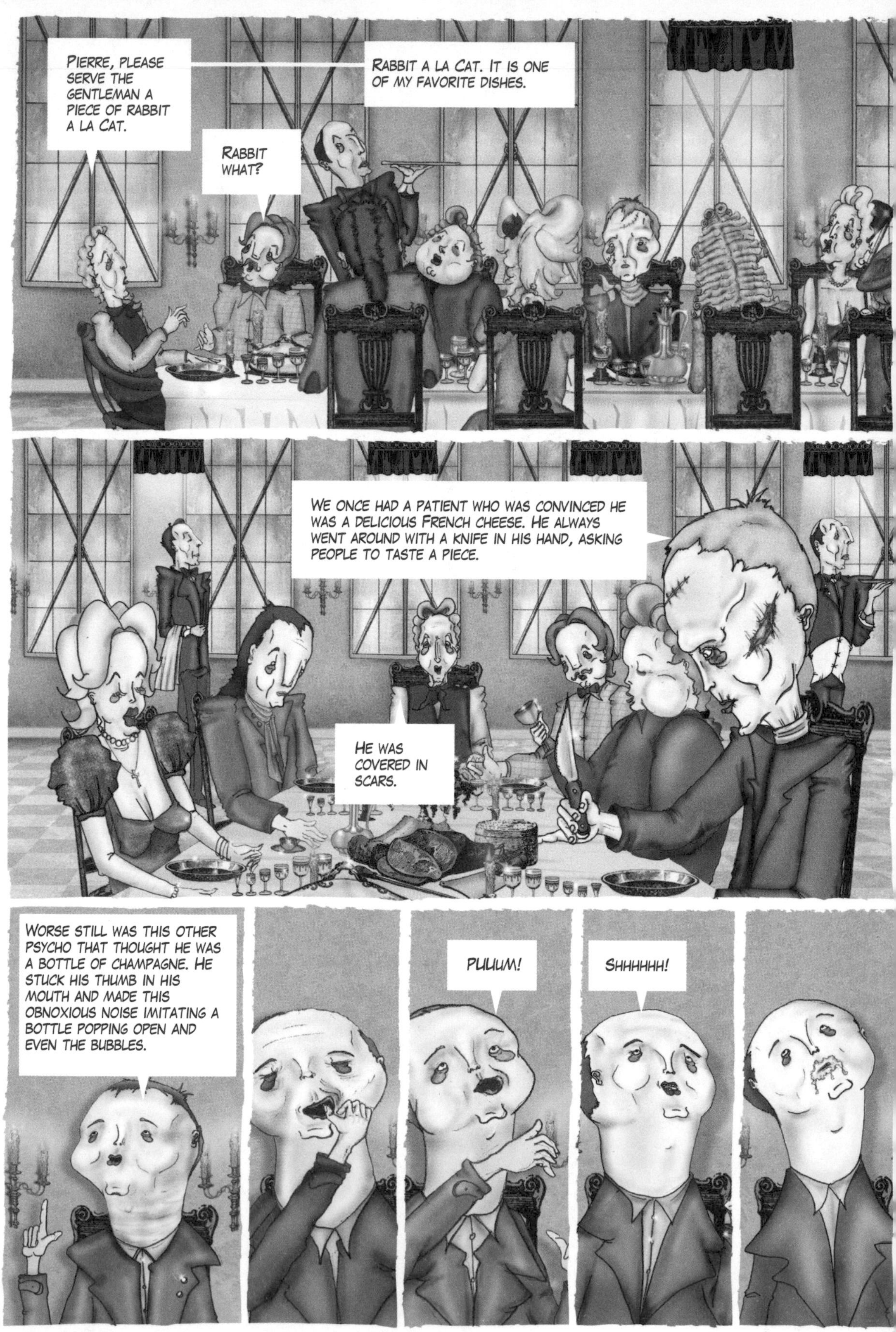
PIERRE, PLEASE SERVE THE GENTLEMAN A PIECE OF RABBIT A LA CAT.
RABBIT A LA CAT. IT IS ONE OF MY FAVORITE DISHES.
RABBIT WHAT?
WE ONCE HAD A PATIENT WHO WAS CONVINCED HE WAS A DELICIOUS FRENCH CHEESE. HE ALWAYS WENT AROUND WITH A KNIFE IN HIS HAND, ASKING PEOPLE TO TASTE A PIECE.
HE WAS COVERED IN SCARS.
WORSE STILL WAS THIS OTHER PSYCHO THAT THOUGHT HE WAS A BOTTLE OF CHAMPAGNE. HE STUCK HIS THUMB IN HIS MOUTH AND MADE THIS OBNOXIOUS NOISE IMITATING A BOTTLE POPPING OPEN AND EVEN THE BUBBLES.
PUUUM!
SHHHHHH!

WELL, I RMEMBER THE FROGMAN, WHO HAD AN EXTRAORDINARY TALENT!

HE CROAKED BEAUTIFULLY IN B FLAT.

CROAAAAAAK!

HE PUT HIS HANDS ON TOP OF THE TABLE AND OPENED HIS MOUTH LIKE THIS...

AND ROLLED HIS EYES BACK LIKE THIS...

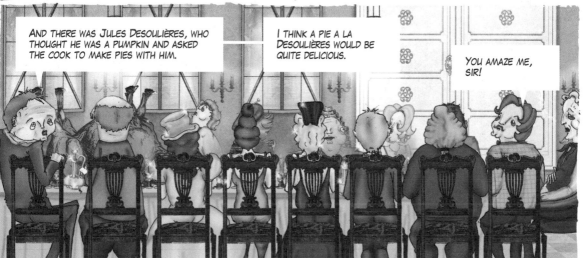

AND THERE WAS JULES DESOULIÈRES, WHO THOUGHT HE WAS A PUMPKIN AND ASKED THE COOK TO MAKE PIES WITH HIM.

I THINK A PIE A LA DESOULIÈRES WOULD BE QUITE DELICIOUS.

YOU AMAZE ME, SIR!

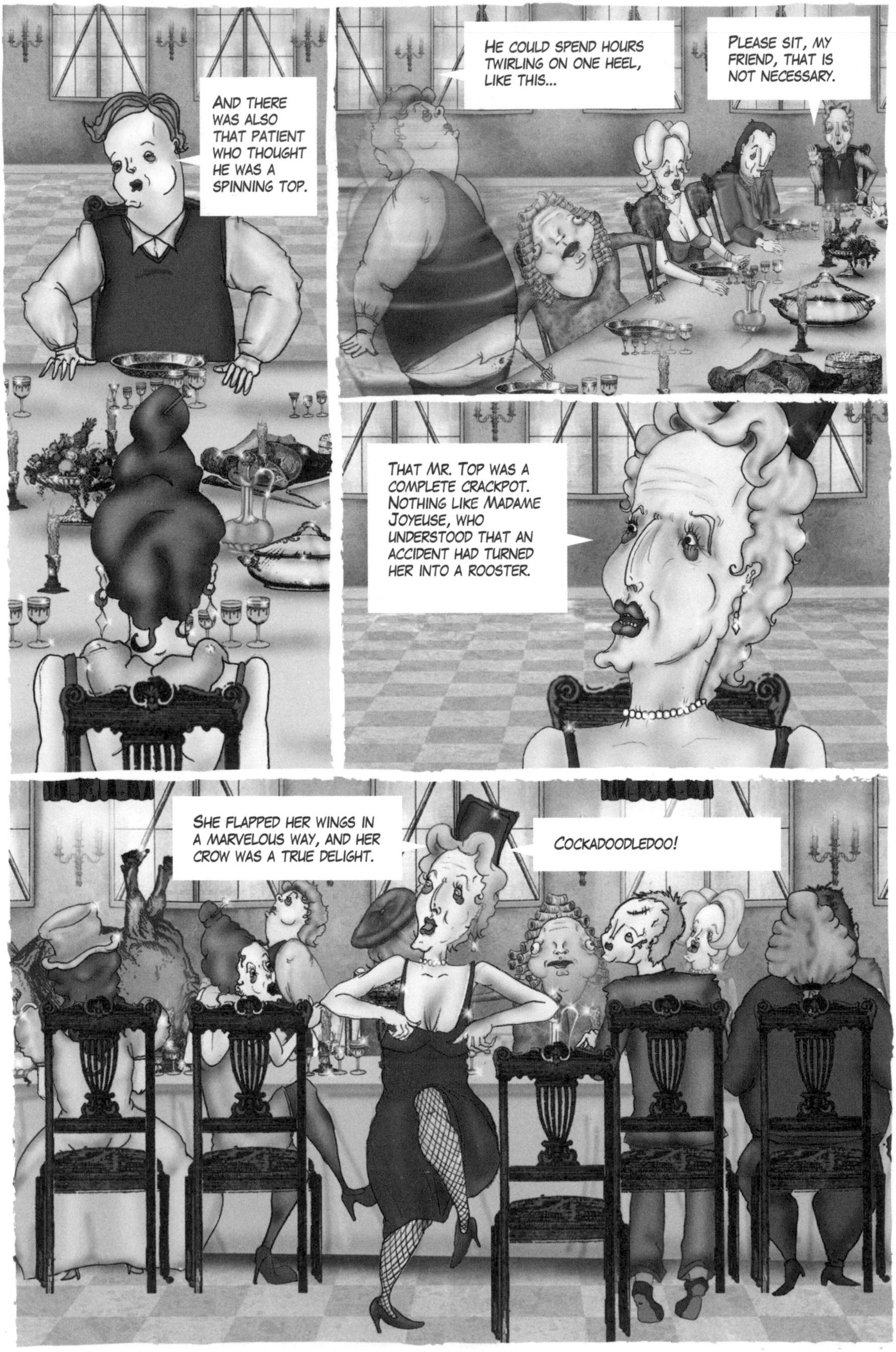
AND THERE WAS ALSO THAT PATIENT WHO THOUGHT HE WAS A SPINNING TOP.
HE COULD SPEND HOURS TWIRLING ON ONE HEEL, LIKE THIS...
PLEASE SIT, MY FRIEND, THAT IS NOT NECESSARY.
THAT MR. TOP WAS A COMPLETE CRACKPOT. NOTHING LIKE MADAME JOYEUSE, WHO UNDERSTOOD THAT AN ACCIDENT HAD TURNED HER INTO A ROOSTER.
SHE FLAPPED HER WINGS IN A MARVELOUS WAY, AND HER CROW WAS A TRUE DELIGHT.
COCKADOODLEDOO!

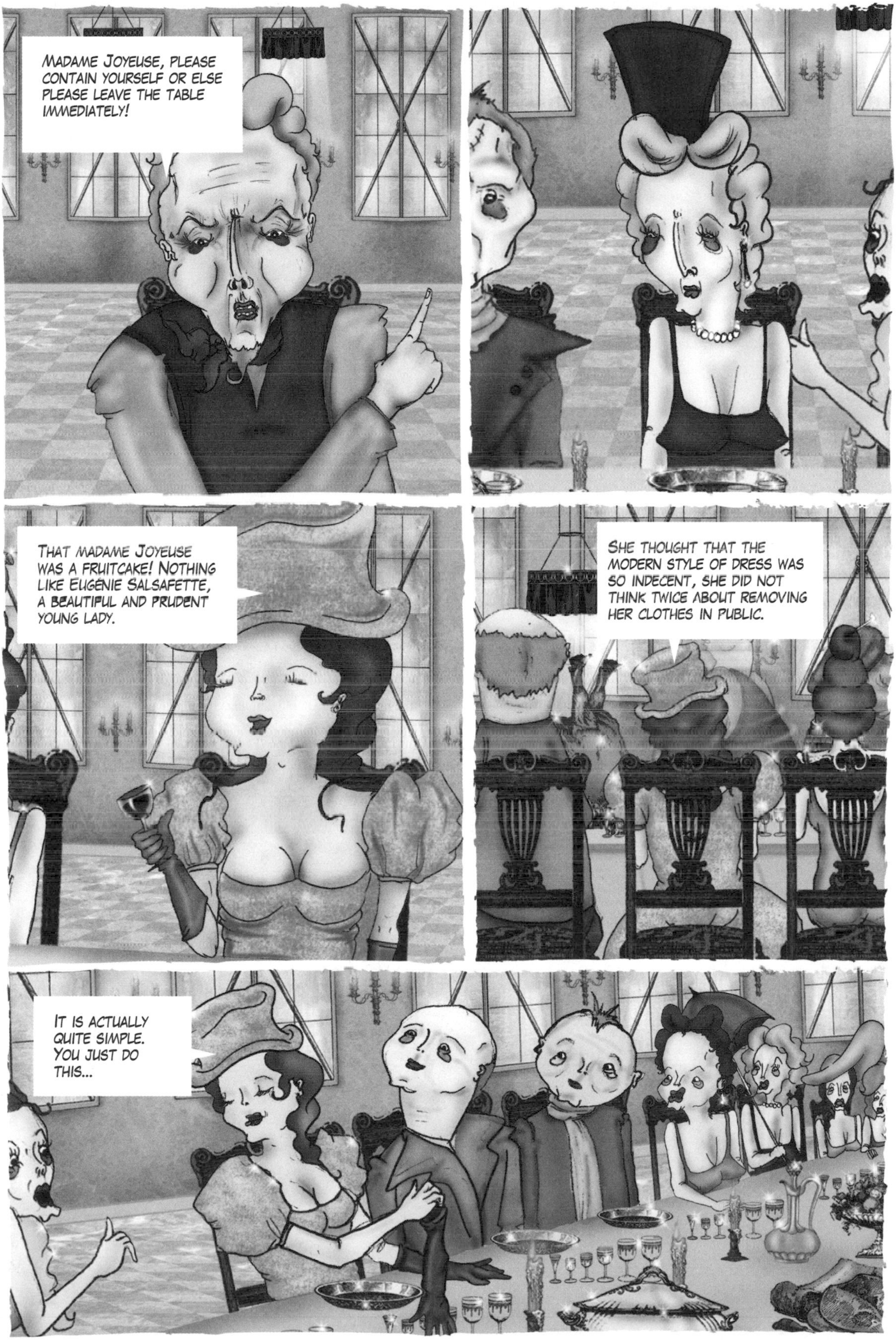
MADAME JOYEUSE, PLEASE CONTAIN YOURSELF OR ELSE PLEASE LEAVE THE TABLE IMMEDIATELY!
THAT MADAME JOYEUSE WAS A FRUITCAKE! NOTHING LIKE EUGÉNIE SALSAFETTE, A BEAUTIFUL AND PRUDENT YOUNG LADY.
SHE THOUGHT THAT THE MODERN STYLE OF DRESS WAS SO INDECENT, SHE DID NOT THINK TWICE ABOUT REMOVING HER CLOTHES IN PUBLIC.
IT IS ACTUALLY QUITE SIMPLE. YOU JUST DO THIS...

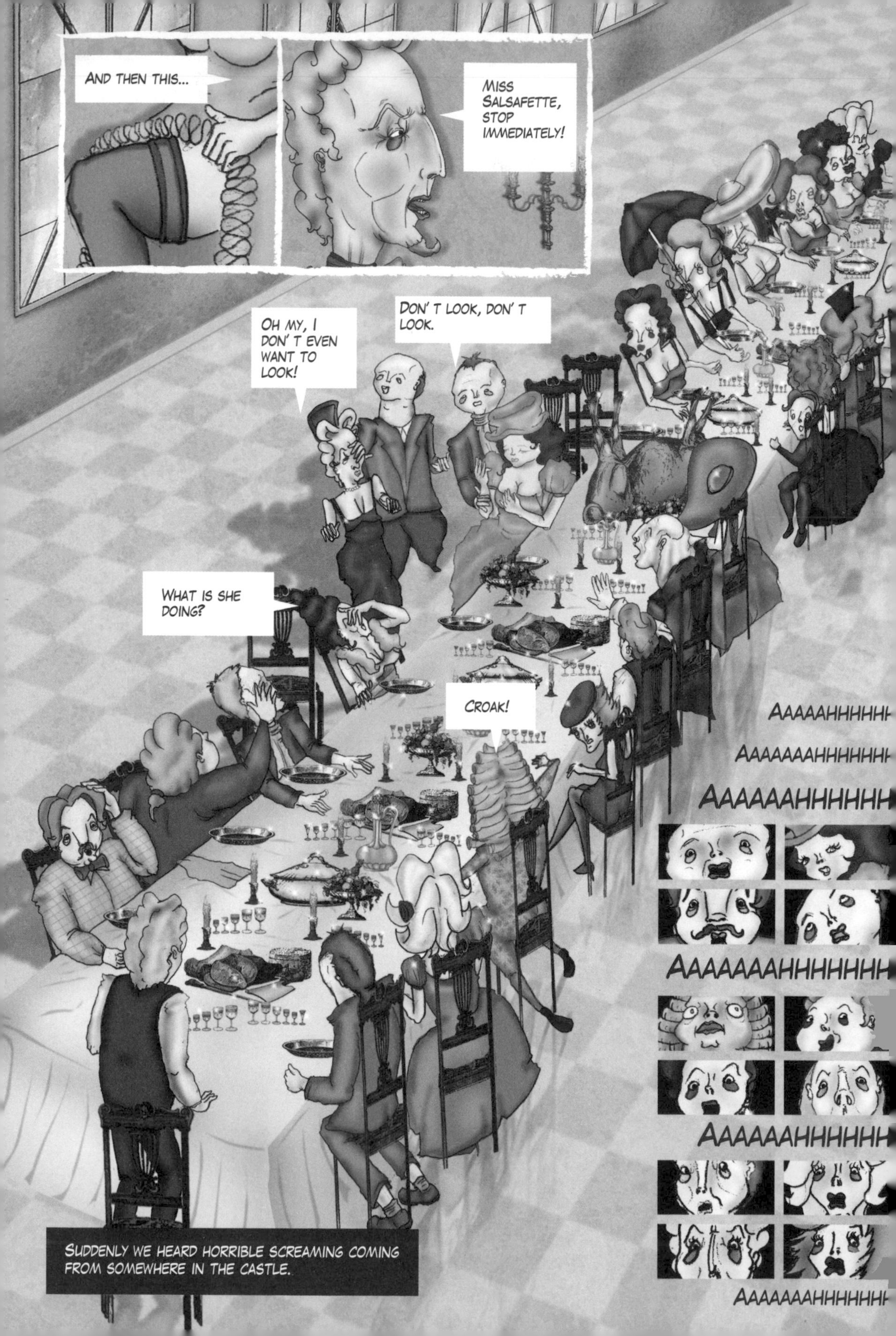
AND THEN THIS...
MISS SALSAFETTE, STOP IMMEDIATELY!
OH MY, I DON' T EVEN WANT TO LOOK!
DON' T LOOK, DON' T LOOK.
WHAT IS SHE DOING?
CROAK!
AAAAAHHHHHH
AAAAAAAHHHHHHH
AAAAAAHHHHHH
AAAAAAAHHHHHHH
AAAAAAHHHHHH
AAAAAAAHHHHHHH
SUDDENLY WE HEARD HORRIBLE SCREAMING COMING FROM SOMEWHERE IN THE CASTLE.

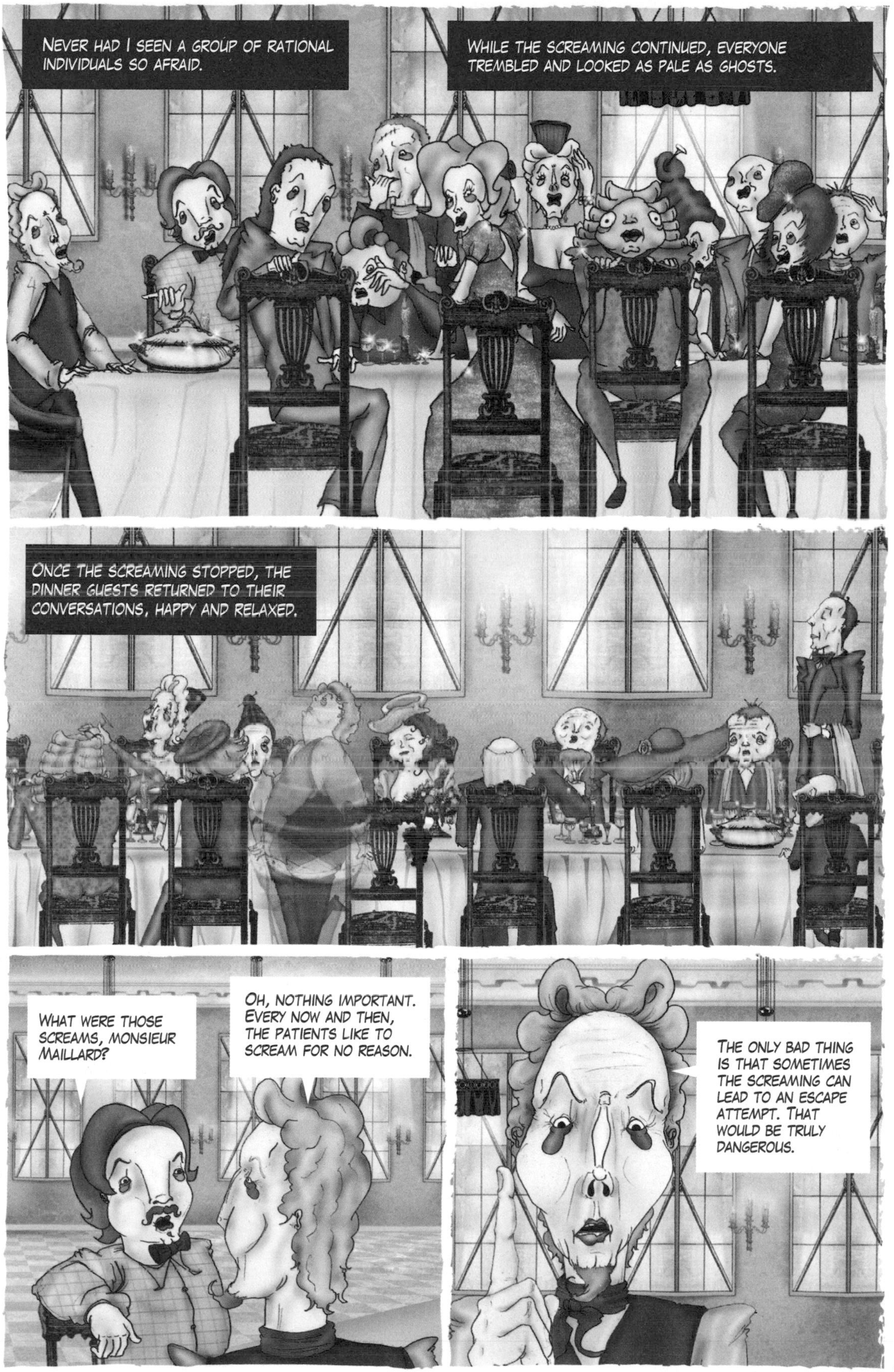

NEVER HAD I SEEN A GROUP OF RATIONAL INDIVIDUALS SO AFRAID.
WHILE THE SCREAMING CONTINUED, EVERYONE TREMBLED AND LOOKED AS PALE AS GHOSTS.
ONCE THE SCREAMING STOPPED, THE DINNER GUESTS RETURNED TO THEIR CONVERSATIONS, HAPPY AND RELAXED.
WHAT WERE THOSE SCREAMS, MONSIEUR MAILLARD?
OH, NOTHING IMPORTANT. EVERY NOW AND THEN, THE PATIENTS LIKE TO SCREAM FOR NO REASON.
THE ONLY BAD THING IS THAT SOMETIMES THE SCREAMING CAN LEAD TO AN ESCAPE ATTEMPT. THAT WOULD BE TRULY DANGEROUS.

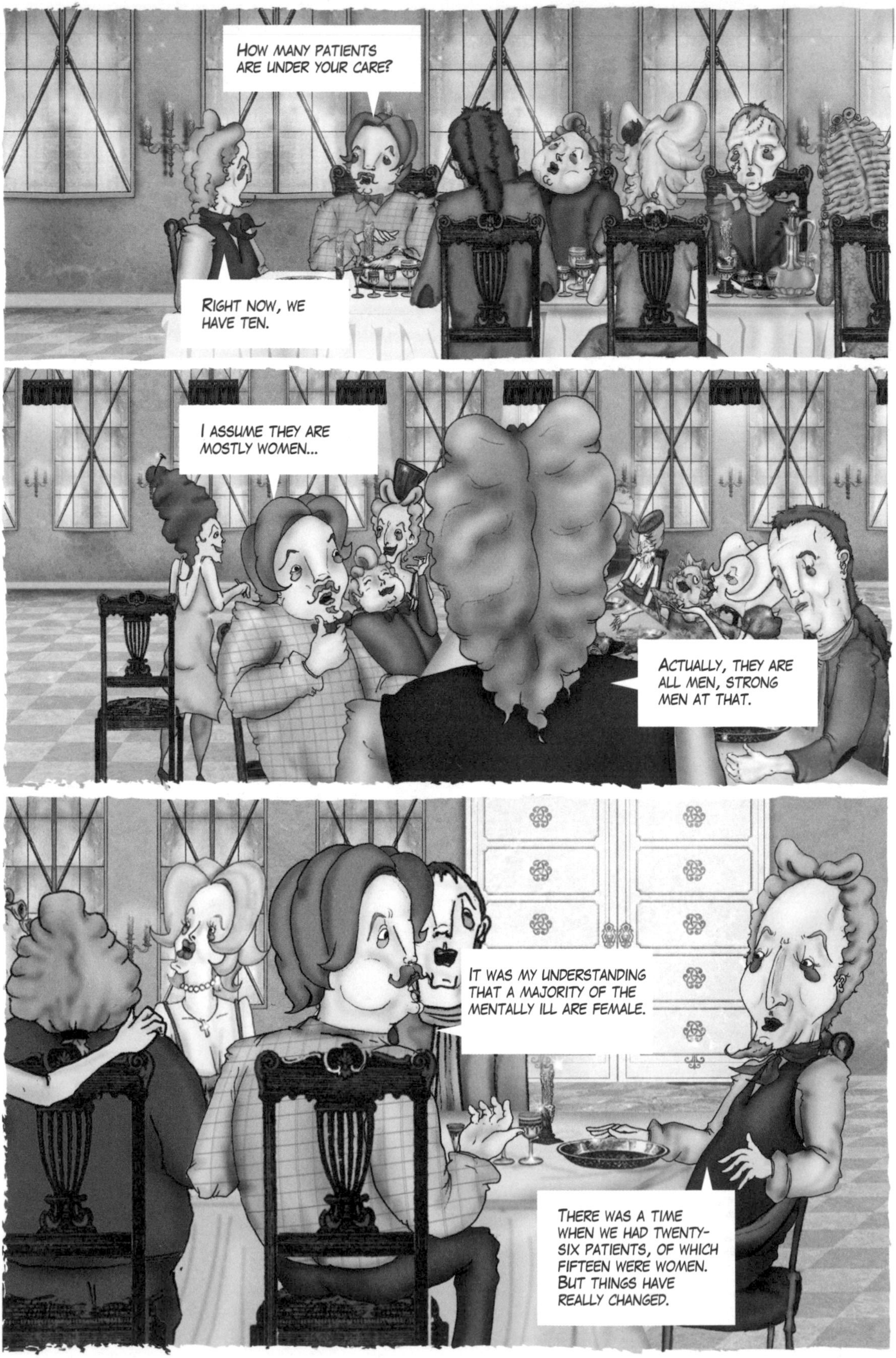
How many patients are under your care?
Right now, we have ten.
I assume they are mostly women...
Actually, they are all men, strong men at that.
It was my understanding that a majority of the mentally ill are female.
There was a time when we had twenty-six patients, of which fifteen were women. But things have really changed.

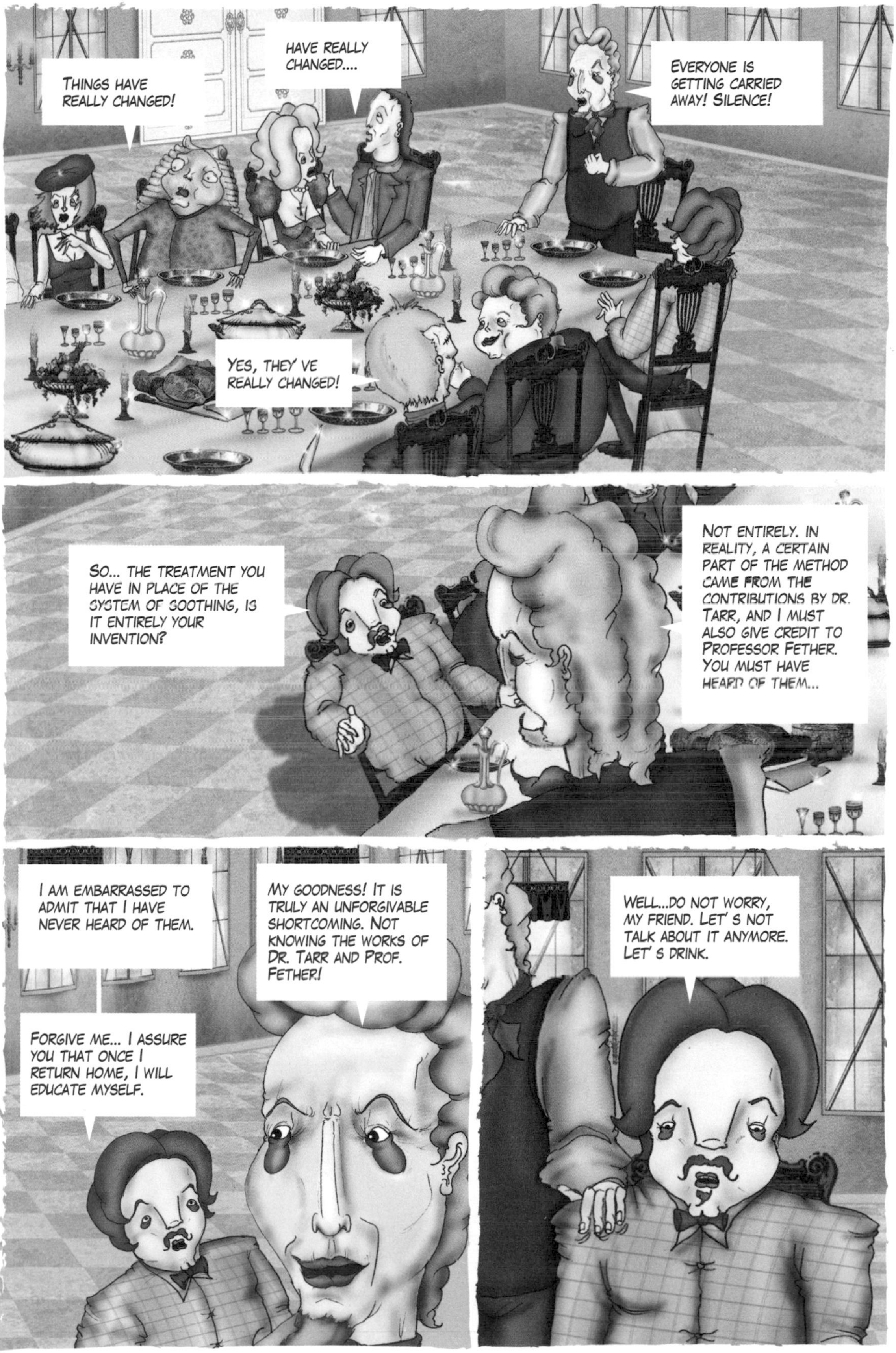
THINGS HAVE REALLY CHANGED!
HAVE REALLY CHANGED....
YES, THEY' VE REALLY CHANGED!
EVERYONE IS GETTING CARRIED AWAY! SILENCE!
SO... THE TREATMENT YOU HAVE IN PLACE OF THE SYSTEM OF SOOTHING, IS IT ENTIRELY YOUR INVENTION?
NOT ENTIRELY. IN REALITY, A CERTAIN PART OF THE METHOD CAME FROM THE CONTRIBUTIONS BY DR. TARR, AND I MUST ALSO GIVE CREDIT TO PROFESSOR FETHER. YOU MUST HAVE HEARD OF THEM...
I AM EMBARRASSED TO ADMIT THAT I HAVE NEVER HEARD OF THEM.
FORGIVE ME... I ASSURE YOU THAT ONCE I RETURN HOME, I WILL EDUCATE MYSELF.
MY GOODNESS! IT IS TRULY AN UNFORGIVABLE SHORTCOMING. NOT KNOWING THE WORKS OF DR. TARR AND PROF. FETHER!
WELL...DO NOT WORRY, MY FRIEND. LET' S NOT TALK ABOUT IT ANYMORE. LET' S DRINK.

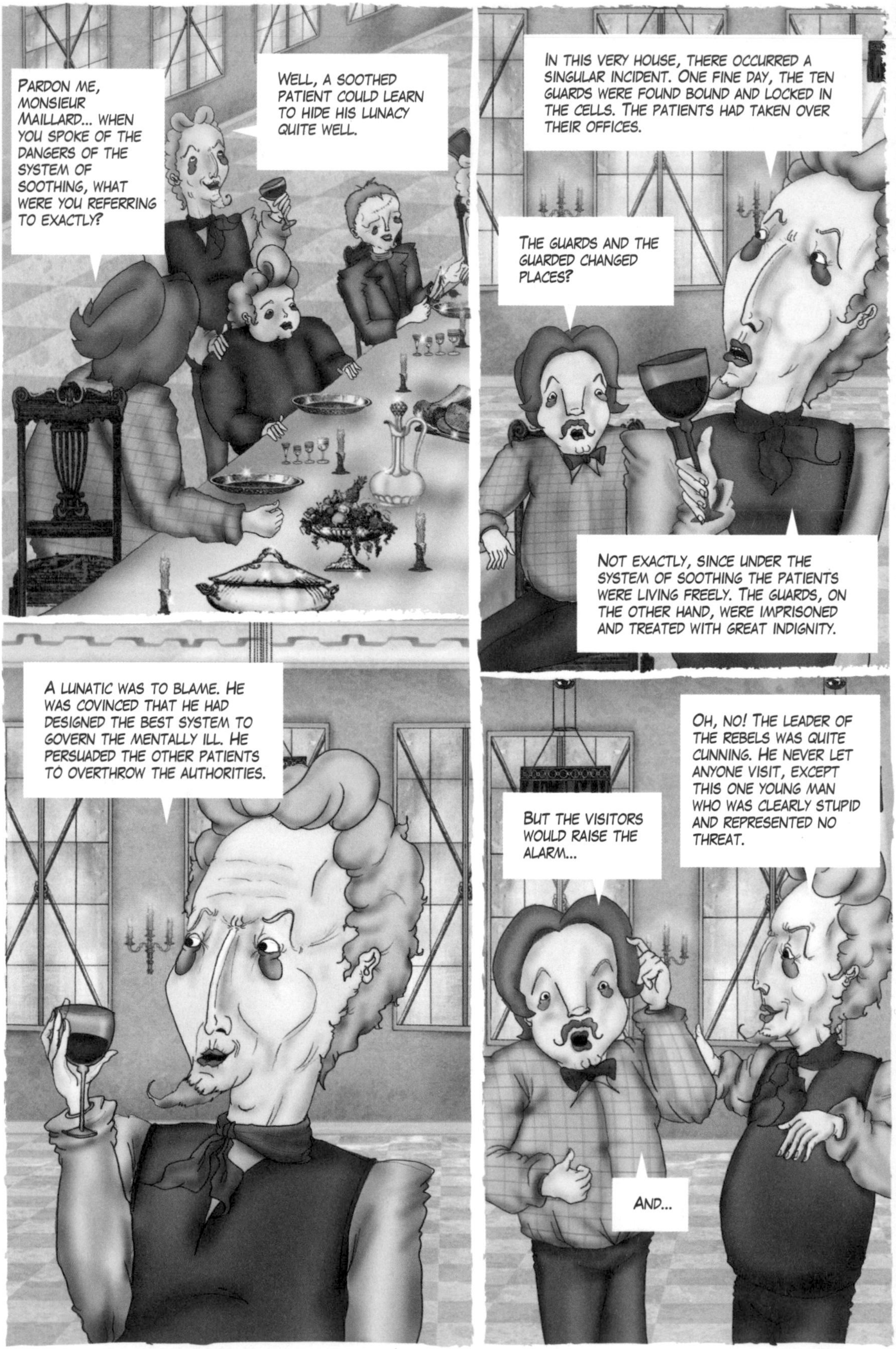

PARDON ME, MONSIEUR MAILLARD... WHEN YOU SPOKE OF THE DANGERS OF THE SYSTEM OF SOOTHING, WHAT WERE YOU REFERRING TO EXACTLY?
WELL, A SOOTHED PATIENT COULD LEARN TO HIDE HIS LUNACY QUITE WELL.
IN THIS VERY HOUSE, THERE OCCURRED A SINGULAR INCIDENT. ONE FINE DAY, THE TEN GUARDS WERE FOUND BOUND AND LOCKED IN THE CELLS. THE PATIENTS HAD TAKEN OVER THEIR OFFICES.
THE GUARDS AND THE GUARDED CHANGED PLACES?
NOT EXACTLY, SINCE UNDER THE SYSTEM OF SOOTHING THE PATIENTS WERE LIVING FREELY. THE GUARDS, ON THE OTHER HAND, WERE IMPRISONED AND TREATED WITH GREAT INDIGNITY.
A LUNATIC WAS TO BLAME. HE WAS COVINCED THAT HE HAD DESIGNED THE BEST SYSTEM TO GOVERN THE MENTALLY ILL. HE PERSUADED THE OTHER PATIENTS TO OVERTHROW THE AUTHORITIES.
BUT THE VISITORS WOULD RAISE THE ALARM...
OH, NO! THE LEADER OF THE REBELS WAS QUITE CUNNING. HE NEVER LET ANYONE VISIT, EXCEPT THIS ONE YOUNG MAN WHO WAS CLEARLY STUPID AND REPRESENTED NO THREAT.
AND...

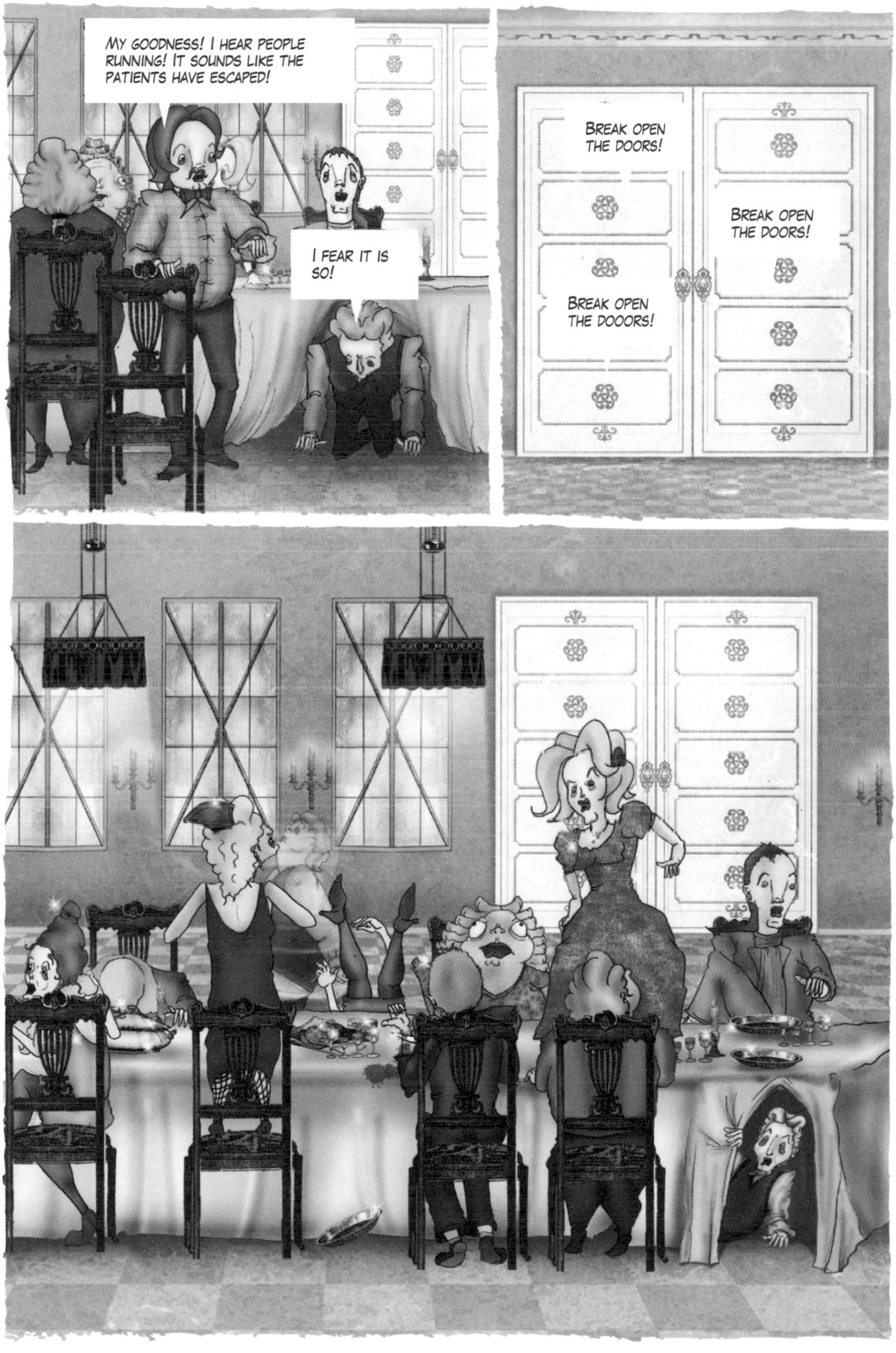

MY GOODNESS! I HEAR PEOPLE RUNNING! IT SOUNDS LIKE THE PATIENTS HAVE ESCAPED!
I FEAR IT IS SO!
BREAK OPEN THE DOORS!
BREAK OPEN THE DOORS!
BREAK OPEN THE DOOORS!

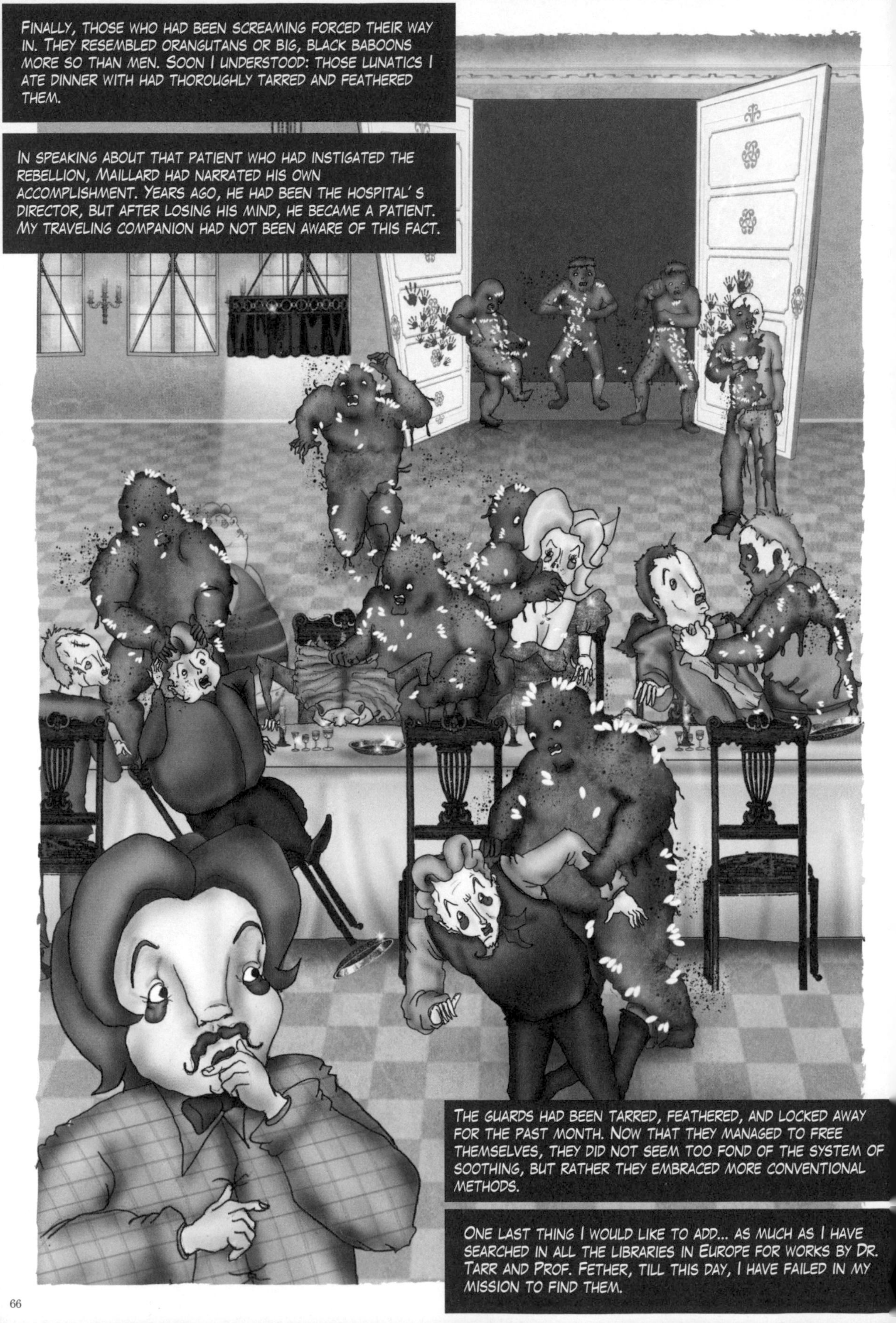
FINALLY, THOSE WHO HAD BEEN SCREAMING FORCED THEIR WAY IN. THEY RESEMBLED ORANGUTANS OR BIG, BLACK BABOONS MORE SO THAN MEN. SOON I UNDERSTOOD: THOSE LUNATICS I ATE DINNER WITH HAD THOROUGHLY TARRED AND FEATHERED THEM.
IN SPEAKING ABOUT THAT PATIENT WHO HAD INSTIGATED THE REBELLION, MAILLARD HAD NARRATED HIS OWN ACCOMPLISHMENT. YEARS AGO, HE HAD BEEN THE HOSPITAL'S DIRECTOR, BUT AFTER LOSING HIS MIND, HE BECAME A PATIENT. MY TRAVELING COMPANION HAD NOT BEEN AWARE OF THIS FACT.
THE GUARDS HAD BEEN TARRED, FEATHERED, AND LOCKED AWAY FOR THE PAST MONTH. NOW THAT THEY MANAGED TO FREE THEMSELVES, THEY DID NOT SEEM TOO FOND OF THE SYSTEM OF SOOTHING, BUT RATHER THEY EMBRACED MORE CONVENTIONAL METHODS.
ONE LAST THING I WOULD LIKE TO ADD... AS MUCH AS I HAVE SEARCHED IN ALL THE LIBRARIES IN EUROPE FOR WORKS BY DR. TARR AND PROF. FETHER, TILL THIS DAY, I HAVE FAILED IN MY MISSION TO FIND THEM.

THE FALL OF THE HOUSE OF USHER

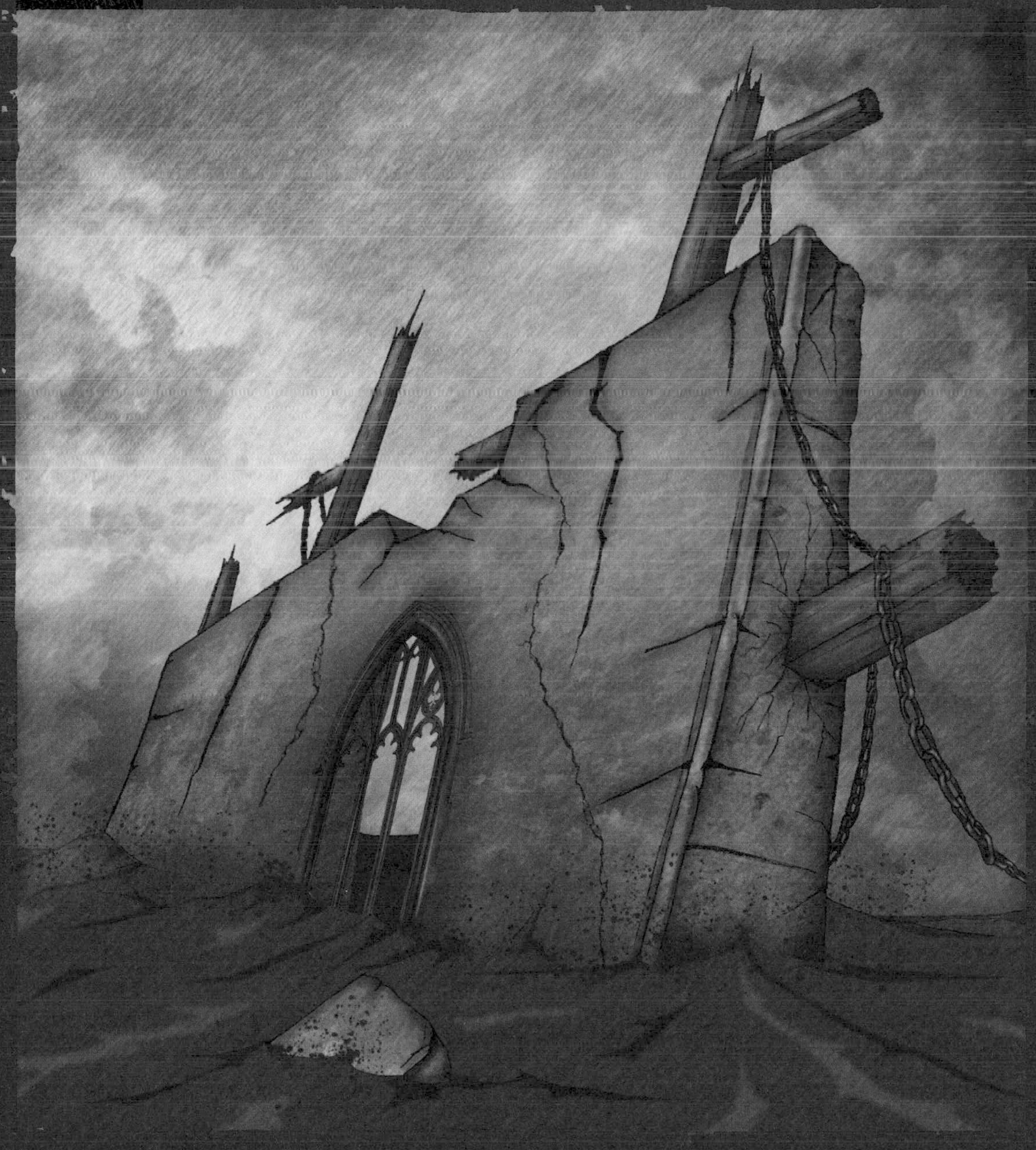

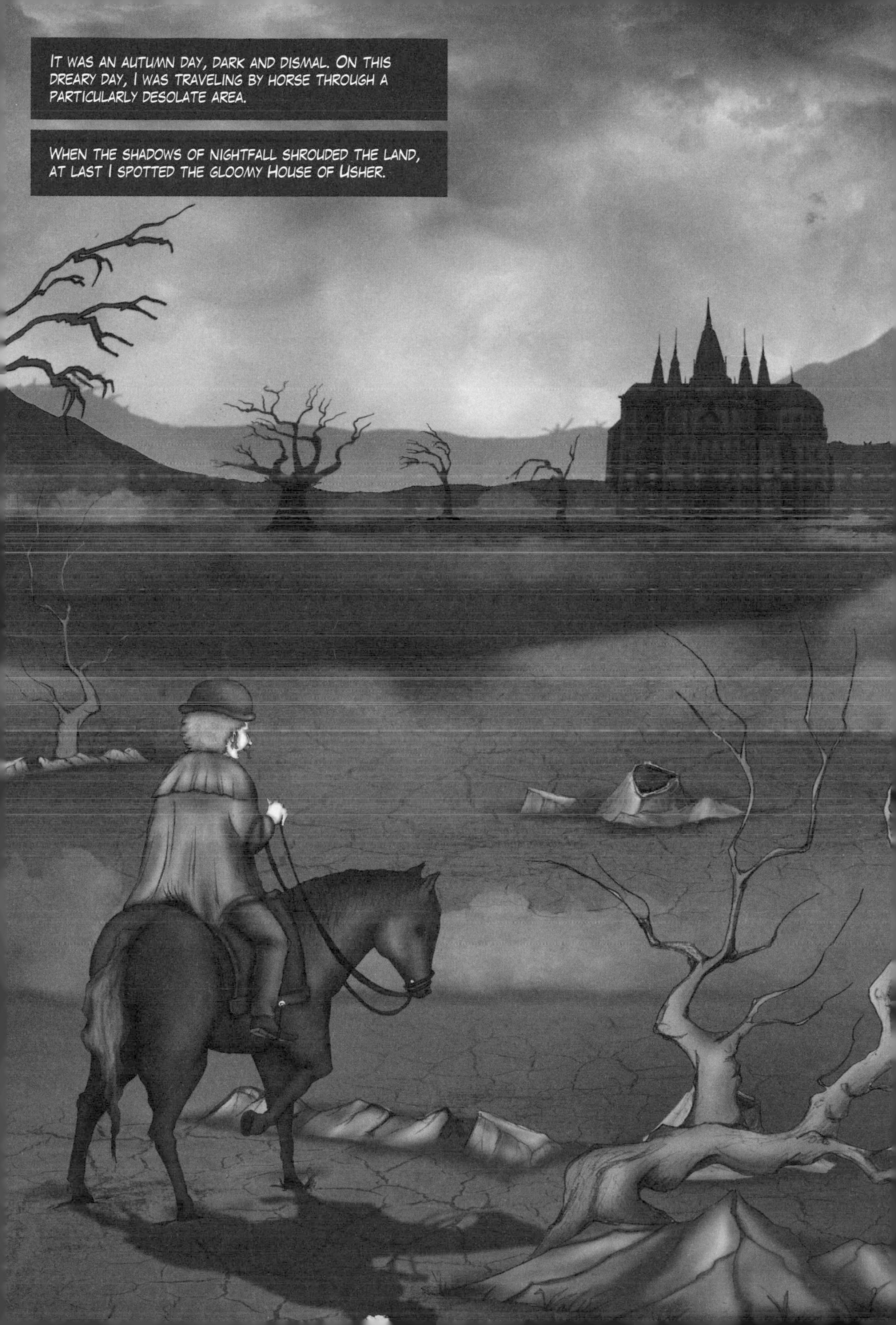
It was an autumn day, dark and dismal. On this dreary day, I was traveling by horse through a particularly desolate area.
When the shadows of nightfall shrouded the land, at last I spotted the gloomy House of Usher.

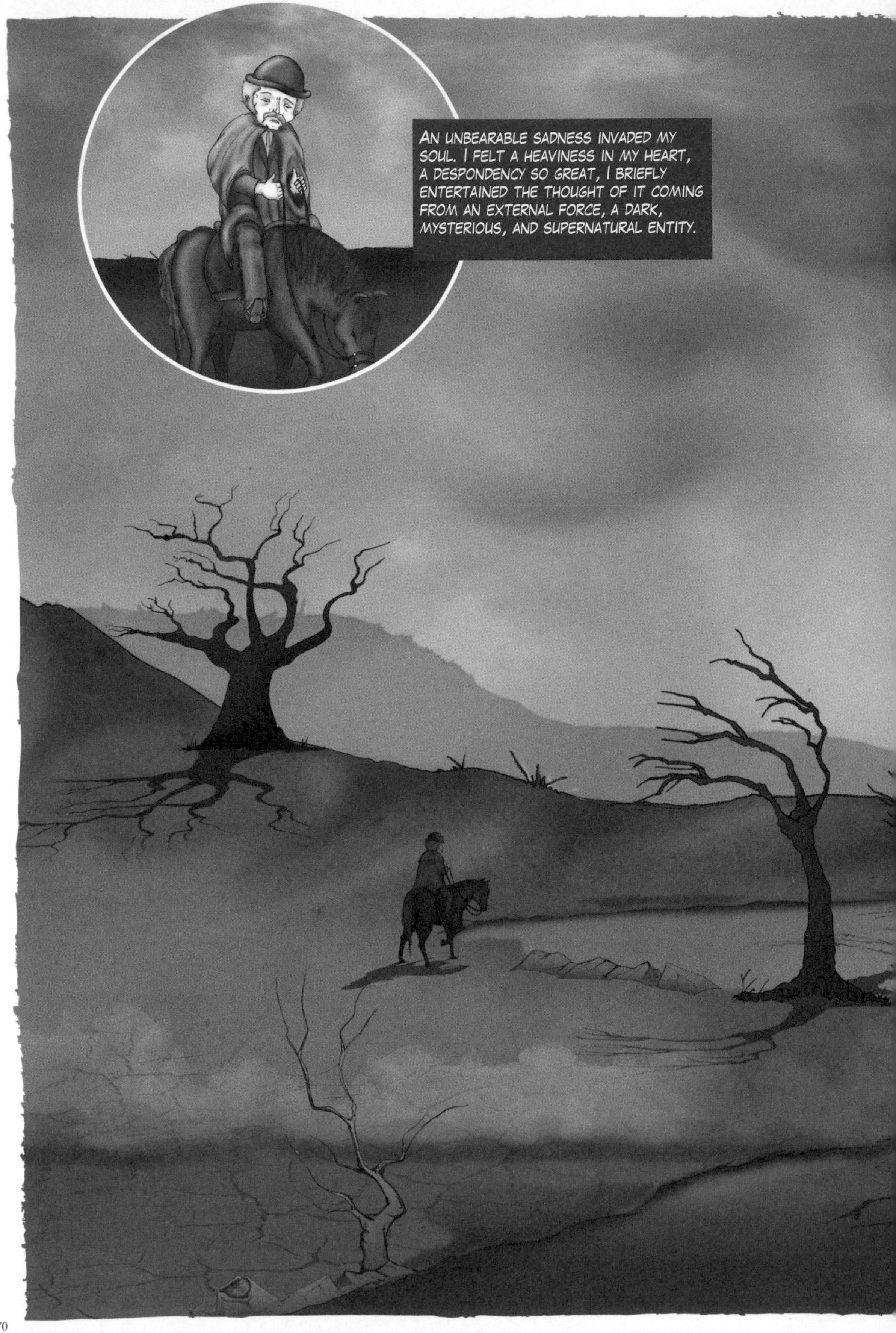
AN UNBEARABLE SADNESS INVADED MY SOUL. I FELT A HEAVINESS IN MY HEART, A DESPONDENCY SO GREAT, I BRIEFLY ENTERTAINED THE THOUGHT OF IT COMING FROM AN EXTERNAL FORCE, A DARK, MYSTERIOUS, AND SUPERNATURAL ENTITY.

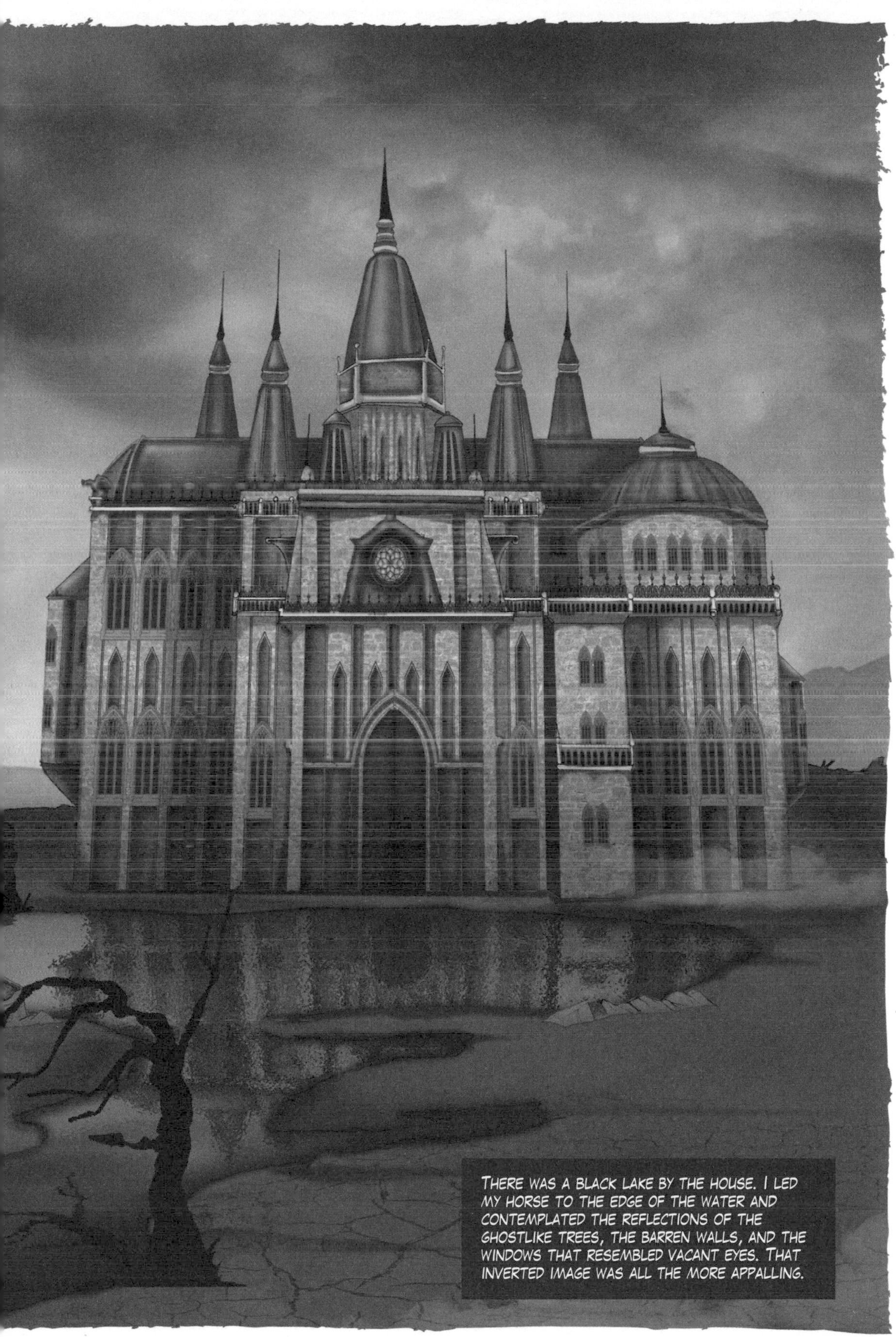
THERE WAS A BLACK LAKE BY THE HOUSE. I LED MY HORSE TO THE EDGE OF THE WATER AND CONTEMPLATED THE REFLECTIONS OF THE GHOSTLIKE TREES, THE BARREN WALLS, AND THE WINDOWS THAT RESEMBLED VACANT EYES. THAT INVERTED IMAGE WAS ALL THE MORE APPALLING.

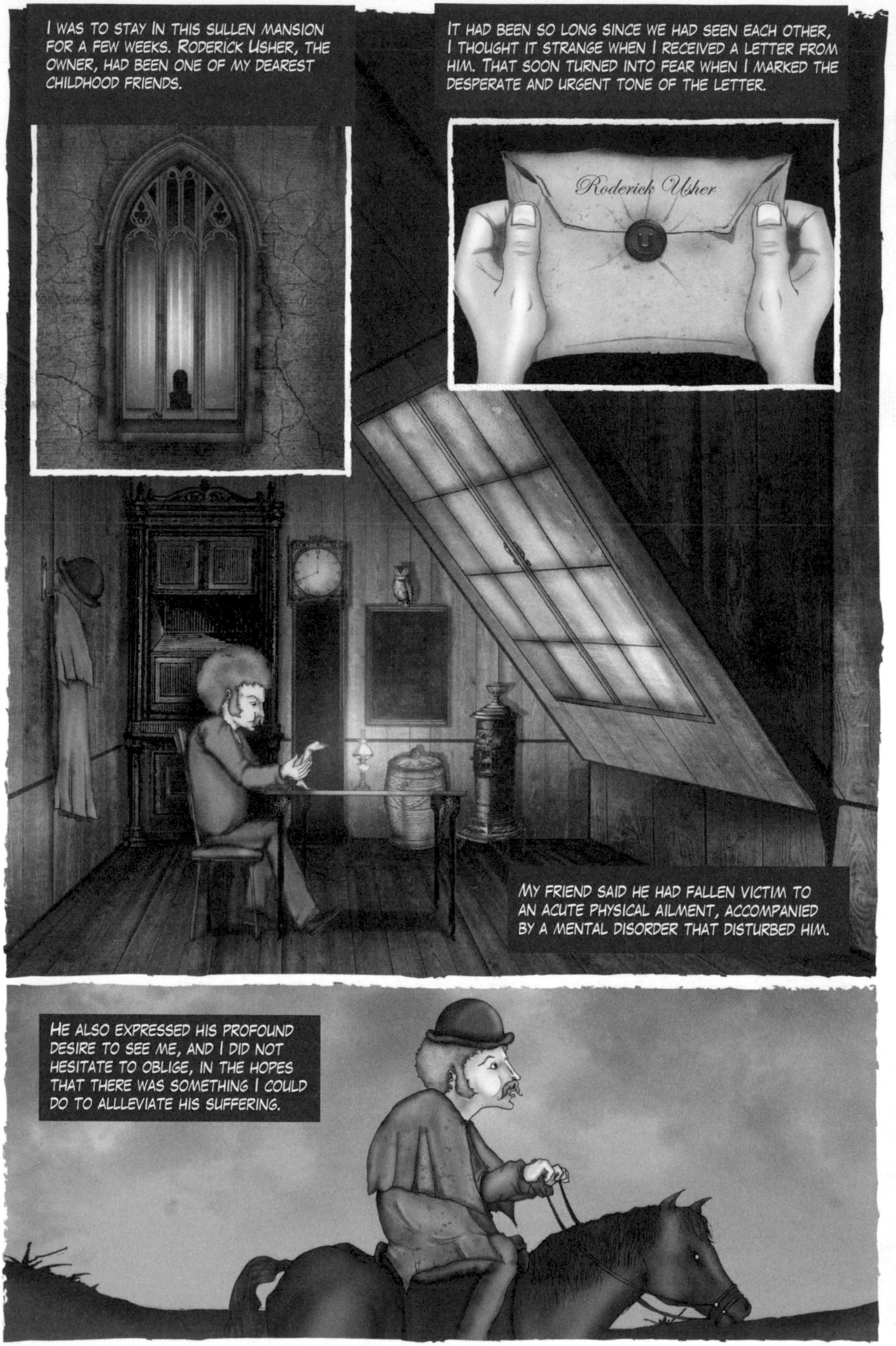
I WAS TO STAY IN THIS SULLEN MANSION FOR A FEW WEEKS. RODERICK USHER, THE OWNER, HAD BEEN ONE OF MY DEAREST CHILDHOOD FRIENDS.
IT HAD BEEN SO LONG SINCE WE HAD SEEN EACH OTHER, I THOUGHT IT STRANGE WHEN I RECEIVED A LETTER FROM HIM. THAT SOON TURNED INTO FEAR WHEN I MARKED THE DESPERATE AND URGENT TONE OF THE LETTER.
Roderick Usher
MY FRIEND SAID HE HAD FALLEN VICTIM TO AN ACUTE PHYSICAL AILMENT, ACCOMPANIED BY A MENTAL DISORDER THAT DISTURBED HIM.
HE ALSO EXPRESSED HIS PROFOUND DESIRE TO SEE ME, AND I DID NOT HESITATE TO OBLIGE, IN THE HOPES THAT THERE WAS SOMETHING I COULD DO TO ALLEVIATE HIS SUFFERING.

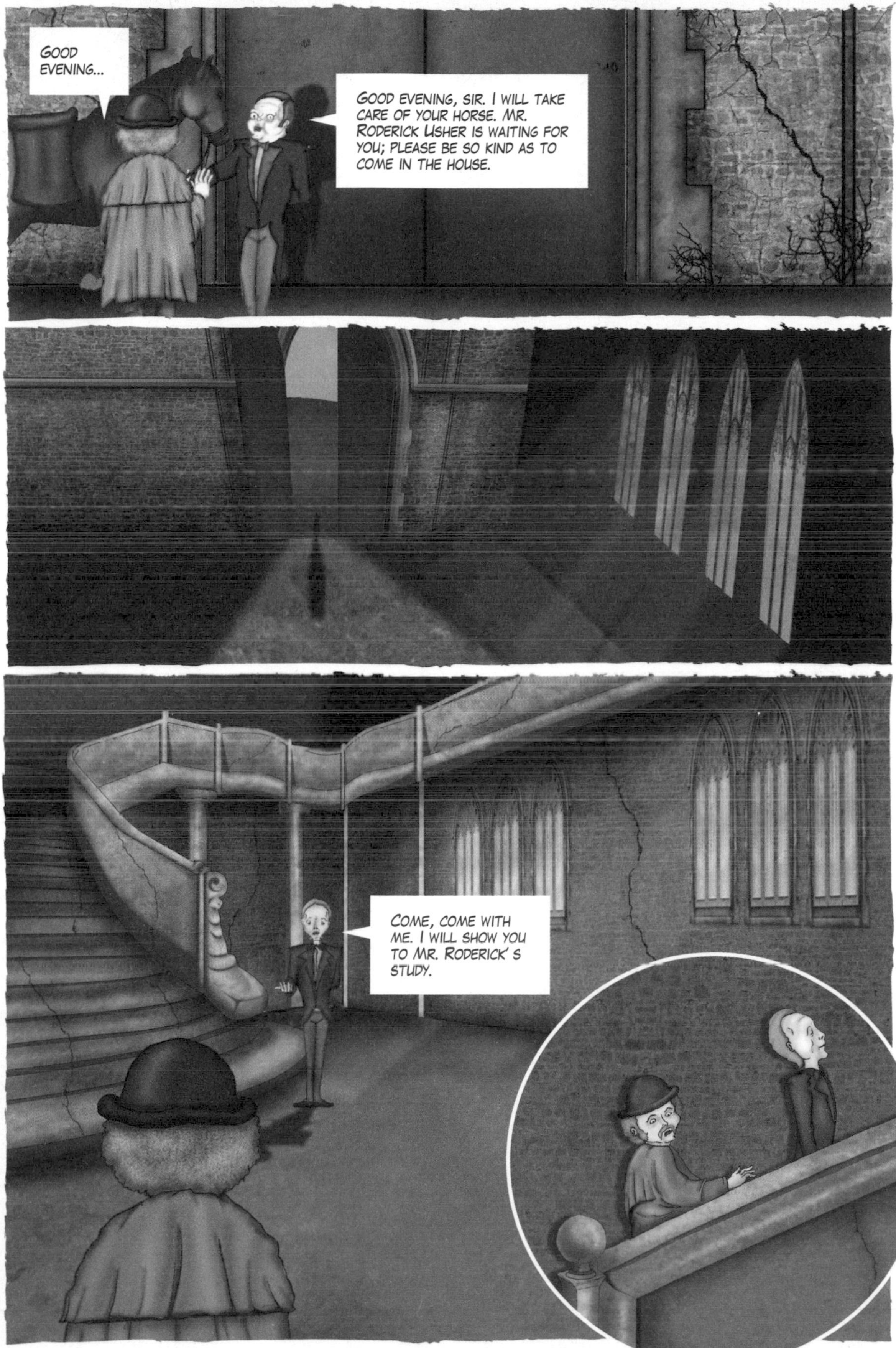
GOOD EVENING...
GOOD EVENING, SIR. I WILL TAKE CARE OF YOUR HORSE. MR. RODERICK USHER IS WAITING FOR YOU; PLEASE BE SO KIND AS TO COME IN THE HOUSE.
COME, COME WITH ME. I WILL SHOW YOU TO MR. RODERICK'S STUDY.

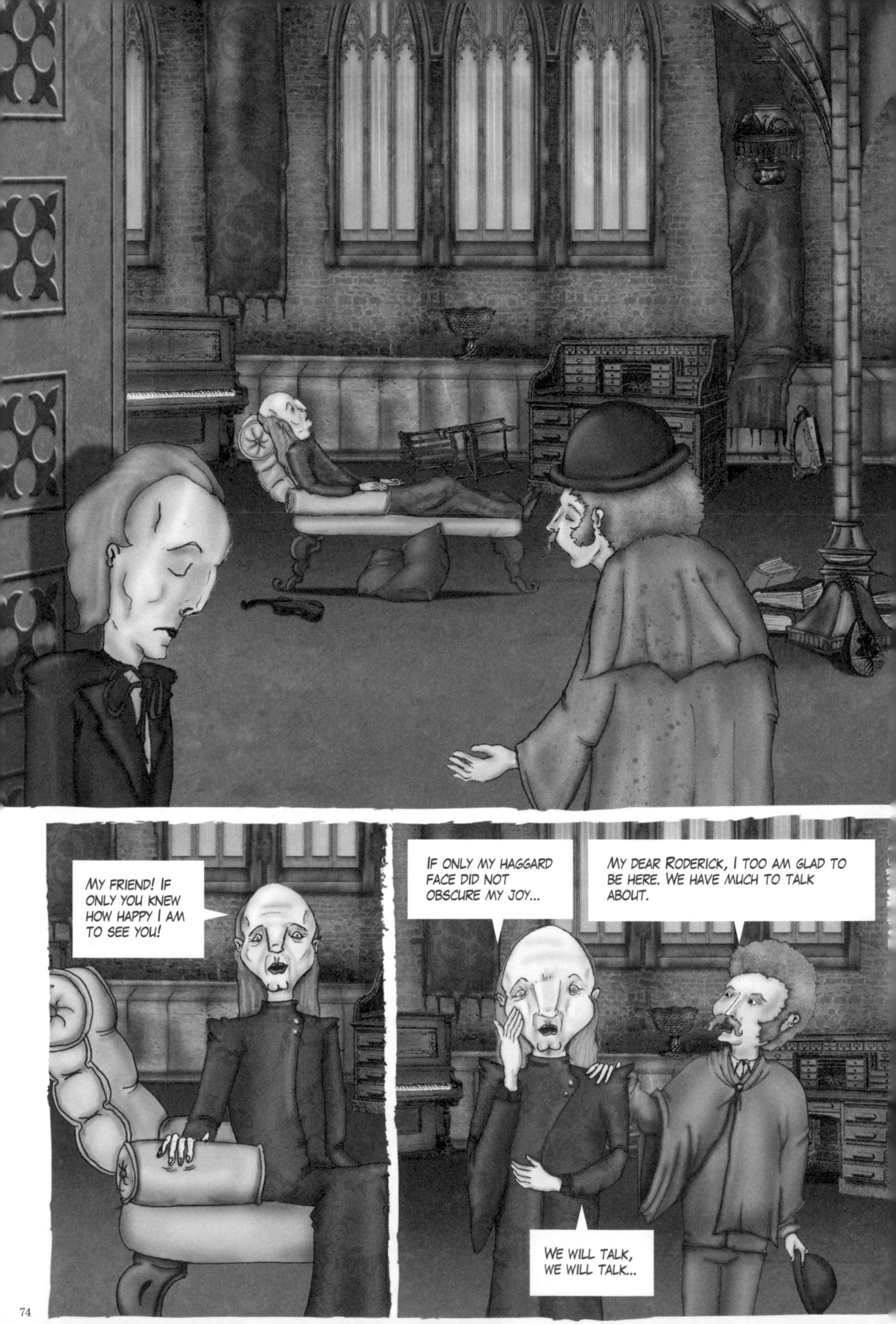
MY FRIEND! IF ONLY YOU KNEW HOW HAPPY I AM TO SEE YOU!
IF ONLY MY HAGGARD FACE DID NOT OBSCURE MY JOY...
MY DEAR RODERICK, I TOO AM GLAD TO BE HERE. WE HAVE MUCH TO TALK ABOUT.
WE WILL TALK, WE WILL TALK...

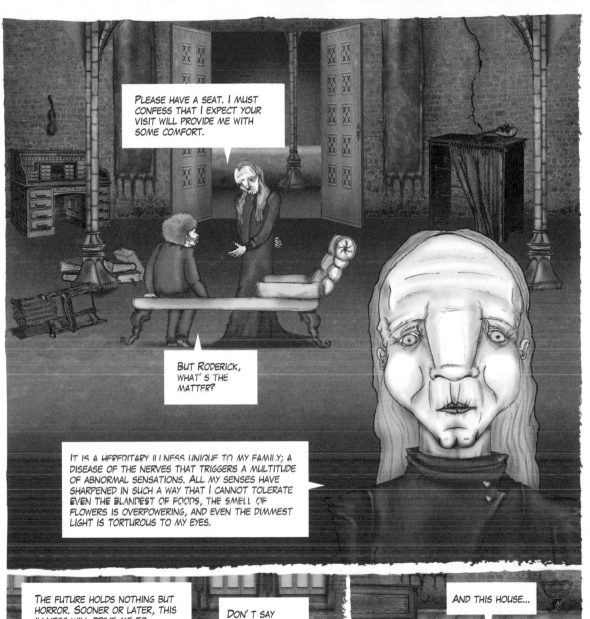

PLEASE HAVE A SEAT. I MUST CONFESS THAT I EXPECT YOUR VISIT WILL PROVIDE ME WITH SOME COMFORT.

BUT RODERICK, WHAT'S THE MATTER?

IT IS A HEREDITARY ILLNESS UNIQUE TO MY FAMILY; A DISEASE OF THE NERVES THAT TRIGGERS A MULTITUDE OF ABNORMAL SENSATIONS. ALL MY SENSES HAVE SHARPENED IN SUCH A WAY THAT I CANNOT TOLERATE EVEN THE BLANDEST OF FOODS, THE SMELL OF FLOWERS IS OVERPOWERING, AND EVEN THE DIMMEST LIGHT IS TORTUROUS TO MY EYES.

THE FUTURE HOLDS NOTHING BUT HORROR. SOONER OR LATER, THIS ILLNESS WILL DRIVE ME TO INSANITY AND THEN THE GRAVE.

DON'T SAY THAT, RODERICK!

YES, MY FRIEND, THE SPECTER OF FEAR CONSTANTLY PLAGUES ME.

AND THIS HOUSE...

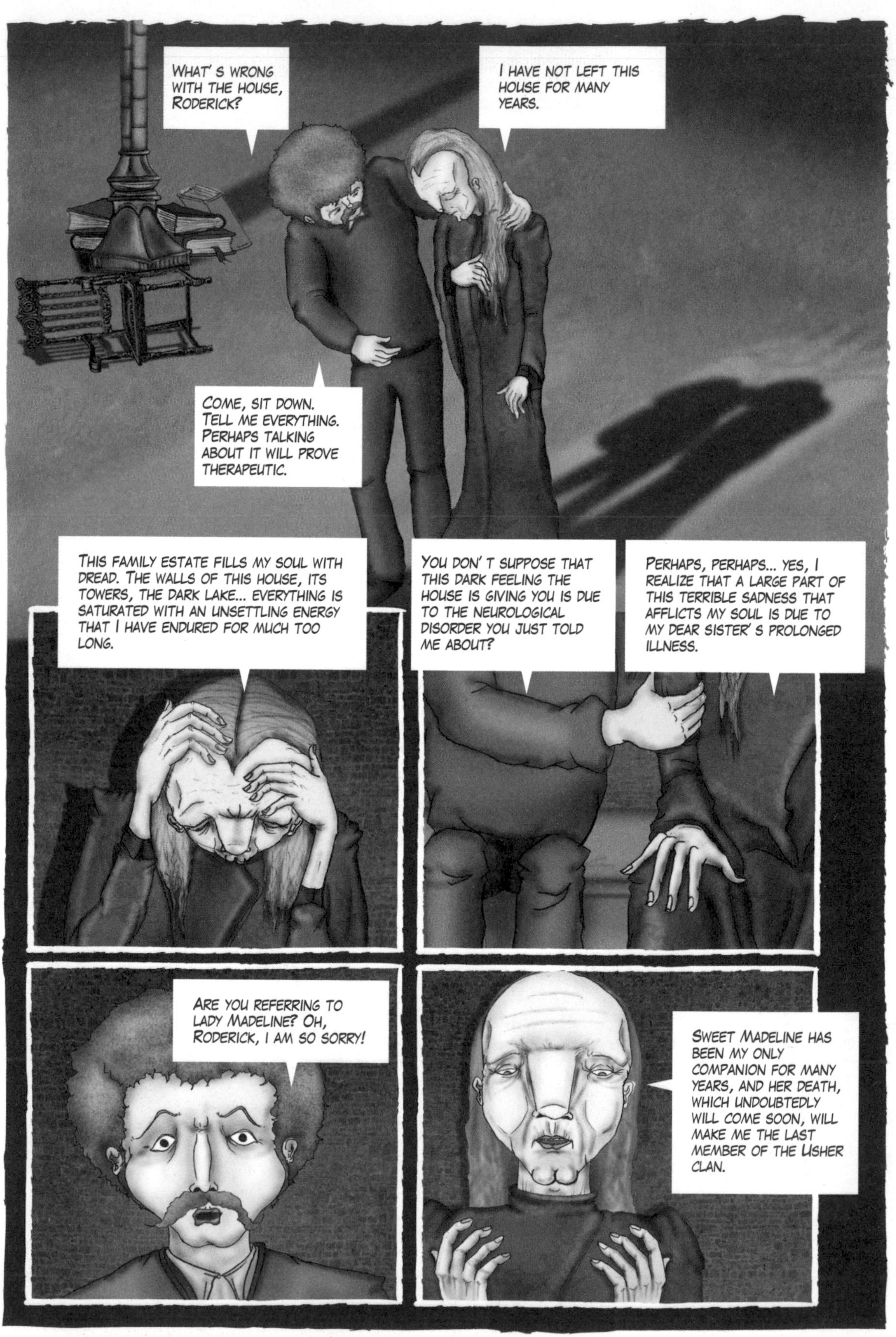
WHAT'S WRONG WITH THE HOUSE, RODERICK?
I HAVE NOT LEFT THIS HOUSE FOR MANY YEARS.
COME, SIT DOWN. TELL ME EVERYTHING. PERHAPS TALKING ABOUT IT WILL PROVE THERAPEUTIC.
THIS FAMILY ESTATE FILLS MY SOUL WITH DREAD. THE WALLS OF THIS HOUSE, ITS TOWERS, THE DARK LAKE... EVERYTHING IS SATURATED WITH AN UNSETTLING ENERGY THAT I HAVE ENDURED FOR MUCH TOO LONG.
YOU DON'T SUPPOSE THAT THIS DARK FEELING THE HOUSE IS GIVING YOU IS DUE TO THE NEUROLOGICAL DISORDER YOU JUST TOLD ME ABOUT?
PERHAPS, PERHAPS... YES, I REALIZE THAT A LARGE PART OF THIS TERRIBLE SADNESS THAT AFFLICTS MY SOUL IS DUE TO MY DEAR SISTER'S PROLONGED ILLNESS.
ARE YOU REFERRING TO LADY MADELINE? OH, RODERICK, I AM SO SORRY!
SWEET MADELINE HAS BEEN MY ONLY COMPANION FOR MANY YEARS, AND HER DEATH, WHICH UNDOUBTEDLY WILL COME SOON, WILL MAKE ME THE LAST MEMBER OF THE USHER CLAN.

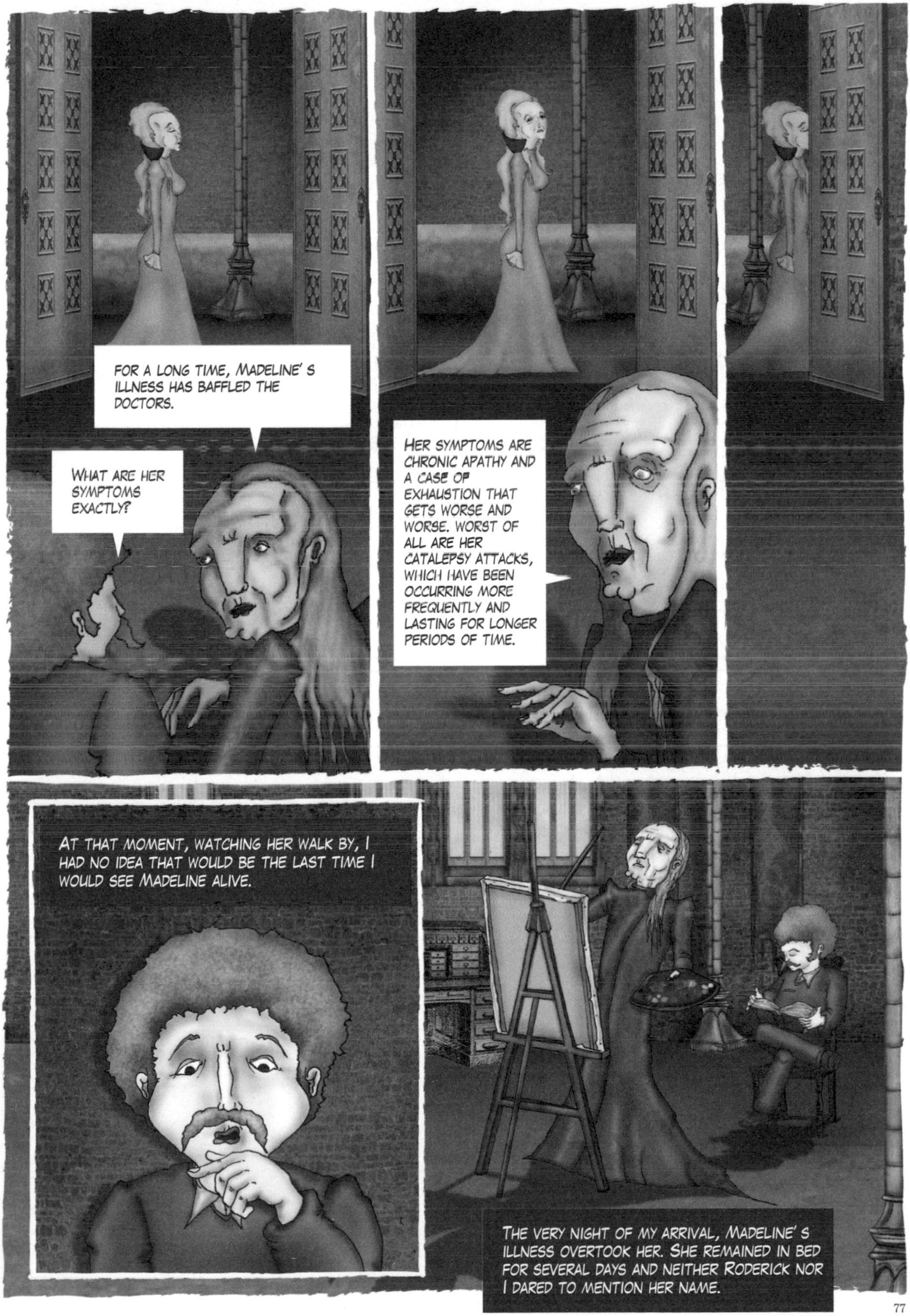
FOR A LONG TIME, MADELINE'S ILLNESS HAS BAFFLED THE DOCTORS.
WHAT ARE HER SYMPTOMS EXACTLY?
HER SYMPTOMS ARE CHRONIC APATHY AND A CASE OF EXHAUSTION THAT GETS WORSE AND WORSE. WORST OF ALL ARE HER CATALEPSY ATTACKS, WHICH HAVE BEEN OCCURRING MORE FREQUENTLY AND LASTING FOR LONGER PERIODS OF TIME.
AT THAT MOMENT, WATCHING HER WALK BY, I HAD NO IDEA THAT WOULD BE THE LAST TIME I WOULD SEE MADELINE ALIVE.
THE VERY NIGHT OF MY ARRIVAL, MADELINE'S ILLNESS OVERTOOK HER. SHE REMAINED IN BED FOR SEVERAL DAYS AND NEITHER RODERICK NOR I DARED TO MENTION HER NAME.

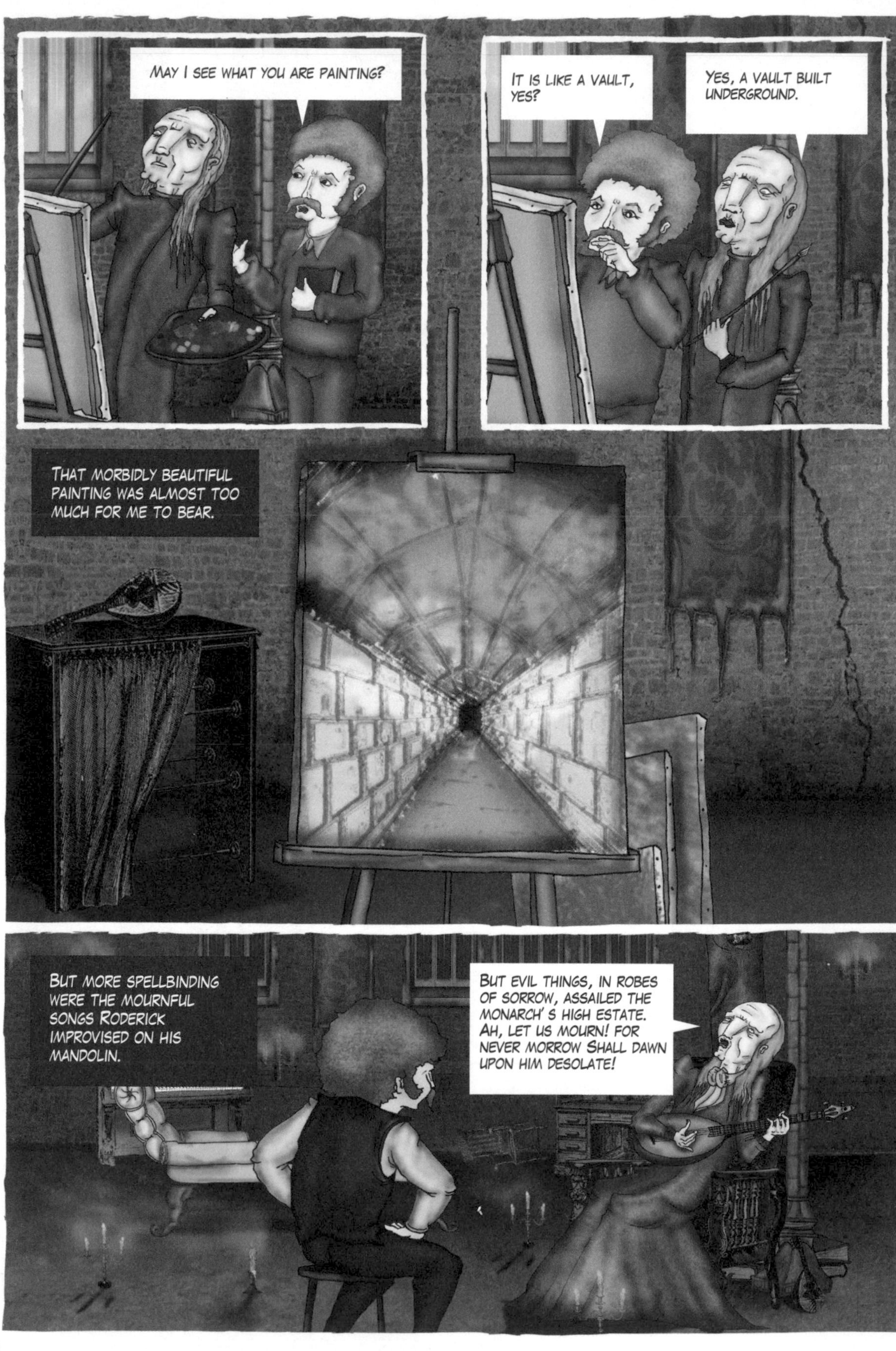
May I see what you are painting?
It is like a vault, yes?
Yes, a vault built underground.
That morbidly beautiful painting was almost too much for me to bear.
But more spellbinding were the mournful songs Roderick improvised on his mandolin.
But evil things, in robes of sorrow, assailed the monarch's high estate. Ah, let us mourn! For never morrow Shall dawn upon him desolate!

I FEEL AS IF EVERYTHING AROUND ME IS ALIVE. THE GRAY STONES, THE MOSS THAT GROWS UPON THEM, THE WITHERED TREES...

AND ABOVE ALL... THAT CONSTANT REFLECTION IN THE STILL WATERS OF THE LAKE.

ONE NIGHT, RODERICK SURPRISED ME WITH A SHOCKING REVELATION.

TODAY, THE LIFE OF MY DEAR SISTER, MADELINE, HAS COME TO AN END.

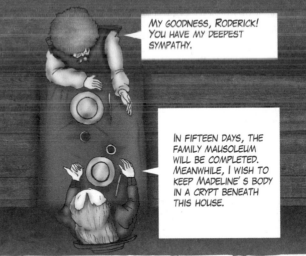

MY GOODNESS, RODERICK! YOU HAVE MY DEEPEST SYMPATHY.

IN FIFTEEN DAYS, THE FAMILY MAUSOLEUM WILL BE COMPLETED. MEANWHILE, I WISH TO KEEP MADELINE'S BODY IN A CRYPT BENEATH THIS HOUSE.

I UNDERSTAND. I WILL PERSONALLY HELP YOU WITH ALL THE PREPARATIONS.

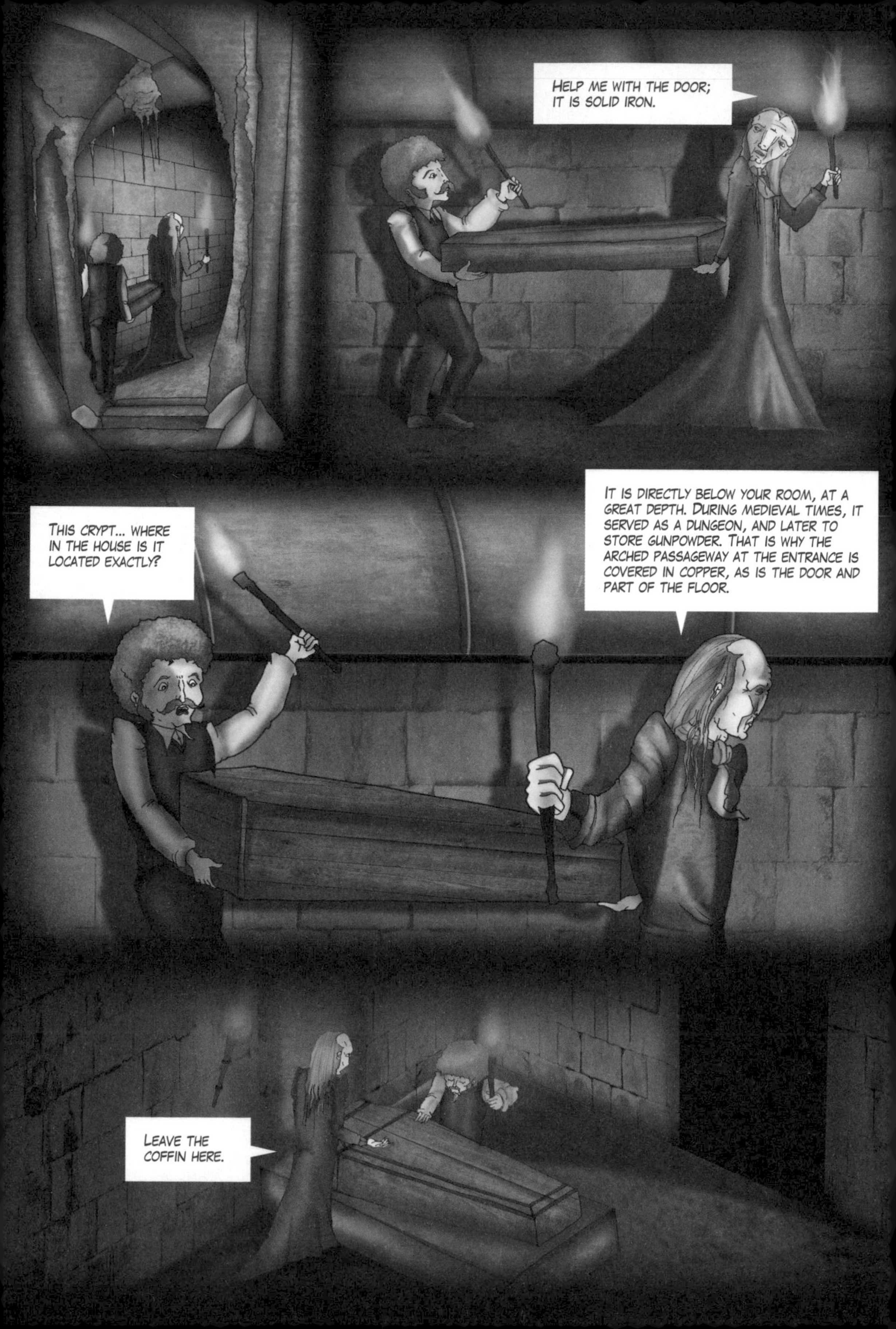
HELP ME WITH THE DOOR; IT IS SOLID IRON.
THIS CRYPT... WHERE IN THE HOUSE IS IT LOCATED EXACTLY?
IT IS DIRECTLY BELOW YOUR ROOM, AT A GREAT DEPTH. DURING MEDIEVAL TIMES, IT SERVED AS A DUNGEON, AND LATER TO STORE GUNPOWDER. THAT IS WHY THE ARCHED PASSAGEWAY AT THE ENTRANCE IS COVERED IN COPPER, AS IS THE DOOR AND PART OF THE FLOOR.
LEAVE THE COFFIN HERE.

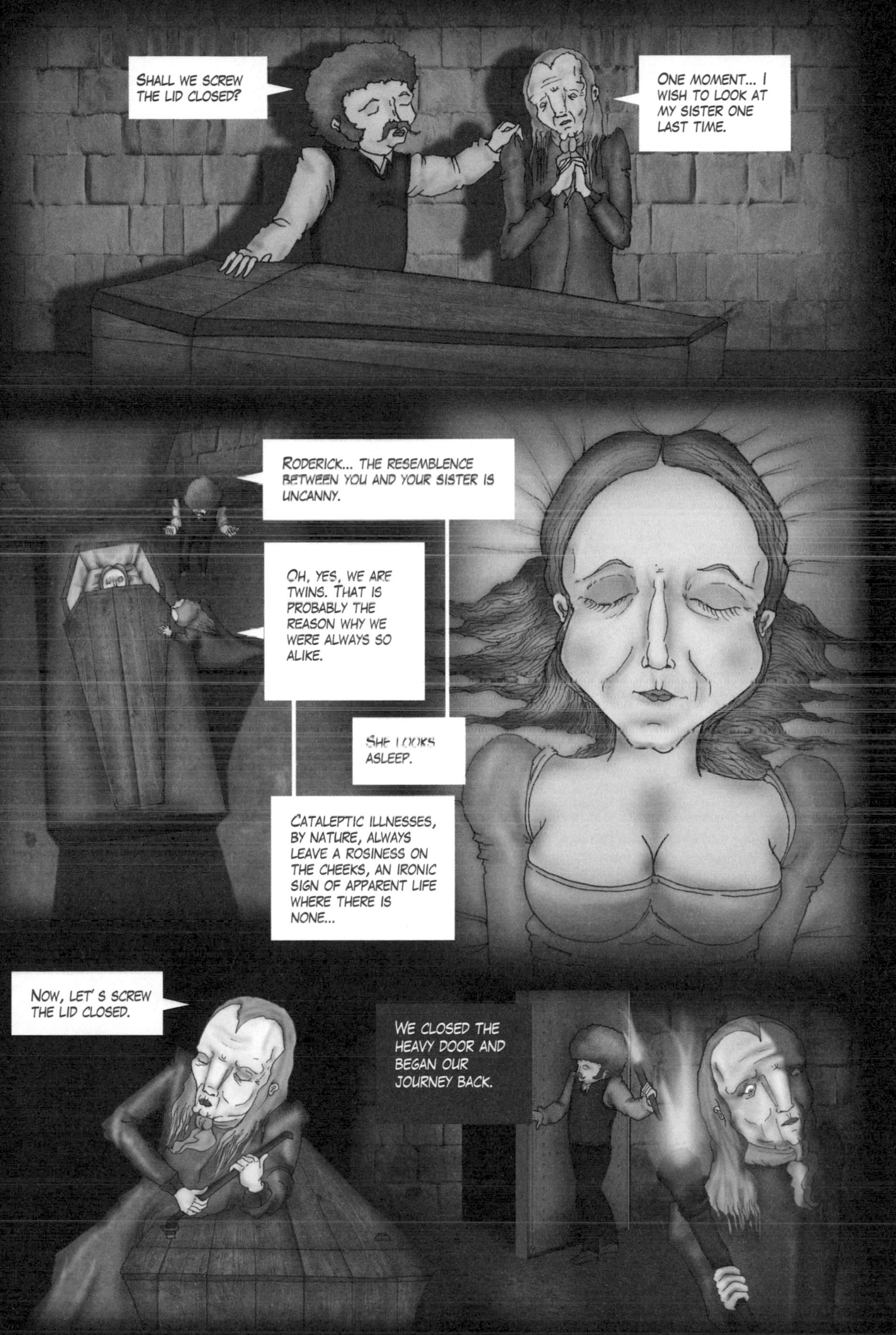

SHALL WE SCREW THE LID CLOSED?
ONE MOMENT... I WISH TO LOOK AT MY SISTER ONE LAST TIME.
RODERICK... THE RESEMBLENCE BETWEEN YOU AND YOUR SISTER IS UNCANNY.
OH, YES, WE ARE TWINS. THAT IS PROBABLY THE REASON WHY WE WERE ALWAYS SO ALIKE.
SHE LOOKS ASLEEP.
CATALEPTIC ILLNESSES, BY NATURE, ALWAYS LEAVE A ROSINESS ON THE CHEEKS, AN IRONIC SIGN OF APPARENT LIFE WHERE THERE IS NONE...
NOW, LET'S SCREW THE LID CLOSED.
WE CLOSED THE HEAVY DOOR AND BEGAN OUR JOURNEY BACK.

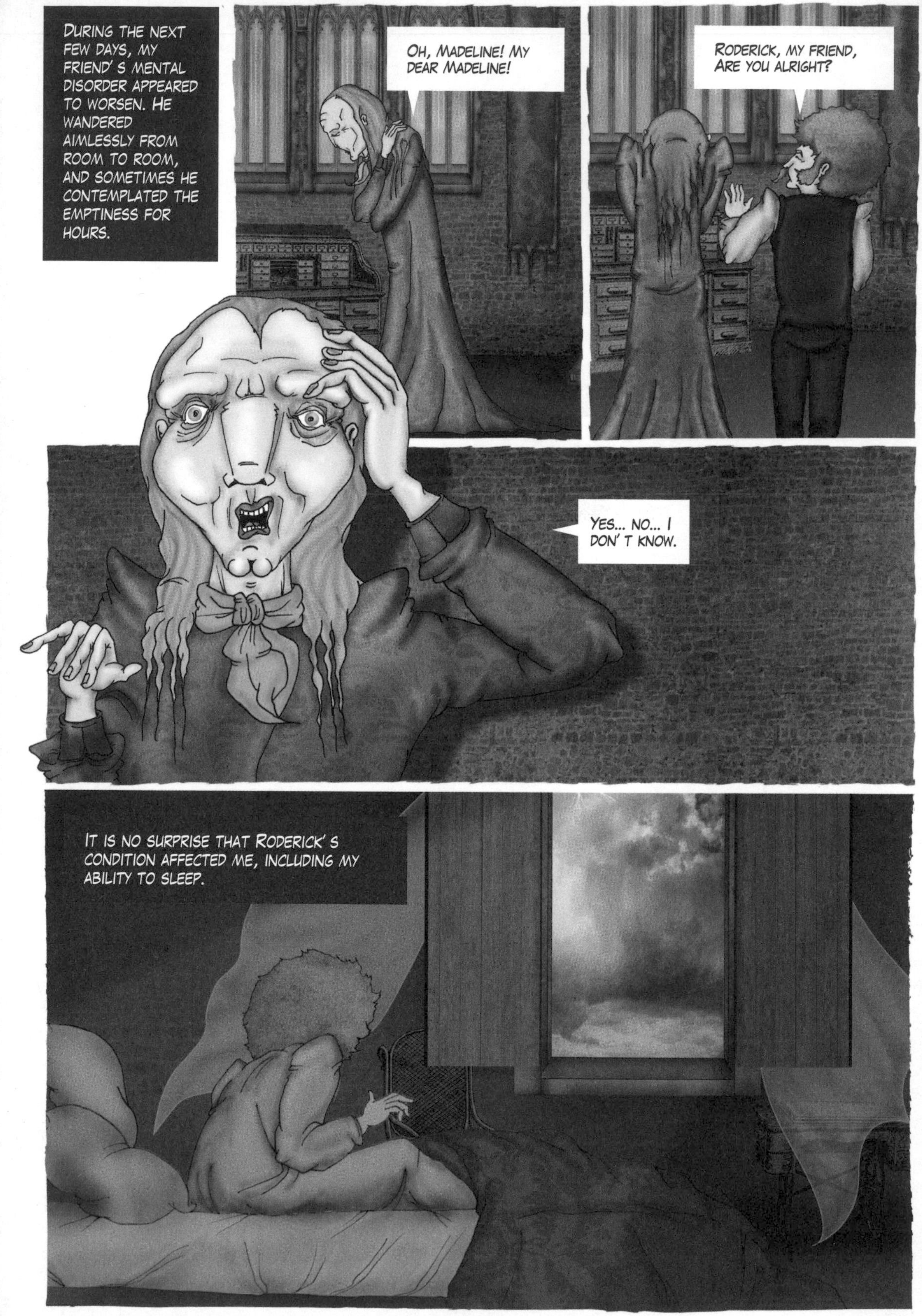
During the next few days, my friend's mental disorder appeared to worsen. He wandered aimlessly from room to room, and sometimes he contemplated the emptiness for hours.
Oh, Madeline! My dear Madeline!
Roderick, my friend, are you alright?
Yes... no... I don't know.
It is no surprise that Roderick's condition affected me, including my ability to sleep.

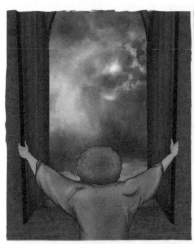

KNOCK!
KNOCK!
KNOCK!

JUST A
MINUTE,
I'M
COMING...

RODERICK...
YOU ARE
SO PALE.

YOU HAVEN'T SEEN
IT? PERHAPS YOU
HAVEN'T SEEN IT.
YOU HAVE TO SEE IT.

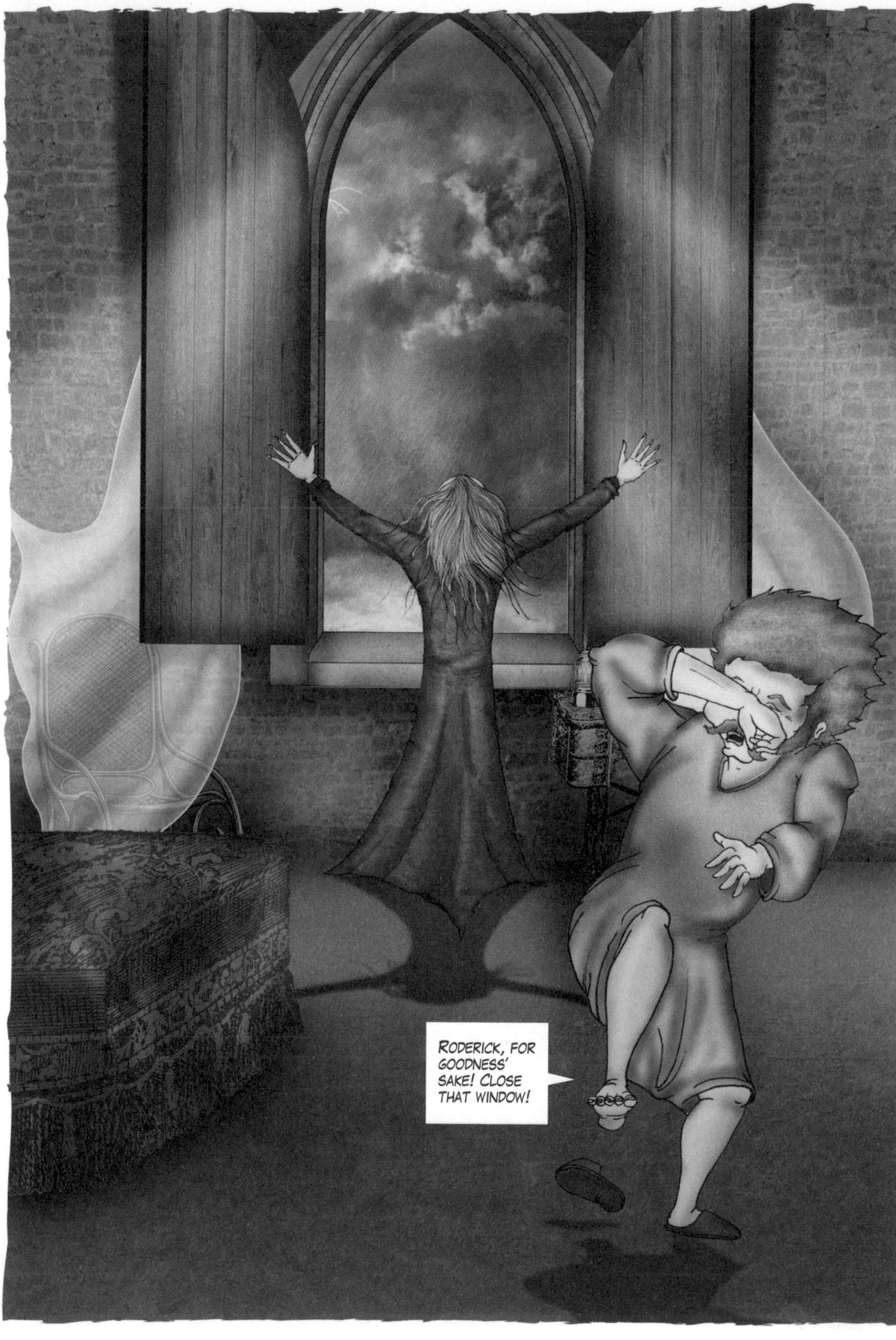
RODERICK, FOR GOODNESS' SAKE! CLOSE THAT WINDOW!

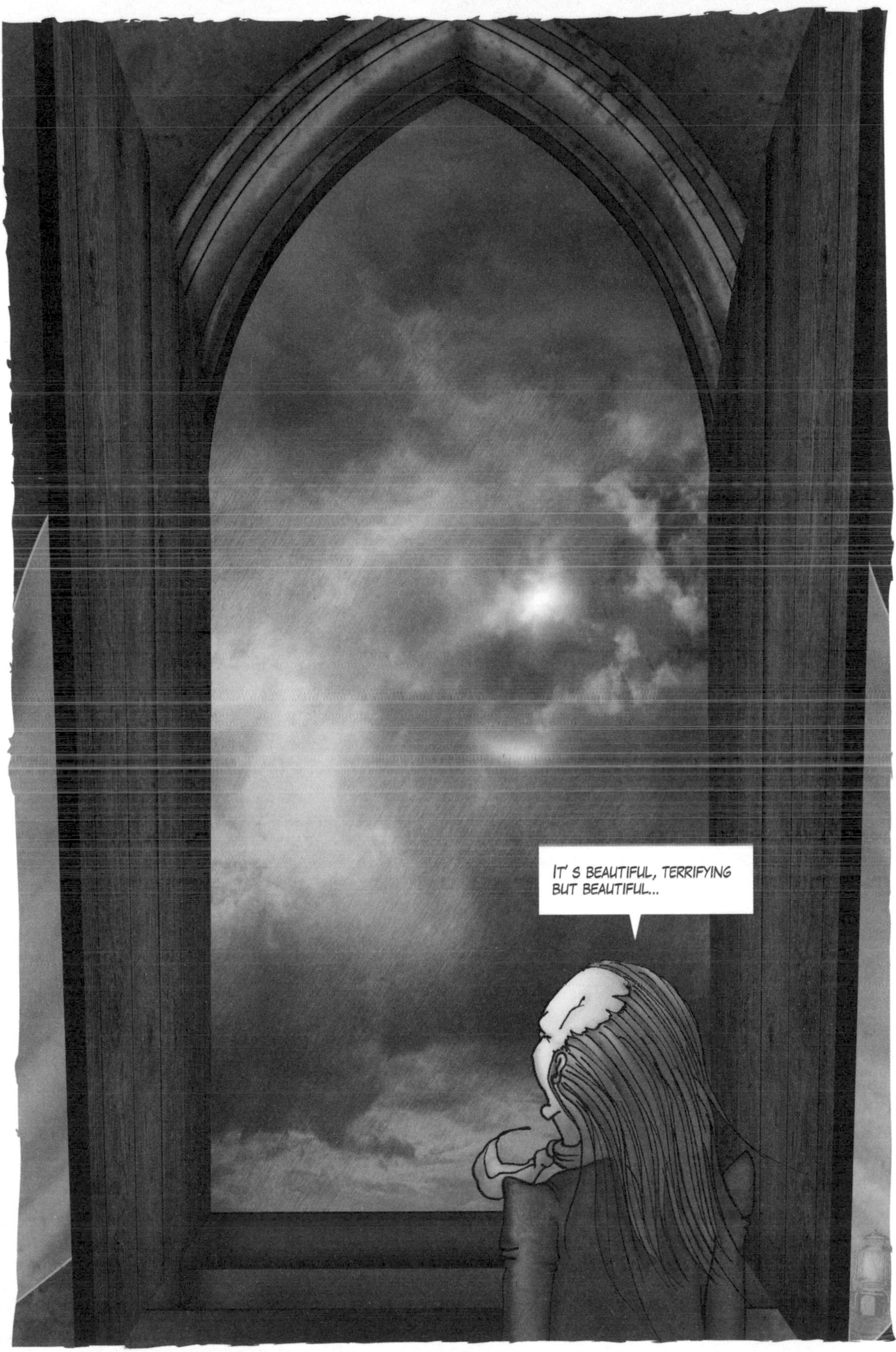
IT' S BEAUTIFUL, TERRIFYING BUT BEAUTIFUL...

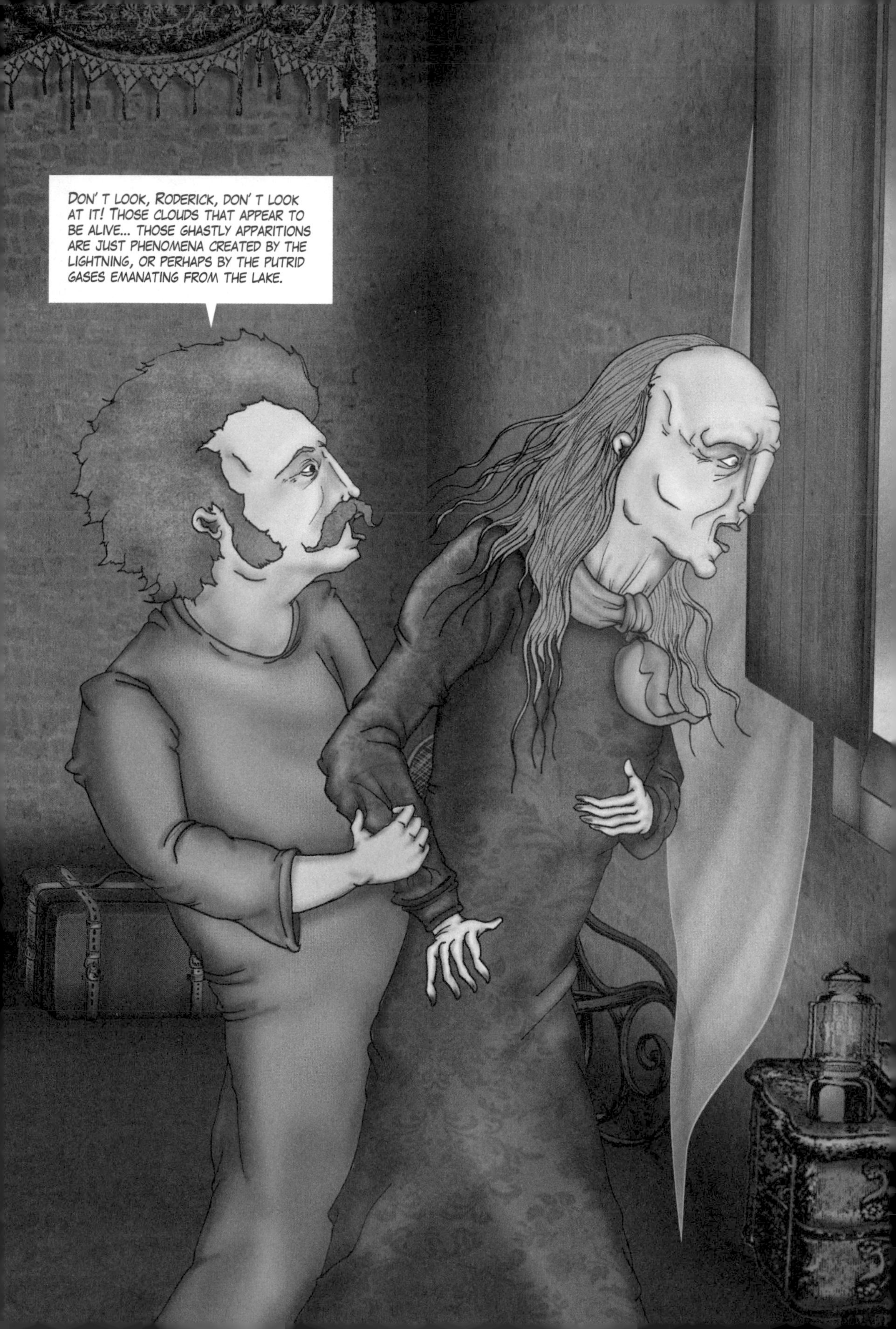
DON' T LOOK, RODERICK, DON' T LOOK AT IT! THOSE CLOUDS THAT APPEAR TO BE ALIVE... THOSE GHASTLY APPARITIONS ARE JUST PHENOMENA CREATED BY THE LIGHTNING, OR PERHAPS BY THE PUTRID GASES EMANATING FROM THE LAKE.

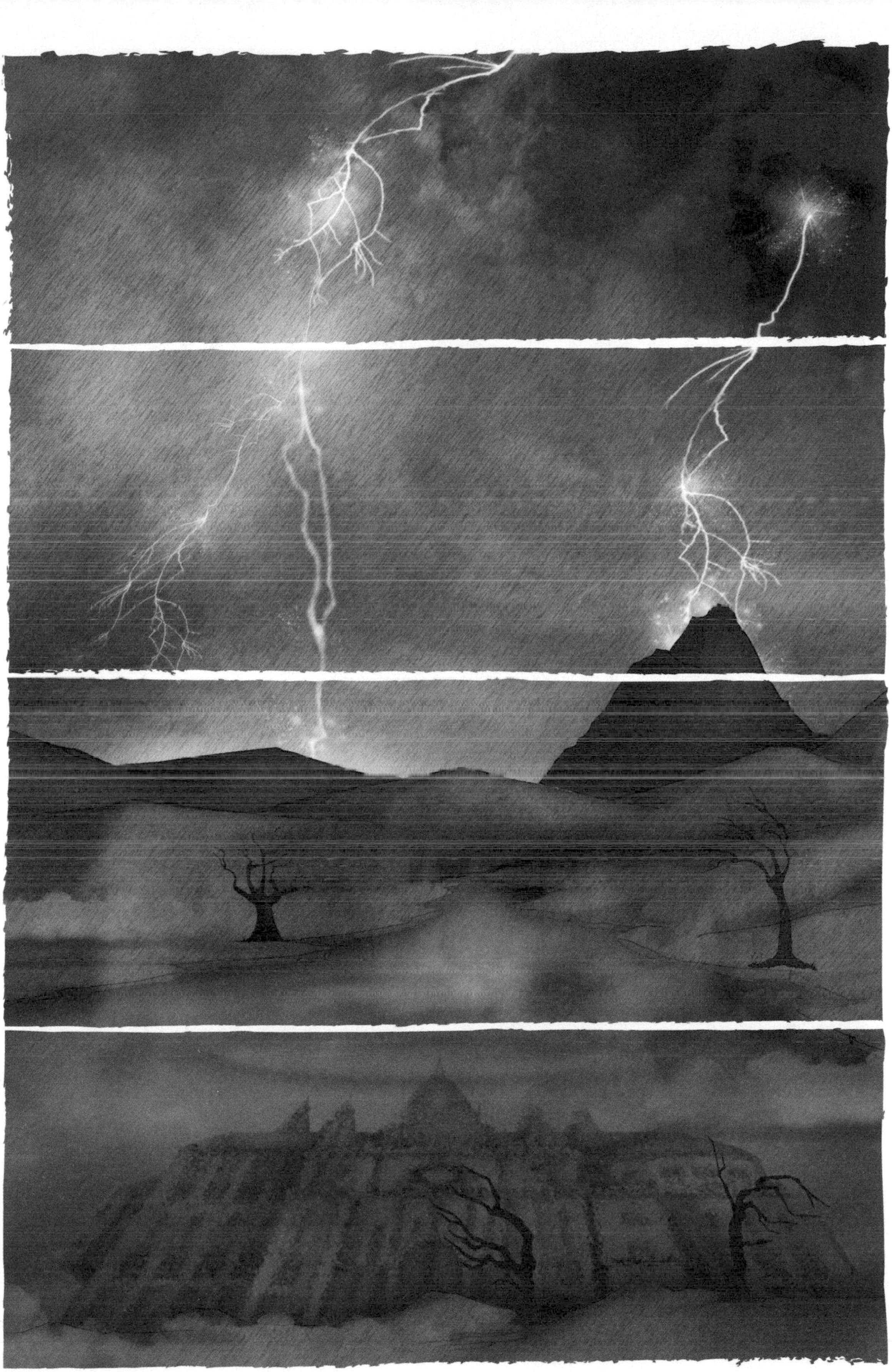

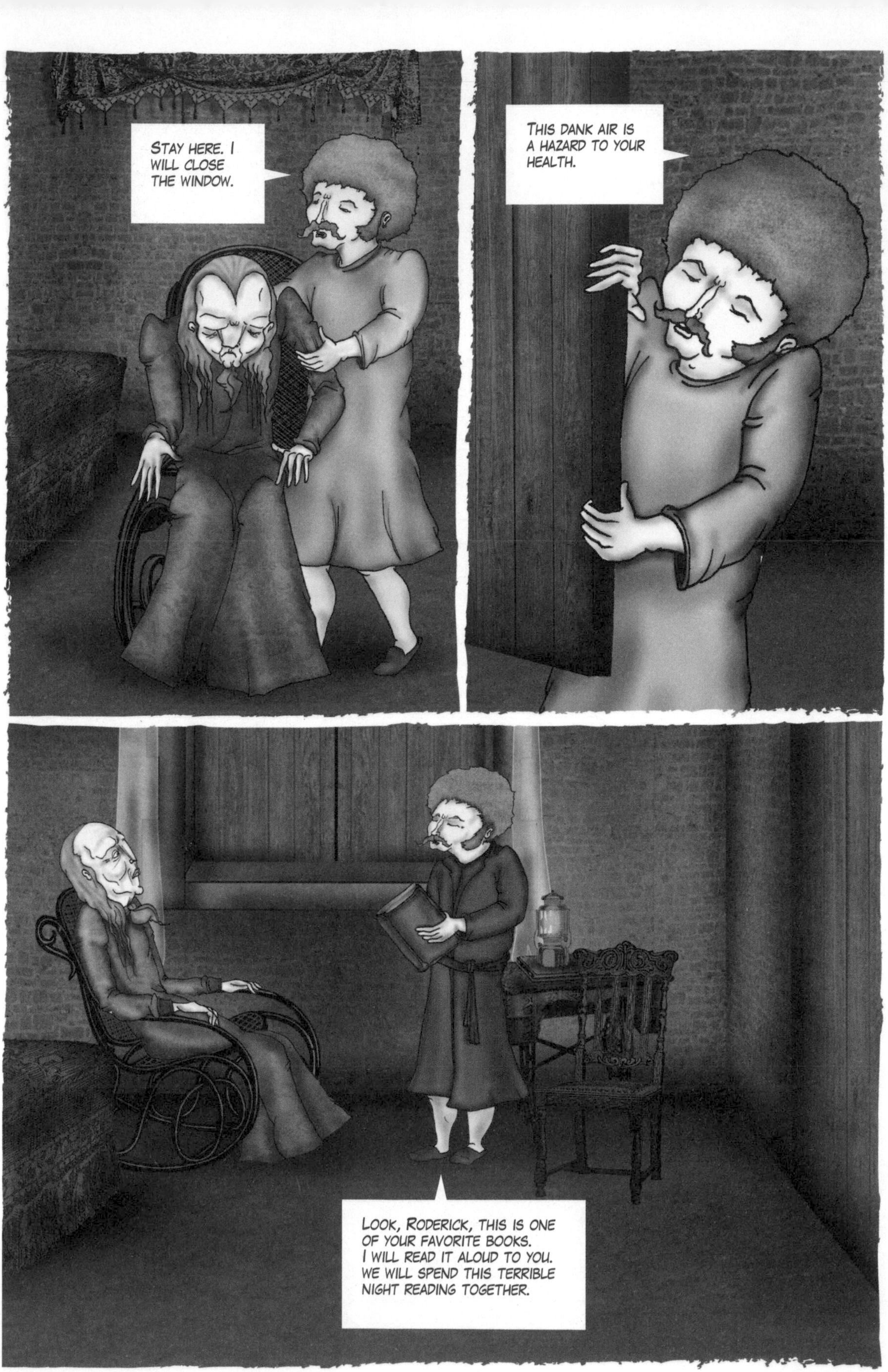
STAY HERE. I WILL CLOSE THE WINDOW.
THIS DANK AIR IS A HAZARD TO YOUR HEALTH.
LOOK, RODERICK, THIS IS ONE OF YOUR FAVORITE BOOKS. I WILL READ IT ALOUD TO YOU. WE WILL SPEND THIS TERRIBLE NIGHT READING TOGETHER.

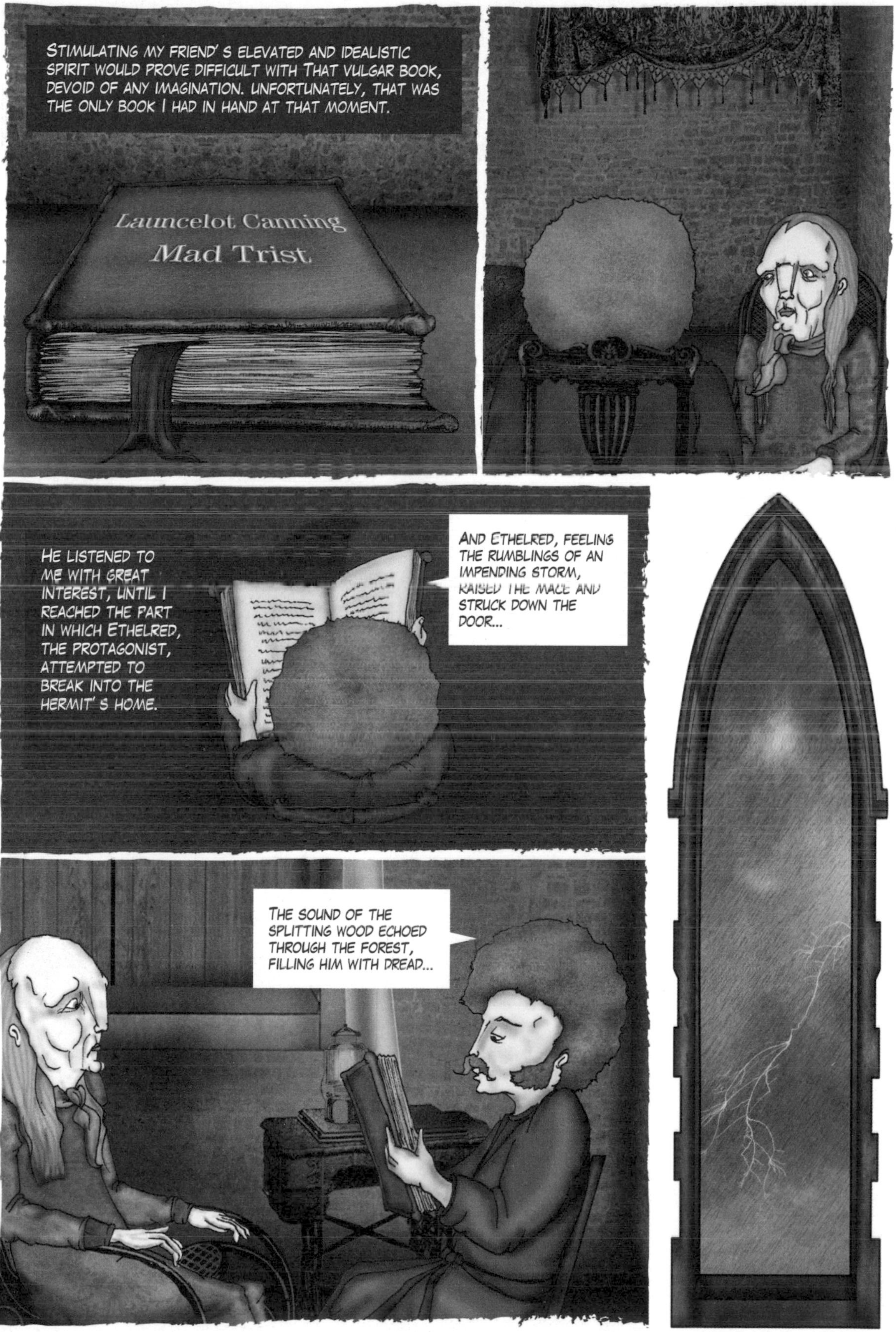

STIMULATING MY FRIEND'S ELEVATED AND IDEALISTIC SPIRIT WOULD PROVE DIFFICULT WITH THAT VULGAR BOOK, DEVOID OF ANY IMAGINATION. UNFORTUNATELY, THAT WAS THE ONLY BOOK I HAD IN HAND AT THAT MOMENT.
Launcelot Canning
Mad Trist
HE LISTENED TO ME WITH GREAT INTEREST, UNTIL I REACHED THE PART IN WHICH ETHELRED, THE PROTAGONIST, ATTEMPTED TO BREAK INTO THE HERMIT'S HOME.
AND ETHELRED, FEELING THE RUMBLINGS OF AN IMPENDING STORM, RAISED THE MACE AND STRUCK DOWN THE DOOR...
THE SOUND OF THE SPLITTING WOOD ECHOED THROUGH THE FOREST, FILLING HIM WITH DREAD...

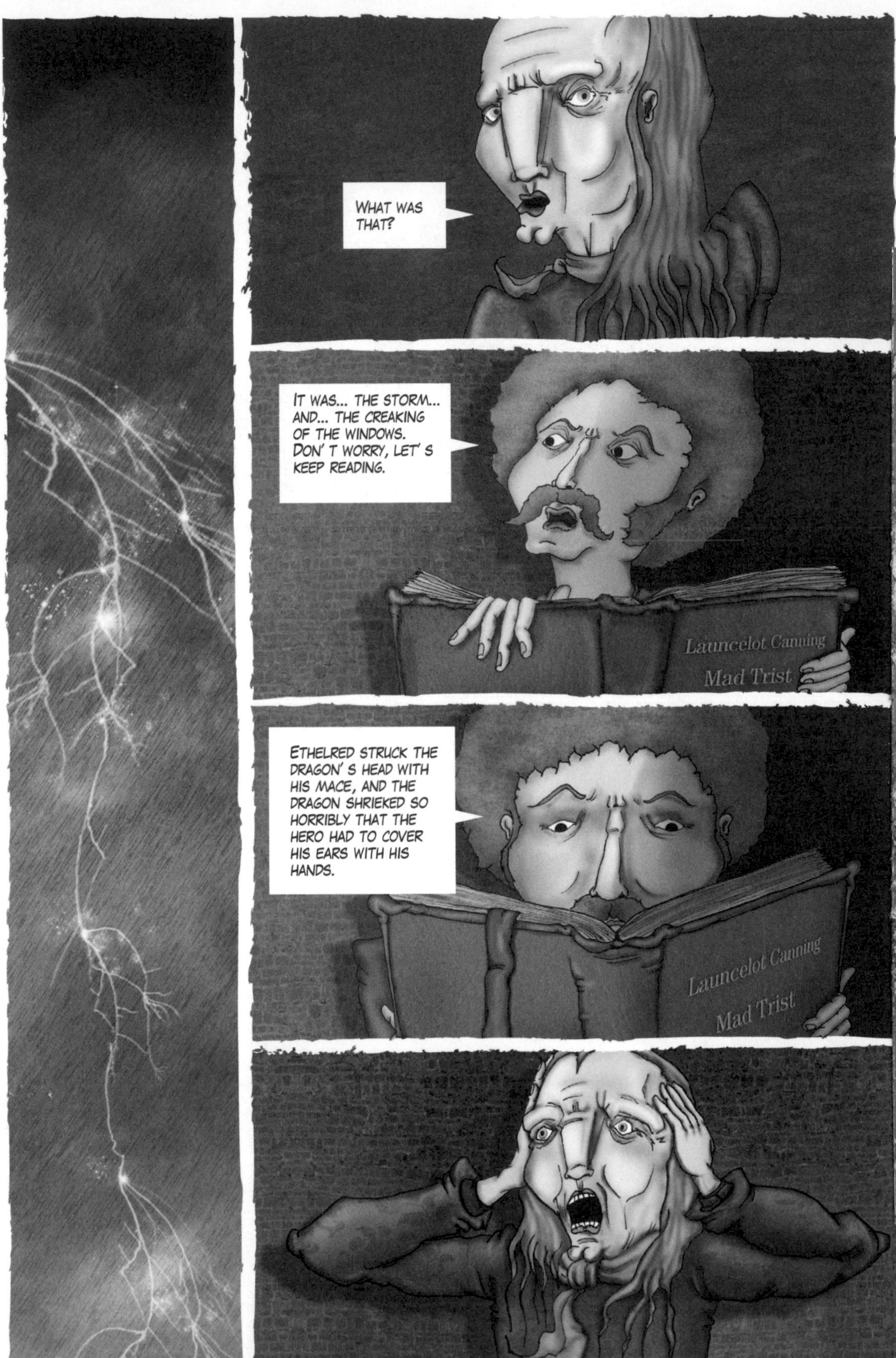

WHAT WAS THAT?
IT WAS... THE STORM... AND... THE CREAKING OF THE WINDOWS. DON' T WORRY, LET' S KEEP READING.
Launcelot Canning
Mad Trist
ETHELRED STRUCK THE DRAGON' S HEAD WITH HIS MACE, AND THE DRAGON SHRIEKED SO HORRIBLY THAT THE HERO HAD TO COVER HIS EARS WITH HIS HANDS.
Launcelot Canning
Mad Trist

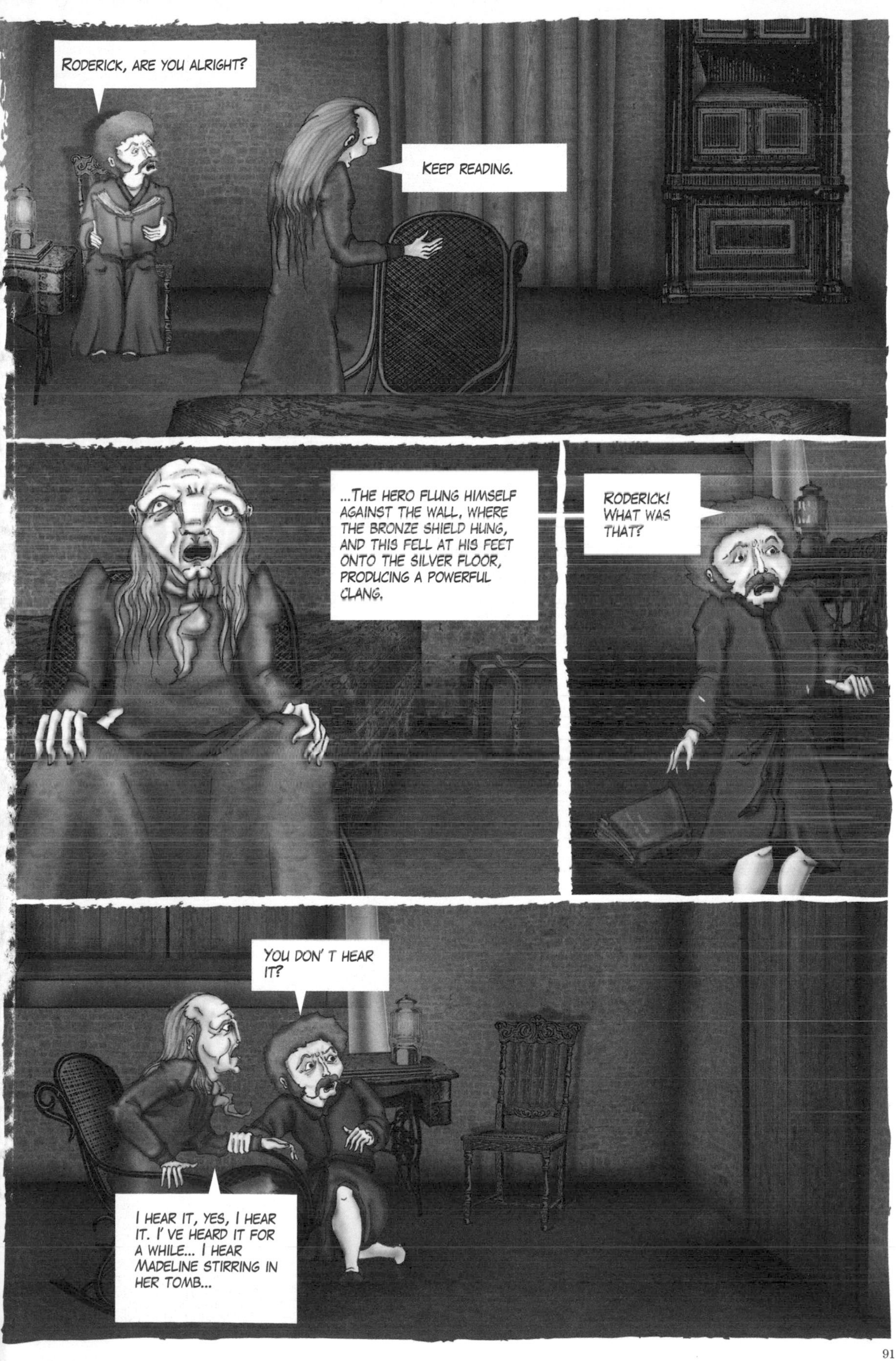
RODERICK, ARE YOU ALRIGHT?
KEEP READING.
...THE HERO FLUNG HIMSELF AGAINST THE WALL, WHERE THE BRONZE SHIELD HUNG, AND THIS FELL AT HIS FEET ONTO THE SILVER FLOOR, PRODUCING A POWERFUL CLANG.
RODERICK! WHAT WAS THAT?
YOU DON' T HEAR IT?
I HEAR IT, YES, I HEAR IT. I' VE HEARD IT FOR A WHILE... I HEAR MADELINE STIRRING IN HER TOMB...

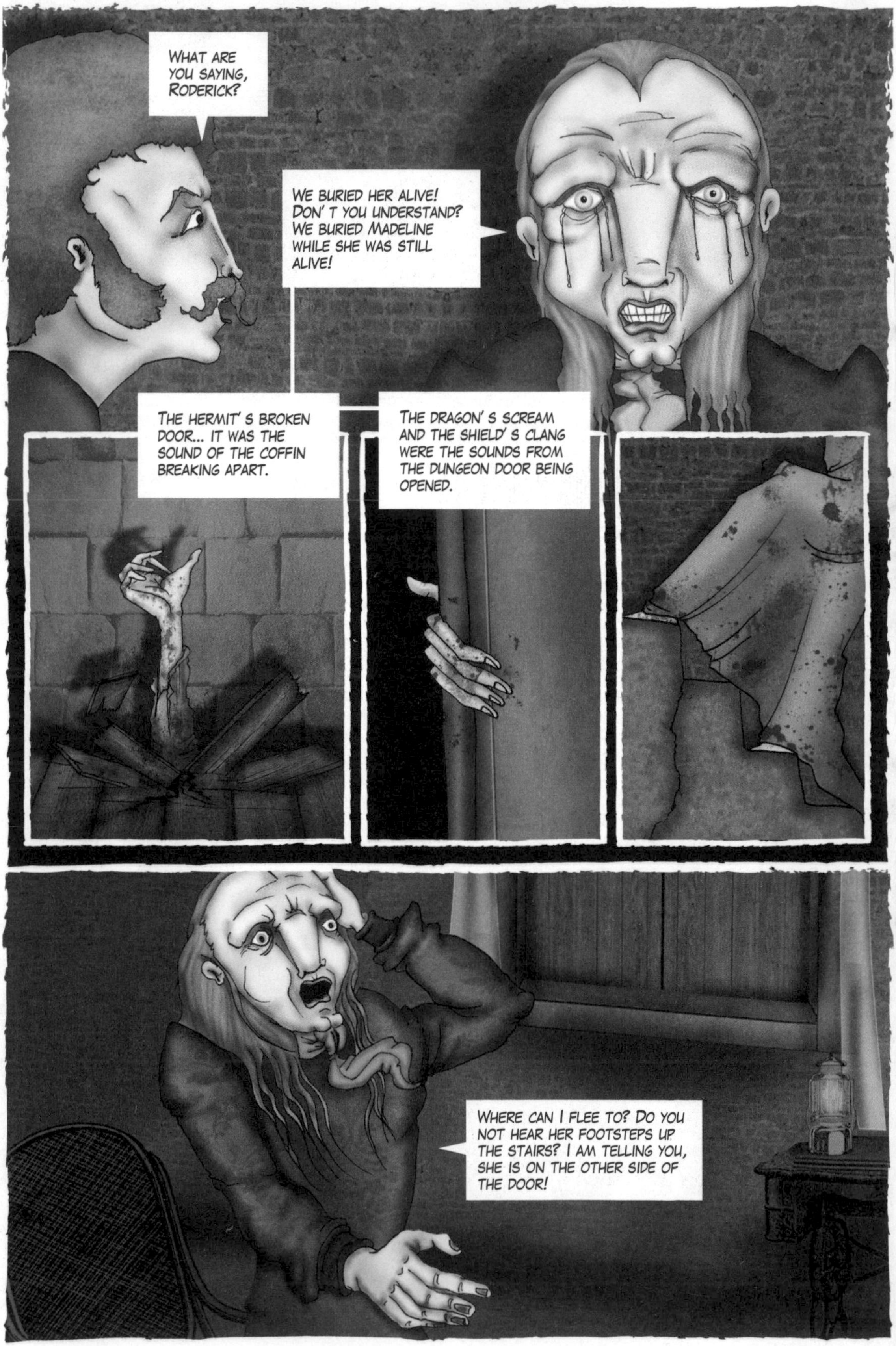
WHAT ARE YOU SAYING, RODERICK?
WE BURIED HER ALIVE! DON' T YOU UNDERSTAND? WE BURIED MADELINE WHILE SHE WAS STILL ALIVE!
THE HERMIT' S BROKEN DOOR... IT WAS THE SOUND OF THE COFFIN BREAKING APART.
THE DRAGON' S SCREAM AND THE SHIELD' S CLANG WERE THE SOUNDS FROM THE DUNGEON DOOR BEING OPENED.
WHERE CAN I FLEE TO? DO YOU NOT HEAR HER FOOTSTEPS UP THE STAIRS? I AM TELLING YOU, SHE IS ON THE OTHER SIDE OF THE DOOR!

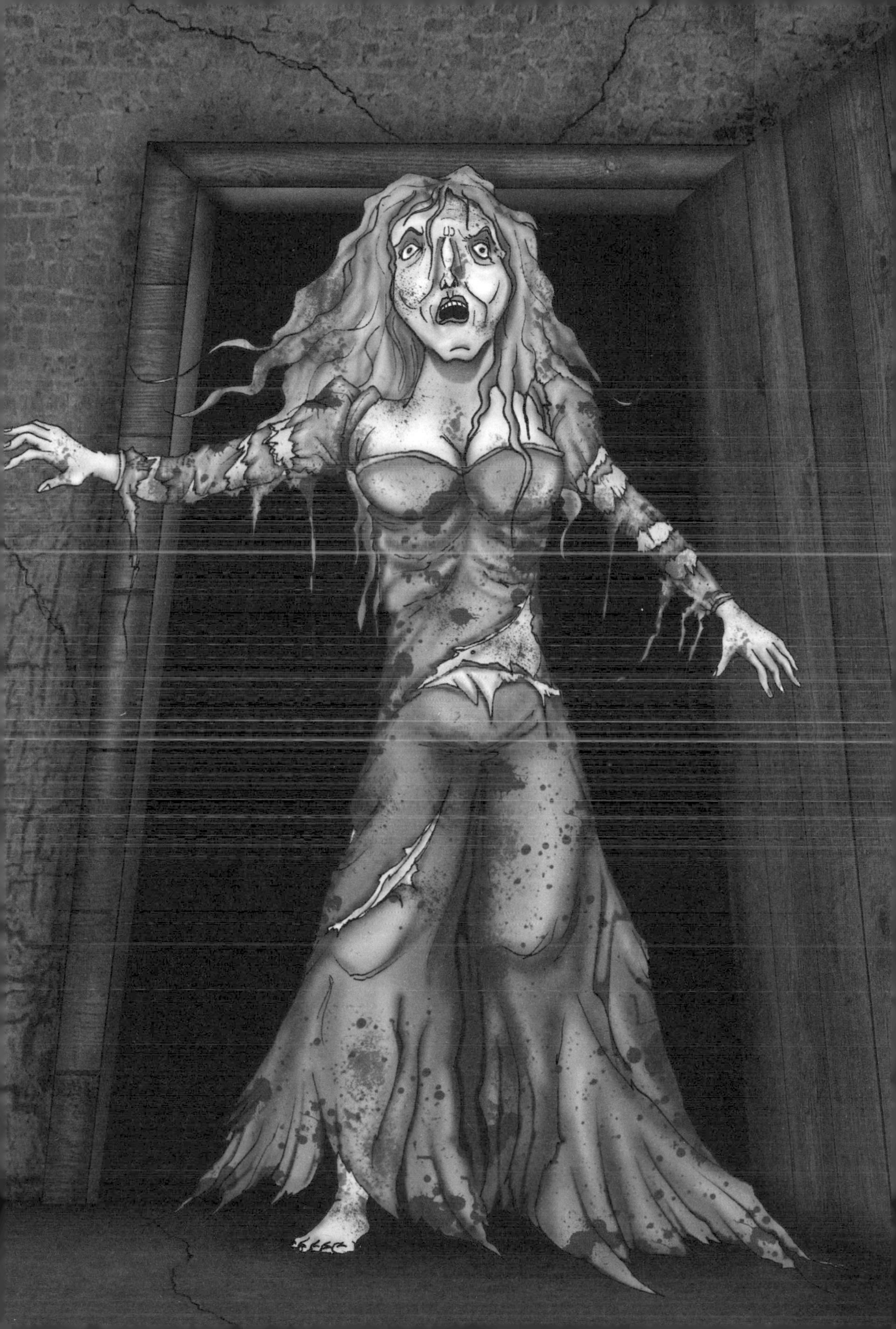

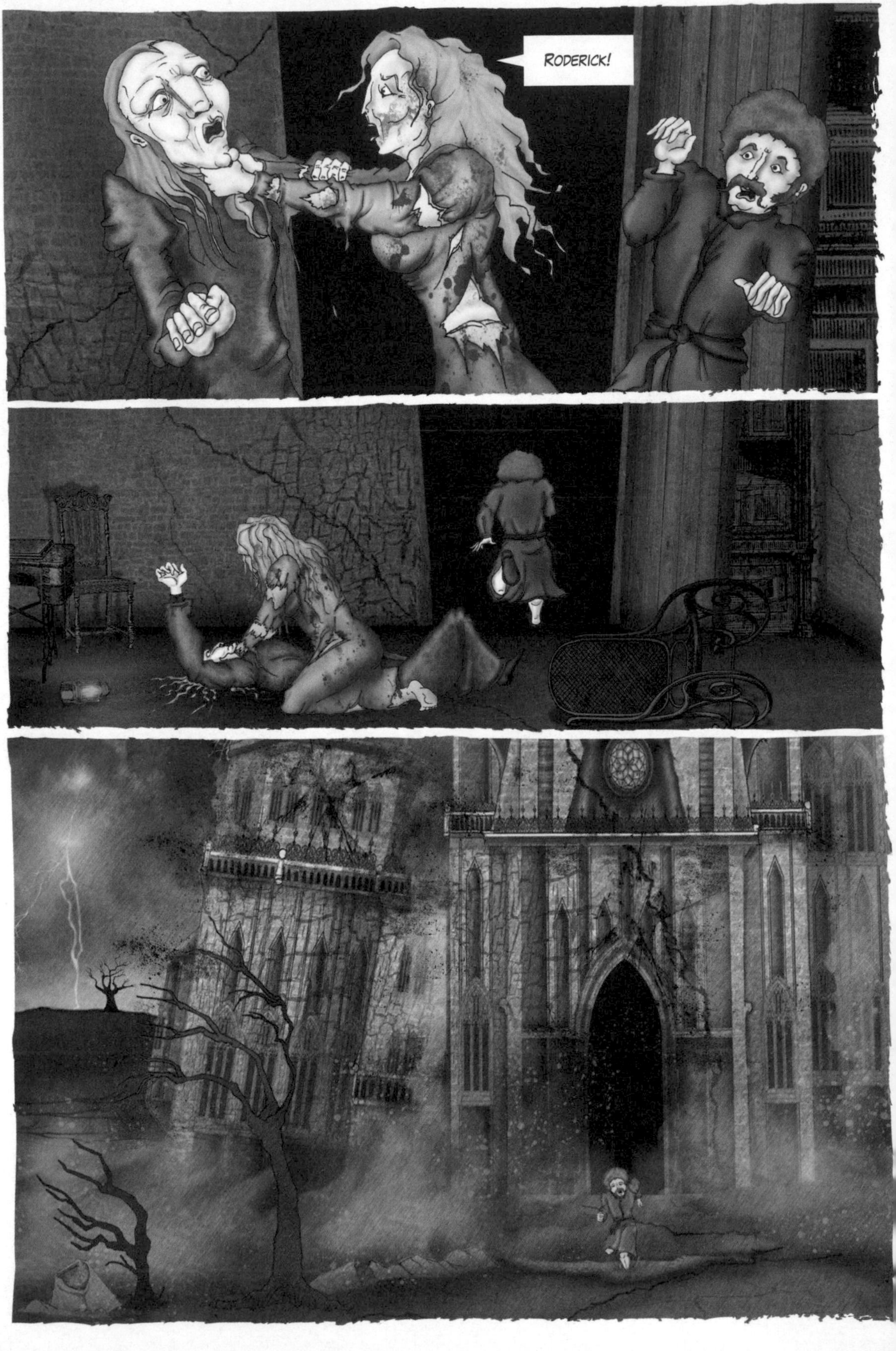
RODERICK!

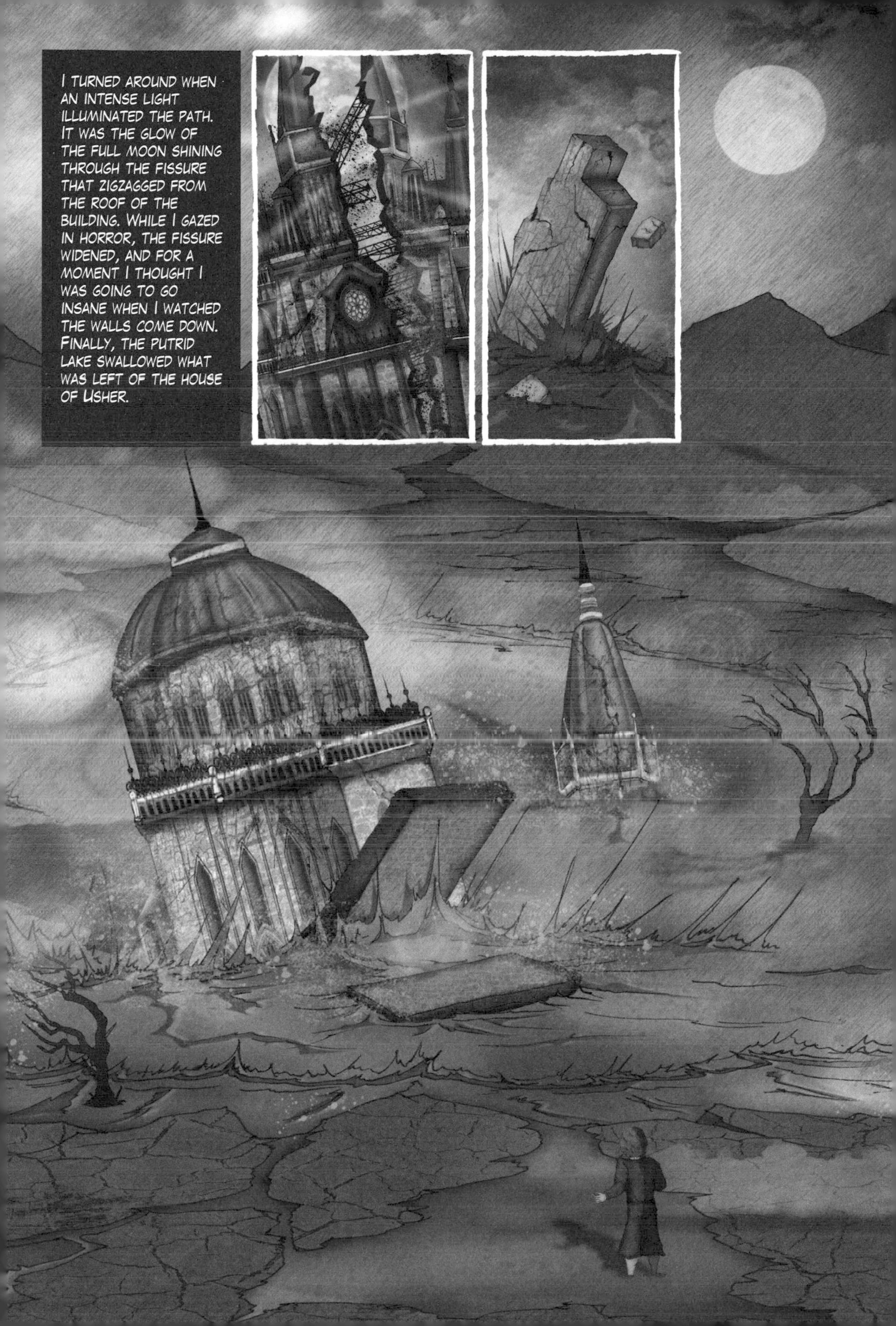
I TURNED AROUND WHEN AN INTENSE LIGHT ILLUMINATED THE PATH. IT WAS THE GLOW OF THE FULL MOON SHINING THROUGH THE FISSURE THAT ZIGZAGGED FROM THE ROOF OF THE BUILDING. WHILE I GAZED IN HORROR, THE FISSURE WIDENED, AND FOR A MOMENT I THOUGHT I WAS GOING TO GO INSANE WHEN I WATCHED THE WALLS COME DOWN. FINALLY, THE PUTRID LAKE SWALLOWED WHAT WAS LEFT OF THE HOUSE OF USHER.

FURTHER READING

BOOKS

Lange, Karen. *Nevermore: A Photobiography of Edgar Allan Poe.* Washington, D.C.: National Geographic, 2009.

Poe, Edgar Allan. *The Complete Poetry of Edgar Allan Poe.* New York: Signet Classics, 2008.

Poe, Edgar Allan. *The Stories of Edgar Allan Poe.* New York: Sterling, 2010.

INTERNET ADDRESSES

The Edgar Allan Poe Society of Baltimore
http://www.eapoe.org/

PoeStories.com
http://www.poestories.com/

The Museum of Edgar Allan Poe
http://www.poemuseum.org/index.php